Books by Lee Charles Kelley

LIKE A DOG WITH A BONE
DOGGED PURSUIT
'TWAS THE BITE BEFORE CHRISTMAS
TO COLLAR A KILLER
MURDER UNLEASHED
A NOSE FOR MURDER

LEE CHARLES
KELLEY

Like A Dog With A Bone

AVON BOOKS
An Imprint of HarperCollinsPublishers

This is a work of fiction. Names, characters, places, and incidents are products of the author's imagination or are used fictitiously and are not to be
construed as real. Any resemblance to actual events, locales, organizations,
or persons, living or dead, is entirely coincidental.

AVON BOOKS
An Imprint of HarperCollins*Publishers*
10 East 53rd Street
New York, New York 10022-5299

Copyright © 2007 by Lee Charles Kelley
ISBN: 978-0-06-073230-1
ISBN-10: 0-06-073230-X
www.avonmystery.com

First Avon Books paperback printing: June 2007

Avon Trademark Reg. U.S. Pat. Off. and in Other Countries,
Marca Registrada, Hecho en U.S.A.
HarperCollins® is a registered trademark of HarperCollins Publishers.

Printed in the U.S.A.

10 9 8 7 6 5 4 3 2 1

For Fred

Acknowledgments

Thanks to Sarah Durand, a wise and verrrrrry understanding editor. And thanks as always to Melanie Weiss, NYPD, Ret., for her invaluable technical input.

Disclaimer

The following is a work of fiction.
Only the dogs are real.

"Dogs are our link to paradise."

—*Milan Kundera*

Like A Dog With A Bone

Prologue

If you're interested, Jamie and I had a wonderful time on our honeymoon in Mexico. We went to Baja. The Yúcatan is closer to Maine, but it was mid-October, hurricane season, and a big storm was brewing down there. Besides, the Pacific has better waves and I wanted to teach Jamie to surf.

She picked it up pretty quickly too. Once I explained the process of counting sets (to get a feel for which swells would turn into the best waves) and showed her how to get in synch with the swell just before it crests, she was doing great.

As for me, I loved sitting on my board, rocking with the ocean's gentle rhythm, and watching as she clenched her jaw, narrowed her eyes, paddled furiously, and caught the wave. Her only problem was she kept trying to fight the wave instead of letting it carry her, so she wiped out more times than not. Still, I think if we'd spent more than four days in Mexico, she would've gotten better at it than I am. But then she *is* nine years younger than I am (she's thirty-four, I'm forty-two), and I haven't surfed since my high school days in San Diego.

Of course it wasn't all surfing. We also spent time just basking in the sun, swimming, walking along the beach, drinking margaritas, eating *enchiladas de camarones* (mmmm . . . yummy), dancing under the stars, all the usual clichés (and a few other fun things we found to do alone inside our hotel room at night).

Our last morning we came back from the beach to find a

coupon on our dresser. It was for free drinks at a cantina up the coast. So we rented a car and drove up the peninsula to a dusty, remote village—no hotels, no bellhops, no room service, just a big tin shack on the beach with a thatched palm roof.

While we were dining al fresco, or whatever they call it, we struck up a conversation with a pale, freckled fiftyish woman with long coral fingernails and a coarse laugh, also from Maine. This resulted in us moving our *platos* and *bebidas* from under *our* beach umbrella to hers, followed by strained laughter, "small world"'s, and that instant yet inane rapport you develop with someone you bump into in a bar in some far-flung corner of the galaxy when the only real thing you have in common is your area code.

Her name was Reggie Durban. And as we sipped sangria and noshed on *sopitos*, she stabbed at her ice with a swizzle stick and told us she was in temporary exile. She'd been staying with her father, a retired general named MacKerry or something, and in a fit of pique he'd thrown her out of his house in Camden, where she'd only been living in the first place, she pointed out repeatedly and a little drunkenly, to take care of the old fool.

Yes, she had her own place in Bar Harbor, thank-you-very-much, and her own money, courtesy of a rich ex-husband, and even her own *casa* in old *May*-hi-co. She pointed toward a white villa that wrapped itself around a distant brown hillside. As she did, our blond, white-shirted bartender caught my eye and gave me a look that said, "*Está loco*," though he looked to be American, not Mexican. (He turned out to be Dutch, but that's another story.)

Jamie finally got a few words in edgewise and told Reggie I was an ex-cop turned dog trainer. She put down her drink, pushed her gold bracelets up her arms, and slid her Italian sunglasses down her nose. "Could you train my father's dog?"

"Sure, if he wants me to. What kind of dog is it?"

"Molly? She's a fox terrier. Though he won't. Ask you, that is. But I'm telling you that dog needs someone like you. And more than that . . . *he* does." She looked around for her purse, found it, got out a checkbook and said, "What's your name again?"

I explained that I couldn't take her check, that I couldn't train someone else's dog without their permission, then asked if there wasn't someone, anyone, among her family, his old friends, or the entire military who could look in on the old guy to make sure he was okay, which is what she really wanted *me* to do.

"No," she said, scribbling. "He won't allow me to even *mention* the army *or* any of his friends. As for our family, my mother ran off twenty years ago. My sister Connie is emotionally detached; she lives in a vacuum. And my father hasn't spoken to my brother Cord since Reagan was in office. What's your name?"

Jamie said, "It's Jack Field."

"Honey . . ." I said vainly.

Then, as Reggie wrote my name on her inane, pointless check, Jamie asked, "Your mother ran off?"

"Twenty years ago," Reggie repeated. "She said she wanted to go to Mexico, to get as far away as she could from my father, and the snow and the mud and the rest of the Maine weather . . ." She stopped writing and looked off at the brightness of the ocean. "Hence my fascination with this damn dusty place."

She sighed, tore off the check, and shoved it at me. I refused it, so Jamie took it instead. Then our "hostess" reached back inside her bag, rummaged around, found a business card, and handed that to Jamie as well. She said to me, "I'll expect regular progress reports, and I always get my way."

"Reports about the dog?" I asked. "Or your father?"

"Both. I'll be back for Thanksgiving; my son's in college and I rarely see him. Anyway, that should give you a good month to teach Molly and Dad how to behave." Then, finished with my instructions, she twisted around and waved at the bartender for another pitcher of sangria, all her bracelets jingling.

"Honey," I complained from the passenger seat on the ride back to our hotel, "why did you let her write me that check?"

"You don't have to cash it."

"I don't intend to."

"Anyway, it wouldn't hurt you to at least meet her father and his dog, would it?"

"Who says it wouldn't? He sounds like a crazy old coot to me. And I think I'd like to stay as far away from that woman and her screwed-up family as possible."

"Yes, but that's not the point." Then she droned on about someone named Morrie and something about life lessons and Tuesday afternoons, but I'd had just enough sangria to give me an excuse to fall asleep so I didn't have to listen to her while she drove.

The next morning it was time for us to de-mariachi ourselves and fly back home while the Maine landscape was still in its last dying flash of October beauty, before it fades into that sad November patina of cold rain, gray skies and even grayer trees. It was time to settle back into our ordinary days and ordinary nights—me happily running a boarding and training kennel between the mid-coastal villages of Hope and Perseverance, and Jamie just as happy being the state's chief medical examiner.

Our ordinary days and nights didn't last long though. With us they never do. But then, life is kind of like a wave that way. You can't fight it. You have to ride it out. . .

1

We arrived at the home of General Lamar MacLeary (ret.) on a cold gray Saturday morning ten days after we'd left for Mexico. It was a big white two-story in the Federal style, with the usual low hedges, tall pines, oaks, and sugar maples scattered around.

I parked near a strip of grass that stood proxy for a curb and we got out. The trees were wet with rain though the clouds—remnants of the hurricane that had hit the Yúcatan—had begun to disperse on our drive over. A light northeast wind still zipped around, though. It danced pretty through Jamie's dark chestnut hair and flapped at the collar of my denim shirt.

We started up a stone-framed cement walk that divided a wide green lawn. A sudden brusque blast rattled the trees and shook hidden raindrops down on our heads, as if the black branches above wanted to let us know they weren't through with us yet.

I shook the rain off. "What do you want to bet that was a bad omen? And I still think I should stay in the car."

"Don't be ridiculous." She shook the rain off of *her* hair. "The only reason *I* came was to make sure *you* did. You're the dog trainer, remember? And since when do you believe in omens?"

"It was a joke. And what does my being a dog trainer—"

"Because this is supposed to be about the dog."

I gave her a cynical laugh.

She gave me a backhand to the belly.

"Besides," she said, "I've never watched you at one of your dog training sessions. Maybe I'll learn something."

I smiled. "That's good. Appeal to my ego."

We climbed three steps up to the wide framed wooden porch, all painted a dull white. I pressed the bell thingie and a dog started barking, a high, shrill sound that came from deep inside the house, maybe upstairs. After a while it trailed off.

"That must be Molly," I said dumbly, then we stood waiting awhile. I said, "Are you sure he's expecting us?"

"Yes. I told you, Reggie called me on my private cell at the ME's office and asked me to speak to him. So I did, and he invited us over. And he's looking forward to meeting you."

"Huh. How did Reggie get your private number?"

"Jack, I told you this already too. She got it from her brother-in-law. Her sister Connie, the one who lives in a vacuum, is married to the deputy state's attorney general."

"No kidding?" I said. "Hey, your hair looks great, all mussed by the wind and rain like that. And with your Baja tan you look like one of Gauguin's Tahitian girls."

She got out a brush and immediately began to straighten it.

"Honey, don't fix it. I just told you it looks pretty."

"Yeah, except I happen to know why *you* like it; it reminds you of the way I look after I've just come out of the shower and I'm naked—like the women in those paintings—and you want to fool around. But I'm about to meet a World War Two hero, not to mention former assistant to the Chairman of the Joint Chiefs of Staff, and I don't want him thinking we just had sex in the car."

Somewhere in the middle of her line about having sex in the car, the front door opened and was suddenly filled by the figure of a white-haired man, standing ramrod straight. He was a few inches shorter than Jamie (she's five-eleven), and he was standing in a wide foyer, though in Maine they call it a mud-room. Another door, standing shut, wasn't far behind him. We could hear Molly on the other side, barking and scratching at the wood.

"It's okay," I told the general with an apologetic shrug.

"I'm her husband. I can have sex with her wherever I want."

"Not around here you can't," he said with a deep, intimidating gravel that made him seem taller than he was.

He was wearing khakis, a tattersall shirt, and a brown tweed jacket. I now noticed that his hair wasn't white so much as it was the shade of pink that red-haired people develop as they age. I also noticed that his eyebrows—which actually *were* white, white as snow—lofted above his blues eyes as if they had a life of their own. He was clean-shaven, his clothes neatly pressed, and he didn't smell of beer, wine, or whiskey. I had to wonder why his daughter Reggie thought she needed me to take care of him.

"Don't mind our little banter," Jamie said, forming a fist beside her left thigh, near to where I stood. "We just got back from our honeymoon—"

"—in Mexico," the old man said, "I know. Which is where you met my daughter, who asked you to see me. Come in."

We went through the second door.

Molly stopped barking and began bouncing high in the air, the way terriers do. She mixed the bouncing in with a little enraptured sniffing of my jeans. (My clothes are always rife with male pheromones, thanks to Frankie and Hooch, my English setter and dogue de Bordeaux, both unneutered.) She also had fun running circles around my feet—sniff, sniff, *boing, boing,* sniff, sniff, circle, circle, sniff, sniff, *boing, boing. . .*

I had to laugh.

The general said, "Don't blame me. I'm no dog trainer. The living room's this way."

He led us slowly yet easily, with no discernible hitch in his gait, through a hall, then down some steps into a large space with a curved bay window that revealed a broad sloped lawn and, past that, the gray, wind-chopped waves at the mouth of Camden harbor. In the center of the grass, surrounded by a semicircle of stones, all painted white, stood a tall, naked flagpole. Its ropes whipped around uselessly in the wind.

We sat on some furniture, and there was the usual offer of coffee and whatnot, which we declined. Then Jamie and Mac-Leary palavered a bit while I fooled around with the dog. She

was black and white, with a little tan mixed in, and seemed to
be about seven months old, with loads of energy.

I used my left hand to playfully bat at her face and snout to
see if she'd try to bite me back in play. She grabbed the sleeve
of my shirt instead, which made me laugh. With my free hand
I produced a tennis ball from my down vest, then looked up
at the general to ask him something. He was in the middle of
interrogating Jamie about how Reggie had seemed when we'd
spoken to her in Mexico. Was she drinking too much, had she
said anything about him or mentioned her mother, was she coming back?

As he spoke I saw some inner disturbance in the man's eyes.
It was hidden by the calm in his voice, but the eyes themselves
reflected a primal conflict of some sort that had apparently sav-
aged his family, his life, and his confidence in his role as a man
of war. He was still sitting ramrod straight, but that angry yet
almost lost quality I'd seen struck at some unknown feelings of
my *own*, which made me suddenly uncomfortable.

"What kind of games does she like?" I asked.

"What kind of *games* does she like?" he repeated, as if he
thought I'd been talking about his daughter.

"Molly. Does she like to play fetch or tug-of-war?"

"No. She won't play any sorts of games. Her favorite activities are chasing squirrels and digging holes in the side yard.
Which is something I'm hoping you can fix."

"Well, we'll see." I teased Molly with the tennis ball. She let
go of my sleeve and I threw the ball past her toward some low
steps that led up to a wood-paneled library/office.

She raced after it. I got a second ball out. She grabbed the
first one and turned around. I showed her the second ball and
teased her with it. She came racing back, dropped the first ball,
and I threw the second one. She went after it.

Jamie and the general were looking at me.

"Don't mind me," I said. "Go on with what you were saying."

Molly brought the second ball back and dropped it right in
front of me, then stepped back, waiting for me to throw it.

I picked it up and threw it, and she went racing after it.

"But she's playing fetch with you," MacLeary said.

"Yep. Cool, huh? This is just beginner's luck, though."

"Beginner's luck? I thought you knew what you were doing."

"Oh, *I* do," I said. "Molly's the beginner. At some point she'll need to complete the hunt, meaning that she'll hang onto the ball instead of dropping it for me to throw again."

Sure enough on the next toss Molly did just that; she even shook her head around as if killing the ball.

"So now what?" the general asked.

I explained that it was a matter of re-arousing her need to *chase* the ball in order to override her impulse to hold onto it and *kill* it. I demonstrated by teasing Molly with the one in my hand, praising her and using a play growl. Sure enough, Molly dropped *her* ball and charged at the one in my hand. I threw it just over her head and she scampered after it.

It went past our line of sight into the shadowed corners of the library. We heard a door open. Nothing happened, then after a bit the ball came bouncing back, with Molly in hot pursuit.

Jamie and I looked at the general. "That's Jervis, my old friend, now also my secretary. He's been helping me with my memoirs." He called out to the man in the library. "Jervis?"

"Yes, sir?" The voice was calm, mannerly, British.

"Everything okay?" MacLeary asked.

"Fine, sir. I was just napping a little." Then we heard him mutter, "Or trying to . . ." and we heard a door close.

"Jervis was up late," MacLeary said with a paternal tone.

Molly began barking at me to throw the ball. I said, "Quiet!" in a hushed, excited voice. She stopped barking for a millisecond. I threw the ball, this time toward the kitchen.

"Well," MacLeary said, "this is all very fascinating, but what does playing fetch have to do with her constant digging?"

"More than you'd think." I explained that dogs dig for two reasons: because there's something under the ground worth digging for—like a prey animal in its hole, or a buried bone—or to reduce tension caused by some inability to satisfy their hunting instincts. "By teaching her to play hunting games, the digging might just go away on its own."

"Really? Just like that?'

"Yes, unless—as I said—there's something worth digging for."

A hint of sunlight teased at the window then slowly died out. The general's eyes went somewhere. Then a faint smile—or the glimmer of one—teased a little at one corner of his mouth the way the sun had graced the window. He remembered who he was. Not a lost, lonely, angry father whose family had come apart, but a patriot, a soldier, a man of tactics, blood, and steel.

"Of course," he said, nodding, "dogs are hunters. When they have no quarry, they're like a soldier with no battles to fight."

"Right. And they need to fill that void somehow. So," I asked, "what do soldiers do when they're not at war?"

"Soldiers train, go on maneuvers, or just dig ditches, which is fitting, I guess, considering Molly's predilections." He stood up. "As for generals, we play war games or retire and write our goddamn memoirs. At any rate, the rain's stopped, so it's time for me to put up the flag. After I'm done, perhaps you'd like to see Molly's handiwork in the side yard."

"Sure," I said, and Jamie and I got up to follow him.

2

The general led us through a large, uncluttered kitchen to a mudroom by the back door, with Molly at our heels. On a shelf near the door was a wooden case made of polished oak with brass trim. He unlocked it and opened it, then took out an American flag, folded in tricorner fashion. He put it under his arm, then held the back door open for us. We all went down the steps, with Molly happily scampering off and sniffing in all directions, loving the smell and feel of the wet grass.

We got to the flagpole, where Jamie and I watched quietly as General Lamar MacLeary (ret.) gently unfolded his American flag. Then—keeping it carefully draped over one arm so as not to let it touch the ground—he attached the hooks on the ropes to the grommets on the flag. Then he ran it briskly up the pole, secured the ropes, stood back, put his hand over his heart and looked up at the flag, which flapped noisily in the wind.

Jamie and I looked at each other. This wasn't a ballgame; were we supposed to put our hands over our hearts too?

We did.

"You don't salute?" Jamie asked when we were done.

"Only when I'm in uniform," the general said simply.

"I didn't know there was a rule," she said.

"You're not alone," he grumped, then gave her a sad smile. "These days too many people *think* they're being patriotic because they fly the American flag twenty-four/seven, yet they have no regard for the proper way to do it."

This precipitated a discussion on flag etiquette. I'm no flag-waver, but I chimed in with a few things I remembered from Boy Scouts. You're supposed to raise the flag briskly at dawn, then bring it down at sunset, slowly and solemnly. Either that or give the flag its own spotlight so it's properly lit at night. And unless it's waterproof, it should never be flown in bad weather. If it's damaged in any way, or even if it touches the ground, it should be taken to a VFW post or a local scout troop for proper disposal. And it should never be used as decoration on clothing except on police and fire department uniforms, etc.

Jamie said, "Not many people know the right way, do they?"

"They do not," MacLeary said. "There's nothing sadder than seeing it blowing in a rainstorm, or flapping in the dark, or flying high, all tattered and stained. And don't get me started on people who run Old Glory up their car antenna. That's the saddest sight of all; a ragged American flag fluttering over a god-damn Toyota."

I chimed in again: "And most of the people who do that are the same ones who want a flag burning amendment, which is ironic since they aren't treating it with any respect themselves."

"You're in favor of burning the flag?" the general asked, his face burning. "You sound just like that goddamn, disloyal son of mine." The anger flared in his eyes again.

"I'm not *advocating* it," I said. "But no matter how offensive it may be to see the flag in flames, it's a symbol of freedom; so, the way I look at it, any law that would restrict freedom would dishonor exactly what the flag stands for."

"Jack . . ." Jamie said, thinking, I guess, and rightly so, that I wasn't paying enough attention to my audience.

"Anyway," I went on, "I say if you're going to pass a flag amendment, fine. Just word it so that any violators will be penalized not only for burning the flag, but for leaving it out in the rain, or tying it to a car antenna, or pinning it to your lapel, which means half of Congress would end up in jail."

"That's enough," he said, shaking. "Do you know how many American bones are buried all across this country and around the world? Bones of heroes who laid down their lives for that flag?"

"Too many. And I apologize if I've offended you with my opinions, sir." Better change the subject. "So, where's Molly?"

"Probably digging up her favorite hole." He took a deep breath to dissipate his animosity toward me. "It's this way."

As the general led us toward the side of the house, charging abruptly ahead of us, Jamie came close to me, pinched the back of my arm and whispered, "You almost gave the man a heart attack."

"Sorry. It *is* a free country, though."

"Yeah, not *that* free."

MacLeary slowed down, began to chuckle a little, turned and said, "You are a reckless and insolent young man, Mr. Field, but I have to say, I agree with your comment on how half of Congress should be put in the slammer."

We started walking again, turned the corner of the house, and found Molly near an azalea bed next to a long, gated trellis that separated the general's property from that of his neighbor. She was digging furiously at a very deep hole. So deep, in fact, that practically all you could see was her curved fox terrier tail sticking up in the air. The rest of her was below ground.

"Molly!" the general said.

Dig, dig, dig!

"Molly, girl!"

Dig, dig, dig!

"Molly, stop that!"

Dig, dig, dig, DIG, DIG!

Finally MacLeary turned to me. "So, Mr. Field, let's see what you can do with your little tennis ball."

"After one, brief game of fetch? I don't think so. I mean, I could give it a shot but it probably won't work."

"So? Fix it somehow! Isn't that what you're here for?"

I had an idea: I could get down on my hands and knees, on her level, and dig the hole *with* her; we'd be partners. Then I would start pestering her, pushing at her, while praising her, turning it into a game where she had to choose between play-fighting with me or digging her hole. That would only work momentarily, of course. I'd have to repeat the game over and over, followed by fetch and tug, until the very desire or need to dig was totally gone.

As I was thinking this over, I looked closer at the crater and thought I saw something no one ever wants to see: the bones of a human hand. My mind froze.

The bottom of the hole was covered in mud, so it was impossible to tell for sure if that's what I'd seen. Maybe it a bunch of roots *shaped* like a hand. But I looked around and saw that the nearest tree was at least twenty yards away. Plus, I had a gut feeling that what I was seeing wasn't plant material but solid bone.

"Uh, General," I said, my knees and my arms beginning to shake, "I think you've got worse problems."

"Such as?"

"Remember I said there are two reasons a dog likes to dig? Well, I don't think she's been doing it because she wasn't getting enough fetch time. I think there's a body down there. And I think it's been there for quite a while."

"What?" He stared at the hole.

I grabbed hold of Molly's collar and pulled her away.

Jamie moved in and said, "I can't see anything."

MacLeary said, "I'll get the hose," and then charged off.

Jamie said, "Show me."

I pointed, still holding Molly back.

She nodded and said, "I see it. It sort of looks like a hand, but it could just be some roots from a nearby tree, right?"

I pointed to the nearest tree.

"Oh, no." She put a hand on my shoulder.

The general came back with the hose, already running. He pointed it into the crater, but it only made matters worse.

Jamie knelt next to the crater, reached down and lifted whatever it was by what would've been the wrist bone slightly out of the muck. The general sprayed some water, and in a flash we saw a long finger bone, with a diamond ring around it.

"Oh my god," MacLeary said, turning white and dropping the hose. "That's Katherine's ring . . . my wife's ring." He trembled a little and began to totter backward. The whites of his eyes disappeared into the back of his head, and he fell slowly and softly onto the azalea bed, landing on his side.

I let go of Molly, who ran over to lick the general's face.

Meanwhile, Jamie clambered out of the pit and ran over to see if she could help the old man. She looked up at me and started to say something.

I was way ahead of her: "Nine one one?" I said into my cell phone. "This is Jack Field from the state ME's office. I'm here with Dr. Cutter. We're going to need an ambulance at General Lamar MacLeary's house, stat." Then I gave them the address. "And we've just found some human remains buried in the yard." Pause. "That's right, human skeletal remains. Send a forensics team."

I clicked my cell phone off and said, "How is he?"

"His breathing and heartbeat are regular." She opened one of his eyelids and looked at the pupil, did the same with the other. "But he's unconscious, and his pupils are nonreactive to light." She pinched one of his nostrils, then ran her fingernail up his sternum. She said, "He's nonreactive to pain. I can't say for sure, but he may be comatose."

"Ah, jeez, let's hope not," I said. I looked into the hole. "Well, it looks like Reggie's mother never made it to Mexico after all, did she?"

She gave me a look. "We don't know for sure yet that those *are* her remains. I have some work to do before it's official."

"Well, at least one thing's official."

"What's that?"

"The honeymoon's over . . ."

3

While Jamie tended to the old man, I hosed Molly's paws, then took her into the house, found a rawhide and gave it to her, then went back toward the library, found the door to the adjoining bedroom and knocked. Loudly. Numerous times.

Finally, Jervis—roughly the general's age, maybe a little younger, with disheveled white hair, a droopy unshaven face, and watery eyes—opened the door. He was wearing light blue pajamas and a dark blue woolen robe with big crimson swirls woven in.

I quickly informed him of the general's condition, then asked him if he knew of any medications the old man was taking, or if he knew the name of the general's primary care physician.

His eyes cleared for a moment, then he went back to being disinterested or in shock or half asleep; it was hard to tell. Either way, I was starting to understand Reggie's concern for her father; Jervis seemed to be of no help to the old man. I also wondered about the relationship between them. MacLeary, from what I'd seen, had a steel backbone; he was like a well-bred German shepherd. Jervis, on the other hand, seemed to be made of tissue paper, the kind of dog who immediately rolls over on his back when you say hello. I had a quick flash that maybe the general was taking care of Jervis more than the other way around. Honor and loyalty seemed important to MacLeary; maybe there was something he felt he owed this flimsy, wobble-kneed Jervis.

Finally, the man spoke. "Where is he?"

I detected the odor of gin, which gave me a little more insight into the man's seeming indifference, and said, "He's passed out next to that big hole in the side yard."

We heard sirens approaching.

Jervis blinked, once. "Is he all right?"

"No. My wife's with him. She's a doctor and she thinks he might have had a stroke." I didn't mention the discovery of Mrs. MacLeary's body—or at least her bones—in Molly's hole.

"I'll get dressed," he said slowly, "and be right out."

"And the information about his medications?"

"I'll . . . I'll see what I can find out and let you know."

He closed the door.

I stood a moment, shaking my head and trying not to scream.

I turned and saw a wall of photographs: family scenes for the most part, with the general, Mrs. MacLeary (who bore a strong resemblance to an old movie star I couldn't name), and what must have been Connie, Reggie, and Cord at various life stages. There were no photos of the general with presidents or heads of state, just the wife and kids: Reggie on horseback, Cord at a lacrosse game, and Connie and her father shooting at a practice range. Connie won a medal that day. MacLeary seemed so proud as he stood next to her. Reggie was in the photo as well. She had one lip curled, pissed off at Connie's glory.

The sirens were getting closer, so I left MacLeary's wall of memories and went out front, where two Camden cruisers squealed to a stop and emitted four uniforms.

Their cars blocked the street, so I vented my frustration on these fine, though unseasoned, young men and one woman; I yelled at them to get their damn automobiles out of the way of the coming ambulance. This precipitated a heated discussion about who I was and what the hell I was doing at the scene, all of which I tried to spell out to them at a rather high volume of speech. While I was thus engaged, several of the neighbors began appearing on their porches and front lawns, wondering what the ruckus was.

I had just gotten around to explaining the general's condition and that the body we'd found had been buried for twenty years, so there was no reason for them to draw their weapons, etc., which is when we first heard the ambulance. The two that had been driving cruisers scrambled back inside and quickly swerved them onto some lawns across the street, ruining the grass.

Jervis then appeared, fully dressed except, I noticed, that he wasn't wearing any socks and his shoes were still untied. He came up to me just as the EMTs were unloading the gurney and tried to hand me a slip of paper. "The list you asked for."

I said, "Give it to them," with a nod to the paramedics.

"Of course," he said, and just stood there.

Exasperated with his zombie attitude, I wanted to yell at him and tell him he was the most inert human being I'd ever met, then realized he needed simple instructions, not valid criticism.

I said, "Jervis, go get in the back of ambulance."

"Beg pardon?"

"Go over to the ambulance and get in the back. You're going to ride to the hospital with the general and stay with him."

He nodded and did as he was told.

Then, once they'd loaded General MacLeary (and Jervis) into the ambulance, Jamie and I had a chance to discuss the situation. She had to wait for the forensics team. Plus, she said, she needed to contact an anthropologist, forensic or otherwise, to supervise the dig; she had no experience in such things.

I, meanwhile, thought my best course was to not hang around, getting in the way, but to take Molly back to the kennel and then to drive Jamie's Jaguar back to the general's house, with my adopted son Leon following me in the Suburban.

I'd found Leon hiding in a closet at a crime scene in Harlem while working a multiple homicide case for the NYPD; a gang of drug dealers murdered his mother and father and two older brothers. He was a witness, which put his life in danger, so I'd given him my own brand of witness protection; I took him with me when I moved to Maine, and eventually adopted him.

"That way," I said to Jamie, "you won't be without transportation and Leon and I can go back home in *my* car."

"That's a good idea, but don't you want to stay here and . . . ?"

"And what? Look at bones? This case is twenty years old.

Whatever trail of evidence there might have been at one point has gone totally cold. Meanwhile, I'll call Reggie in Mexico and let her know what's happened. Maybe I can reconstruct some fragment of the case by talking to her and her sister and brother."

I got Molly back to the kennel, which is an old barn that sits slightly downhill and to the left of my Victorian two-story. A guest cottage—which is where Leon lives with his computer, his Game Boy, and his wheaten terrier mix, Magee—sits recessed between the house and the kennel. The barn had been rebuilt from the inside with cinder blocks and a cement floor, though after I bought the place, which was about four years ago, I'd had the cinder blocks covered over with knotty pine. It looks "Mainey."

Each cubicle has its own doghouse and Maine-themed décor: a pine motif in one; lobsters, sailboats, or lighthouses, in the others. The dogs could care less, but my clients like it. In fact, some ask that their dog always stay in one particular kennel based on nothing more than its ornamentation.

I put Molly in the "moose" kennel then called Reggie in Baja. She didn't answer. I got her brother Cord's and her sister Connie's numbers from information, then called them. Connie didn't answer, so I tried her brother. Him, I got. But as soon as I mentioned the general's condition, he said, "It serves the old bastard right," and then hung up on me.

Nice family; no wonder MacLeary had sad/angry eyes.

I roused Leon (he was still in bed even though it was well past noon) and we drove down to Camden.

There were a dozen news vans and whatnot parked along the perimeter, a few blocks up the street. We had to circle awhile before finding a place to park in the Sharp's Wharf lot.

When Leon and I arrived on foot at MacLeary's house, Jamie was still cooling her heels, waiting for an anthropologist to show up. She told me she'd talked to someone she knew of from one of the local colleges, but she hadn't arrived yet.

Also on hand were Jamie's ex-uncle-in-law, Horace Flynn, the outgoing sheriff of Rockland County. His replacement, Peggy Doyle—mid-thirties, medium build with a bit of heft to her, but not too much—was with him. Flynn was in uniform; Doyle was in jeans and a sweatshirt. A few deputies were helping the Camden PD and the state police with the canvass and crowd control.

"You're taking over already?" I asked Doyle.

"November first," she said, smiling. A sudden breeze tousled her red curls. "I'm a deputy for now, just observing."

"I'm breaking her in," said Flynn proudly.

Flynn had just won a hard-fought recall election but had gotten sick of the politics of the job, so he'd turned around and announced his retirement, leaving Katie Doyle, who'd come in second, as his replacement. The voters loved Doyle; she'd recently helped me and Jamie put a serial killer behind bars.

Also on hand was Trudy Compton and her brother Jeffrey. Trudy was a deputy. The last I'd heard, Jeffrey was a law student who'd volunteered to spend a night in jail with a racist white police chief named Colbern, just as a sociological experiment.

I smiled and said to him, "You here to do another experiment on white cultural values in small-town New England?"

"No, I'm with the attorney general's office now."

"Oh, you graduated," I said, nodding. "Congratulations. So, is the attorney general going to be handling this case?"

"Could be," he said. "I'm just keeping an eye on things."

Then we all traded information, or the lack thereof, and I found that I was enjoying myself, shooting the bull at a crime scene, just like the old days in New York. I'm always resistant to getting involved in Jamie's little murder cases—I'd much rather be working with dogs. But though I hated to admit it, there was a part of me that liked being back in the game.

As I was ready to leave, Jamie said, "What is it, Jack?"

"Nothing."

"No, I know you. Something's wrong."

"Well, don't you think it's odd," I said finally, "that the DA isn't handling this, that the attorney general is?"

"I'm not sure. I know Allan Forbert. He's a good guy."

"Maybe so, but criminal cases aren't the AG's purview; they handle class action suits, government corruption, that sort of—"

"I thought about that too. But after all, this *is* going to be a high profile case."

"Yeah," I said, then gave back her car keys. "But the victim's son-in-law is the deputy AG. If there was any case Forbert's office shouldn't be involved in, this is it."

When Leon and I got home, he and Magee went back to bed, while I called Reggie again; this time she answered. I told her what was going on with the general, but before I had a chance to explain about her mother's bones being found in the side yard, she hung up on me, intent on flying back home tout-suite.

I tried Connie but she didn't answer, nor was there an answering machine. It didn't matter. I was pretty sure her husband knew about the discovery of the bones by now.

My next call was to Otis Barnes, publisher and editor of the *Camden Herald*. He wasn't home, but since the crime scene was just down the street from his office, I figured I might be able to reach him at work, and I did.

We got the usual chitchat about last week's poker game out of the way—I'd won over fifty dollars off him Thursday night and he was still bellyaching—then I told him about Jeffrey Compton.

"Yeah," he said, "I saw him there earlier. He wouldn't make a comment, but he seemed to be keeping an eye on things."

"Funny. That's what he told me he was doing, word for word. Look, you know more about how they run things up here, but in New York I never came across a single case that was handled by Albany. They were all run out of the Manhattan DA's office."

"Things are a *little* different here," he said, "but I have to admit, it's unusual. You got any inside stuff to give?"

"Not really. The general's dog found the body, or what was left of it, but you probably already knew that."

"Yeah. Nobody's been able to find the dog, though."

I laughed. "Why would anybody want to find Molly?"

"Are you nuts? Do you have any idea how much circulation goes up when you put the picture of a dog on the front page?"

"All right," I said. "You can have one of your photographers come up here and get your facackta picture."

"She's staying with you?"

"Yeah, but don't let anybody else know she's here."

"Are you kidding? That's the last thing I'd do." A pause. "You know the *Herald* only comes out on Thursdays, right?"

"Yeah?"

"So, do you mind if I sell the photo to the Portland and Augusta papers, or to one of the wire services?"

I sighed. "Fine, you can do what you want to with it, just promise to quit whining about losing to me at poker."

The rest of the day involved dodging phone calls from the media, including Lily Chow, my producer at the Portland station where I do a biweekly training segment on Saturday mornings.

I also had some kennel business to take care of, which meant taking what dogs I had staying with me that weekend—along with Frankie, Hooch, Molly, and Magee—down to the play yard, a fenced-in area roughly the size of the infield at Fenway Park that sits downhill from my house and the kennel building.

Around three, while I was still out with the dogs, Otis Barnes, tall, lanky, around sixty, with hair the color of French bread, arrived and brought along a female photographer named Ellie Something—Green or Brown; it was some color. She was of medium height and build, about forty, and had short hennaed hair and a face like a fist. Otis had apparently told her I'd moved to Maine from New York City, because she beamed when she jumped out of his tan Land Rover, and couldn't wait to tell me that she had too.

"I mean, don't you love it up here?" she said, looking around in a kind of crazed happiness.

Ellie said, "I mean, don't you just love the whole state of Maine? Isn't it just fabulous?"

"Yeah. It's great."

"Yeah, but I bet you miss being able to get good bagels, though, right? Right? And take-out pizza? Ooh, and Chinese?"

"Actually, there's a great bagel place in Camden. In fact, they make better bagels than anyplace I've been to in New—"

"Which one's Molly?" she said, pulling a camera out of a canvas bag, but looking at the dogs as she did it.

I pointed Molly out, and Ellie stomped down the hill, then began circling her and snapping her picture—click, click, click.

I said to Otis, "Did she forget to take her Ritalin?"

"I know," he said with a shrug. "But she was available."

Poor Molly! She immediately barked at the madwoman, and when that didn't work, she ran away, keeping one eye on Ellie over her shoulder. Ellie just ran after her, her eye up to the lens, and kept taking pictures—click, click, click—while racing after Molly. By now they were at the far end of the play yard.

"Okay," I said to Otis, "that's enough. She's scaring the crap out of that poor little dog."

"Sorry," he said to me, then called out to the crazy woman. "Okay, Ellie! That's enough!"

"What?" she said, one eye still against the viewfinder.

"You're scaring the dog! We've got enough pictures."

"Oh." She stopped, then looked at Molly. "Okay," she said, then immediately put the camera back up to her eye and took another ten pictures. It was as if she couldn't help herself.

I shouted, "Hey! Stop taking pictures! Now!"

She stopped, said, "Okay." She stood there. "Okay." She just stared at the ground with the camera in her hand. Molly was still barking. Every time Molly barked, Ellie's hand twitched, as if she were about to put the camera up to her eye again.

All the dogs were staring at me, wondering what to do. I praised them in a high, silly voice, and they all went back to playing. I called Molly, and she came running. When she arrived, I praised her and threw a tennis ball for her to chase. She went after it, followed by Frankie and Hooch. Ellie, meanwhile, was trying to put the camera back in her bag, her hands trembling.

This was too much. I wondered what kind of games God or evolution had been playing with the human race to give us someone like Jervis, with no energy at all, and Ellie, with way too much of it. Hasn't anybody in charge ever heard of proportionality?

I said to Otis, "Where did you find her?"

"I went down to the crime scene after you called. I gave her fifty bucks to come up here and shoot the dog. Sorry. I didn't mean she'd actually shoot the dog. Anyway, if you think *this* was bad, you should've been in the car on the ride up."

"So who the hell *is* she?"

"She was a paparazzo, working the hotels on Central Park South, had a nervous breakdown and came up here to recuperate."

"And to inflict herself on the rest of us?"

"I guess." He gave me an earnest look. "How about one last shot of Molly digging up something?"

"Oh, you've got to be kidding."

"Come on, that's how she found the body . . ."

"Yeah, but I don't have any skeletons on the property."

Ellie was coming toward us, waving. "I got some really good shots!" She was grinning, waving her camera, which she'd been unable to stuff in her bag. "Good stuff, really good stuff!"

"Fine," I said to Otis, thinking it couldn't hurt Molly to download some of her energy. "There's a couple of sand pits in the play yard. But I'll take the damn pictures myself."

I borrowed Ellie's camera—while she sat in the car, her energy spent now—and got some great shots of Molly digging furiously at the sand pit in the far left corner of the play yard. It actually felt good to see her having so much fun.

After Otis left, I got the dogs settled back inside their kennels, and as I was taking Frankie and Hooch up to the kitchen, I noticed most of the clouds had disappeared, and that the few that were left had taken on a rosy color. I realized there was something important I had to do back at General MacLeary's house.

I got in the Suburban and drove there as fast as I could.

The crowd had gotten bigger in my absence, though with the waning light and the lack of access to the scene, many of the reporters and photographers were starting to head home to dinner, or whatever they head home to.

I nodded to a deputy on crowd control, then ducked under the yellow tape and crossed to MacLeary's yard.

Jamie was crouching next to a canvas tarp where a number of bones, including the skull and a pair of hand, arm, and shoulder bones, were laid out. A woman I assumed to be the anthropologist was knee-deep, digging carefully in Molly's hole.

Jamie smiled to see me, brushed her hair out of her eyes with the back of a gloved hand, and said, "So did you come all this way just to find out how we're doing?"

"No," I said. "It's almost sunset, and someone's got to take down the general's flag."

"Oh. That's so thoughtful. I'll come with you."

"Good," I said. "I'll probably need you to help me fold it afterward."

"Okay, if you'll show me how." She stood up and brushed the dirt off her knees. "Hey, we've got the COD."

"No kidding. Already?"

"Yep." She took her gloves off and we walked to the back of the house. "The poor woman was shot in the back of the head with a .22. The bullet was still inside the skull."

"Odd," I said. "It sounds like it could either be a mob hit or the work of a professional assassin."

"That's what one of the cops said. Ballistics is going to run what's left of the slug through IBIS."

"They probably won't find a match." I explained why hit men and assassins like using .22s: they're cheap, they're easy to conceal, they don't make a lot of noise, you can muffle them easily with a makeshift silencer made from a plastic soda bottle filled with cotton, and you can easily ditch them afterward.

"Yes, the detective I spoke to said the same thing. Or part of it; he didn't say anything about any soda bottles. They're going to run the slug anyway. Did you get any ideas or leads from Reggie?"

"No," I said, then told her about our brief conversation.

"Well, hopefully, something will turn up."

"After twenty years?" I scoffed. "I wouldn't count on it."

Something did turn up, though. The next day, in fact. But I didn't know it was related at the time.

4

Sunday morning was bright and cold. Jamie'd had a long night, poring over old bones, so I got out of bed quietly, went downstairs, made some slow-cooked oatmeal with blueberries and walnuts, and some coffee, making sure to leave plenty for her.

After breakfast I got the dogs fed and exercised, then decided to wash and detail my cars: a midnight blue Suburban—five years old—and a 1938 Ford station wagon—cream paint with oak and mahogany trim, the kind of ride known to surfers as a "woody."

That's when I found a roach in the ashtray of the Suburban. At first I just stared at it, not sure if it was real. Then after the truth, and the distinctive odor, hit me, I began to turn over the possibilities in my mind.

I was pretty sure it wasn't Leon's. Yes, I'd let him use the car the night before to go to a dance at Camden Hills Regional High. But he's been violently antidrug since the night his family was killed by drug dealers. There was no way, I thought, that he would've been the one to smoke that joint.

So how did the damn thing end up inside my car?

Another possibility presented itself: my kennel manager Farrell Woods used to deal marijuana. He'd been a handler with the K–9 corps during Vietnam and was great with dogs. He had his own pack of ten beagles, and from the moment we first met he'd been bugging me to give him a job at the kennel, which I wouldn't do; not until he agreed to stop dealing *and* smoking grass.

He was also in love with a math professor named Amy Beckwith (a.k.a. Tulips), who had her own drug problem. He got her into treatment and stopped selling and using grass, which is when I'd finally hired him. But here's the real kicker: he drives the Suburban on a daily basis, doing pickups and drop-offs for dogs who come to the kennel for day care. So if he'd picked up old habits, he could've easily left the offending object behind.

Unfortunately, Leon and Magee were still asleep, and Farrell had the weekend off. So neither of my two main suspects was available for questioning. And even though Leon had been the last one to use the car, I didn't want to wake him up and confront him with what I'd found until I talked to Farrell first.

"Great," I said to Frankie and Hooch as I scooted out of the Suburban, holding the joint between my thumb and forefinger. "And to think I left New York to get *away* from drugs and crime."

The dogs looked up from where they lay among the narrow yellow willow leaves. Frankie, who was lying with his front legs straight out in front and his head erect, gazed at me and wagged his tail. Hooch, who was lying on his side, lifted his head slightly then dropped it again as if it weighed a ton.

Good, I thought, holding the joint away from my body, I can still laugh at Hooch's antics; my day isn't entirely ruined.

I whistled the dogs up to the house. They followed me into the kitchen, where I put the roach in a Baggie, put the Baggie in the trash, then called Farrell Woods.

He said he wouldn't lie; he'd started again, but not all the time, only once or twice, at home after the dogs were asleep.

"That's okay," I said sarcastically. "Unless one of them suddenly starts throwing up blood in the middle of the night and you have to drive them to the vet while you're wasted . . ."

"Oh, I see. So it's all right to have a nightcap or two but not to smoke weed."

This started a debate about grass versus booze, which ended, I thought, by me saying, "Okay, so maybe I have a glass of scotch before bed once in a while, but I never get stoned."

He saw my point then swore again that he hadn't left the doobie in my car. "Could I come take a look at it?" he asked.

"Sure, I guess so," I said. "Why?"

"Maybe I could figure out where it came from."

"Okay, fine. And bring the super group for a play."

He arrived an hour later in his blue '75 Bronco pickup, with a tan camper shell on the back. He had someone with him. They got out and I saw it was Tulips, a slim, pretty Eurasian girl who's not only a professor, but a great singer too. In fact, she sang at my wedding. It had been a while since we talked, and I could feel my face break into a smile to see her.

She shyly smiled back.

Her black hair was pulled into a bun and she was clad in jeans, a red turtleneck, and a conservative brown leather jacket with notched lapels. Woods was dressed in his usual jeans, flack jacket, and Boston Red Sox cap (to hide that he's bald).

He said something in her ear. She pulled away with an annoyed look. He shrugged then went around to open the tailgate.

Tulips and I said our hellos and how-was-the-honeymoons, etc., while Frankie and Hooch came over, wagging their tails.

"I've run into a snag on that computer program," she told me, putting the back of her hand out for the dogs to sniff.

Before she could finish telling me about it, Farrell's ten beagles swarmed out of the camper and raced, baying loudly, toward the play yard. Frankie and Hooch followed after them, barking and leaping around.

Tulips and I laughed at the sight, then Farrell rejoined us and we walked down to the gate and I let the dogs in for a play.

Most of Farrell's dogs are named after his favorite musicians, which is why I refer to them as "the super group." They're Lucy (she came with the name), Grace, Janis, Petey (named after Peter Green, a founding member of Fleetwood Mac), Wampus (another mystery), Maggie (named for the Rod Stewart song), Jimmie Rodgers, Smokey Robinson, B.B. King, and Townes Van Zandt.

One of the dogs—I think it was Smokey Robinson—was barking at Farrell, or if not him personally, at one of his pockets. Farrell produced a scuffed baseball from the pocket, held it firmly in his left hand, did a wind-up like a pitcher—which caused Smokey Robinson to back away while staring, laserlike, at his pitching arm. Then Farrell threw a hard, low fastball past Smokey Robinson's nose, and the dog went racing after it.

While they were playing fetch I asked Tulips what the snag was with the computer program she was working on for me. It's a kind of Sims-style thing, only it involves developing software to prove, mathematically, that a wolf pack is a bottom-up, self-emergent system, not a top-down hierarchy.

"Oh," she said, "well I've noticed that when the virtual wolves are at the den—before they go hunting—they sometimes act like the captive wolves did in those outdated studies."

"You mean they exhibit dominant and submissive behaviors?"

"A little bit. I mean, you were absolutely right. Once they start hunting, there's none of that; they're in synch." She smiled broadly. "I haven't got it totally down yet, but I'm starting to see these beautiful patterns start to emerge."

"That's great."

"Yeah, but I don't get why they're exhibiting this kind of dominant and submissive behavior when they're not hunting."

"Maybe that's *why*."

"What is?"

"They're not hunting. There may be an emotional resistance to it, especially hunting large prey. It's kind of dangerous, after all. Maybe the tension has to build to a certain level before they'll leave the safety of the den and go do it."

She broke into a big grin. "Of course," she said, beaming, "they have to reach the tipping point." She looked down the hill toward a brake of aspens on the neighbor's property. But she wasn't looking at the scenery; she was seeing something in her mind. "I see exactly how those dominant and submissive behaviors aren't what they seem to be at all—they're actually a template for the hunt. I can see similarities in the patterns."

"Cool. I can't wait for you to show me what it looks like." I looked over at Farrell, who was rubbing the baseball. I told him, "Hey, you've got pretty good form for an old war vet."

He laughed. "I actually thought I was going to have a career in the majors at one point, back in college."

"What happened?"

"You mean besides Vietnam?" He rubbed his left shoulder. "I had a hanging curve. I just couldn't get it to snap."

I nodded. "That's funny. My dad had the same problem. He was a southpaw too."

"Really? He was a pitcher?"

"He wanted to be, when he was younger." I watched the dogs a bit. Smokey Robinson was racing around the pea gravel, holding the baseball in his mouth and teasing some of the others with it. "You think they'll be okay by themselves for a minute?"

"Sure," Farrell said. "Why?"

I said that I wanted to have him look at the roach, as he'd suggested. I asked Tulips if she wanted to come but she said she'd rather stay and watch the dogs. She wanted to see if she could detect patterns in the chaos.

So I took Farrell up to the kitchen, got the Baggie out of the trash and gave it to him. He examined it, sniffed it, opened the paper, and spread the ashes on the counter.

"Well," he said, holding the rolling paper with his right hand and pushing the ashes with his left forefinger, "this isn't just grass, it's chronic, meaning it's got crack cocaine mixed in. And the only person who sells this shit is Eddie Cole."

"You mean Eddie Cole is back in business?"

"It sure looks like it."

"Jesus," I said. "It was bad enough when he was making threats about killing Jamie, and then he kidnapped her . . ."

"You saved Tulips's life that night."

"Yeah. How's she doing?"

"She's okay. I've been going to meetings with her. We've got one in an hour in Rockland. The thing is, though . . ."

"What?"

He shrugged. "I think she's been messin' around with this professor friend of hers."

"The one who played piano at our wedding?"

"Yeah, but he's married. And I think he's leading her on."

Yeah, and you're jealous, I wanted to point out, but said, "I'm curious. I never asked Tulips about this, but . . ."

"What?"

"Well, I don't know, it never made sense to me that she would get herself addicted to heroin."

"Why not?"

"Well, for one thing, she was raised by a middle-class family in suburban Washington State."

"Yeah? So was Curt Cobain."

"Okay, yeah, but he was a rock singer. And Amy's got two Ph.D.'s, one in math and the other—"

"—in computer science, I know. But so what? Just because she grew up with a white-bread family you think that makes her immune? Besides, her birth mother was a Vietnamese hooker, remember? She was probably addicted to heroin while she was in the womb and had her first withdrawal the day she was born."

"God, that's awful."

"Yeah." He gave me a long look. "And I'm not jealous of this jerk of a professor, if that's what you were thinking. But he's got a wife, and I don't want Tulips getting hurt is all."

"Yeah, okay. Hey," I changed the subject, "let's go back down to the play yard and see how the dogs are doing."

As we left the house I filled him in on the honeymoon in Mexico, and meeting Reggie Durban, and how she'd tried to hire me to train her father's dog.

"You mean General MacLeary? The one who lives in Camden?"

"That's the guy. You've heard of him?"

"Oh, hell yeah."

He told me that when Lamar MacLeary was just a fresh-faced, twenty-two-year-old lieutenant, he'd been the only officer in Patton's Third Army to get away with disobeying a direct order from the hot-tempered general. Patton's directive had something to do with leaving a bridge to the Nazis and putting MacLeary's entire platoon out in the open, which he stoutly refused to do.

Patton vowed to have MacLeary court-martialed once the battle was over but was talked out of it by Omar Bradley. It turned out that young Lieutenant MacLeary and his brave group of men held the bridge for three days with no provisions, and no support from the air or from the artillery.

That bridge, and that small unit of men, turned out to be instrumental in winning the entire Battle of the Bulge.

"So, MacLeary was quite a young upstart, huh?"

Woods laughed and said, "I knew you'd relate to that."

We passed Tulips, who was walking toward the truck. "I want to make notes," she said. "There's a pen and pad in the car."

We went on down the hill and I said, "I see why you like her. She's smart *and* pretty."

"She reminds you of Jamie, huh?" he asked.

"Yep."

We got to the gate, and he told me that MacLeary had been severely reprimanded for his insubordination and put on report, but when Patton died suddenly, he was promoted and eventually worked his way up the ladder to three-star general, and had even been on a short list for the Joint Chiefs after Vietnam.

I remembered something that Reggie had told us in Mexico. I said, "This Reggie woman said the general hadn't spoken to his son—Cord, I think his name was—since the Reagan administration."

"Yeah, Cordell MacLeary was a big anti-Reagan activist. I know him, sort of. He used to . . . well, never mind."

I laughed. "I get it. You used to be his dealer."

He said nothing.

Then Tulips came back with a steno pad and a pen.

"Can I observe them from inside?" she asked.

"Yeah, but your being there will change their behavior."

She gave me a look. "Yeah, I know. But I think I've already figured out how to factor that in."

I smiled, let her in, and she went down to the middle of the space and stood alternately watching the dogs and scribbling.

"She really *is* like Jamie," I said, then the conversation turned back to Eddie Cole and how he'd been arrested, not only for kidnapping Jamie, but for raping and almost beating Tulips to death. But he'd escaped from jail and disappeared.

"I don't know if I ever told you this," I said, leaning on the fence rail, "but last summer I could've sworn I saw him outside the courthouse in Portland, getting into a limousine."

"Huh. Maybe the Koreans are backing him."

"Why would you say that?"

"The leaves in that joint were grown hydroponically. That means they probably came from one of the houses in Portland run by one of the Korean gangs. They might run around in limos."

"And you can tell that just by looking at the ashes?"

He shrugged. "Except for these beagles, marijuana used to be my whole life. But I always got my supply from people who were only selling me their crop so they could stay offa welfare."

"Yeah, you were a real working-class hero."

"Hey, some people saw it that way. Some still do."

I regretted my sarcasm, remembering that Woods had also supplied cancer patients, including my late friend and attorney Jill Krempetz, with the drug, free of charge. I can't say I admired him for it, but I had to admit he wasn't in the same dirtbag category as Eddie Cole.

"So," he changed the subject, "didn't you tell me once that your old man served in the army?"

"The navy. He fought in Korea." Then I explained that meeting the general had made me realize what little contact I had with members of the armed services.

He nodded. "Just guys like me and your dad that the military swallowed up, used, and spit out, huh?"

"I guess so." I suddenly realized something I'd never known about my father. I'd hated him in some ways, his drinking, his fooling around with barmaids, his fits of anger. I now realized, though, that some of it wasn't his fault; he'd been through something in Korea that the army had never prepared him for.

I said to Woods, "They teach you to shoot, but they don't train you how to deal with the emotional part of war, do they?"

"They try. But nothing can prepare you for what it's like when the bullets start flying, or you're walking through a mine field and your best buddy screams when his leg gets blown off."

"Or when the enemy kills your dog," I suggested.

A sudden well of tears rose in his eyes. "Yeah," was all he could say as he remembered the story of how his mine-sniffing German shepherd Champ was shot by a Viet Cong sniper forty years earlier. Forty years and the tears still come that quickly.

We watched the dogs awhile and I studied Farrell while he gazed at Tulips. I saw such longing in his eyes, while she just watched the dogs and scribbled in her notebook.

I wanted to tell him to give it up, to say, "She's never going to love you back," but I knew it wouldn't do any good.

I thought about the dynamic between them. Unfortunately for Farrell, he was the "nice guy," which from where I stood wasn't what Tulips wanted. Yes, he was a little rough around the edges, but that didn't make him the bad boy type she was attracted to.

I thought about her and that married professor. And while it was a recipe for disaster in some ways, it might be good for her. She could flirt with danger without going completely off the deep end and losing her battle with addiction. She could twist in the wind of all kinds of negative emotions, shame, guilt, longing, anger, the whole gamut of love's worst side. It wasn't healthy but it was a lot safer than putting a needle in your arm.

I thought how lucky I was to have Jamie, and how I'd been neglecting to let her know how I felt since we got back from Mexico. I wondered if she saw me as the bad boy or the nice guy. (It's always easier to see someone else's dynamic than your own.)

My musings were interrupted when Farrell asked: "So what does watching dogs running around have to do with this computer program she's developing about wolves?"

"Huh? Oh, she's looking for any similarities between how dogs play and wolves hunt. You see that?" One of the beagles was doing a play bow. "He's trying to start a game of chase. A wolf will do something similar to make a prey animal run."

"Huh. That's interesting. But is it really important?"

"I think so." I explained that some experts believe that even though dogs are descended from wolves and have many of the same instincts, impulses, and reflexes, they don't think wolf behavior has any relevance to dog training. "In fact," I said, "they like to say that learning from wolves about how to interact with dogs makes about as much sense as trying to learn parenting from a chimp."

"Well, I can kinda see their point . . ."

"Except that humans and chimps aren't the same species; dogs and wolves *are*. And dog training involves interspecies communication, which parenting doesn't. Plus, if a trainer doesn't understand why wolves have social instincts, how can he understand what makes dogs want to be social, not to mention learn and obey?"

"You're right, that *is* relevant. So, let me ask you something: do you think Leon smoked that joint in your car?"

"I doubt it, but I'll bet you one of his friends did."

A light went on in his eyes. "Hey," he said excitedly (or as excited as he gets), "do you remember the time you almost tore me a new one, accusin' me of sellin' my stuff to high school kids?"

"Yeah. And you said you'd never do that."

"Right. But it turned out that there was this college kid, Brent Pfleger, who was buying from me and selling it to his little brother Kurt. And he goes to Camden Hills High."

"You think that's where this came from?"

He shrugged. "Who knows? But this guy Brent was always asking questions about where to get ecstasy and shit like that."

"And Eddie Cole deals ecstasy?"

"Yeah, and Oxy and H and Vitamin K." He scratched his beard, thinking it over. "Look," he said finally, "I ain't no nark, but if you want my help finding Eddie Cole, let me know. If nothing else, I'd like to nail him for what he did to Tulips."

"All right, but be careful. If Eddie Cole's got someone backing him, it may not just be the Koreans. It could be somebody inside the criminal justice system."

"That little creep? I hardly think so."

I reminded him that Cole had been blackmailing Judge Merton, a state superior court judge, which Jamie and I had uncovered when we worked on the Marti MacKenzie case. "It fits his M.O.," I said. "Plus, it's the only thing that explains how he's been able to stay out of jail for so long. So be careful."

"Didn't you know?" he said. "I'm *always* careful."

He waved at Tulips, then pointed to his watch. She nodded, closed her notebook, and came up to the gate. Farrell gave a whistle. The beagles stopped playing and came running. Tulips was suddenly up to her knees in beagle tails; they were all wagging like metronomes, each set at a different tempo.

I asked her, "Did you get what you wanted?"

"Not totally. I wish I had slow-motion vision."

I said, "Maybe one of your students would volunteer to come videotape them. Then you could review the tape in slo-mo. Why are you looking at me like that?"

"No one uses videotape anymore, Jack. It's all digital." She touched my arm. "But that's a good idea."

Farrell opened the door for her and said, "You know, she's got kids lining up to work on the project with her."

"Nobody's lined up," she said, annoyed.

"That's great," I said to her. "Let me know if you want to tape them—or whatever you call it." She said she would.

Farrell said, "Beagles, ten-hut!" and the dogs all sat in formation, in a near perfect line. Townes Van Zandt almost lifted one front paw, like a good soldier trying to salute.

As they drove away I had a minor epiphany. It started with a thought about how some alpha theorists believe there are as many as three to five alpha wolves during the hunt, which makes no sense; alpha means first, so how can there be more than one?

Then I thought about Farrell's beagles and how in some ways a canine pack is like a platoon of soldiers, except that wolves will follow a certain pack member because he's best suited for a particular task at a given moment, not because he's the sergeant and they're all privates. (The main reason they followed Farrell just now was because he was the one with the car keys.)

Then I recalled the five-step sequence that all predators go through: the search, the eye-stalk, the chase, the grab-bite, and the kill-bite. And even though a dog's prey drive has been modified over the years to suit various tasks humans have wanted them to do, all five steps are still encoded into their DNA.

So why isn't there at least one alpha wolf who leads the pack through these five steps whenever they hunt?

Because each wolf has a different approach to prey, based on his own individual temperament. As the hunt progresses, one wolf might be in closer proximity to the prey, or more in synch with its movements, or better able to anticipate what it's going to do. There will always be at least one wolf during each part of the hunt who will have the magic ticket for killing that prey animal at that time; he'll be the one with the car keys. As a result, the others will become galvanized to him. This gives the impression that they're following his every move, and to a certain extent they are. But it has nothing to do with his superior rank; it has to do with his superior skills and access to prey.

Then, if there's a change in terrain, or the "first alpha" gets tired or the prey does, a *new* wolf may be best suited for the next gambit. The rest of the pack will be galvanized to *him*. This explains perfectly why alpha theorists believe there's more than one alpha during the hunt, but the truth is, no wolf ever leads the hunt; the prey does.

As I walked up to the driveway to finish detailing the cars, I made a mental note to tell Tulips this. I also made a silent prayer that she'd stay alive long enough for me to do so.

5

Half an hour later I was crouched in front of the woody, polishing the chrome on the front bumper, when Leon appeared bleary-eyed and yawning, with Magee in tow.

"Aren't you going to have some breakfast?" I asked as they headed past me toward the play yard. "It's almost ten."

"Nah, I'm cool. I had a candy bar."

"Well, that's not breakfast. And we need to have a talk. So take Magee up to the kitchen, have some oatmeal, and I'll be there in five minutes." An errant breeze brought me a quick whiff of the rag I'd been using to polish the bumper. "God, don't you love the smell of chrome polish on an October morning?"

He looked at me like I was crazy, then said, "What do we gotta talk about?"

"Kurt Pfleger. You let him smoke dope inside my car."

He tried to look casual but couldn't pull it off. "Okay, first off, I didn't know that's what he was gonna do. When I *did* find out what he did, I bitched him out good. And, second, how the hell did you know about it?"

"I used to be a detective, remember? And watch your tone with me, Leon. We'll talk about it over breakfast. Now, go!"

That evening Jamie and I went to a movie in Rockland. She needed a diversion to take her mind off the skeletal remains in her morgue. I thought it was a good idea, and suggested we also refrain from talking about the case. She agreed.

Since it was late October, Hollywood wasn't putting out their best product. And since I wasn't in the mood for mindless crap left over from summer, I picked a movie with Steve Zahn in it.

On the drive down Jamie said, "Why does our movie have to have Steve Zahn? And, now that I think of it, who's Steve Zahn?"

"Just an actor almost nobody's heard of, but he somehow always makes any bad movie he's in less bad."

"But why not just go to a *good* movie?"

"I'd love to but there aren't any playing right now."

"You're impossible."

The movie *was* bad, but Steve Zahn was fun to watch. Even Jamie agreed that he made the film better. Afterward we stopped in at a nearby pizza joint, and shortly after we sat down to eat our slices, I looked over her shoulder and said, "Uh-oh."

"Uh-oh, what?"

"Look behind you."

She did and saw her two best friends, whom we refer to as Eve Arden, waving at us through the glass. They'd been her maids of honor. (She couldn't decide who to ask, so she had them both do it, which was fine with them; they do everything together.)

While Jamie waved them inside I said, "They look different."

"That's because Ardyth dyed her hair red."

"Good. I'll finally be able to tell her apart from Evelyn." She kicked me under the table. "Hey, you've known them your whole life; can I help it if—"

The girls appeared—poof!—at our table, and I said, "Hello, Evelyn," to the blonde, and "Hello, Ardyth," to the redheaded one. They were shocked—it was the first time I'd ever called either of them by name—then said, "Hello, Jack," in unison.

"We didn't want to intrude on the newlyweds," Evelyn chirped at Jamie, lying through her artificially whitened teeth.

"But we just had to say hello and find out about Mexico!"

So they bought some slices and Diet Cokes, and pulled up a couple of chairs to our table, sat down, and started a gabfest, with pepperoni and black olives. It didn't really involve me so

I went to the counter and bought another beer. When I came back, Jamie was telling them about the movie we'd just seen.

"Why'd you go see *that*?" said Evelyn, scrunching her face.

"I heard it isn't very good," said Ardyth, doing likewise.

"It wasn't," said Jamie. "But Jack wanted to see it because it had—" She turned to me. "What's that actor's name again?"

"Steve Zahn."

"Because it had Steve Zahn in it," she said to the girls.

Eve Arden looked at each other with blank faces, then shrugged at Jamie to indicate they'd never heard of him.

"Well, anyway," she said, "Jack was right. He's great."

They nodded as if they knew what she was talking about, then began asking about Mexico and what it was like to be back. They didn't ask about the murder. I strapped on a big smile, thanks in large part to the beer, and listened and nodded until the pizza was gone. (Don't get me wrong; I love female energy—I just prefer when it's relevant to my own.)

After they left I put the pizza crusts into a doggie bag.

"What are you doing?" Jamie asked.

"I was thinking of making a tomato soup with pepperoni, black olives, and mozzarella. These'll be croutons."

"Pizza soup? What happened to your lobster bisque or your French onion? You know, you're really turning into such a guy."

"What do you mean? I always *was* a guy. Or don't you think Leon would like soup with his favorite pizza ingredi—"

"Maybe. You were great with Eve Arden just now, I'm just worried that the next thing I know you'll be camped out on the sofa watching football and drinking a six-pack every weekend."

I chuckled at the thought. "I doubt that'll ever happen."

"So, how long did you ground him for?"

"Leon? A month."

"A whole month?"

"Honey, he let some friends of his smoke dope in my car."

"Who were they?"

I told her about Kurt Pfleger and his older brother. I didn't mention Brent by name, or his connection to Eddie Cole.

"But if Leon didn't know this kid was going to smoke the—"

"It doesn't matter. He has to learn that when he uses other people's things he has to take responsibility for what happens."

"I guess you're right." She looked at the pizza crusts. "Can't you just make your own pizza dough at home?"

"I can make any kind of dough. I just can't bake it."

"Oh, right. I forgot. You're afraid of the oven."

"I'm not afraid of it, I just—"

"I can bake them, if you want. I mean, next time,"

"You know how to bake?"

She shrugged. "Who's the greatest cook you know?"

"Your mother."

"So? The apple doesn't fall far—"

"Then how come I've been doing all the cooking?"

"Because you're a great cook and I'm always too busy. Besides, I don't enjoy it the way you and Mom do."

"I *do* like it; it relaxes me. Still, we could be making some things together. Enchiladas, frittatas, lasagna."

"That sounds nice. But I'm still worried about your posthoneymoon behavior. You know, you used to be this charming, wonderful man, and now you're turning into—I don't know how else to put it, but you're turning into a typical boring husband."

I laughed. "That's ridiculous. How?"

"Well, for one thing, you don't listen to me when I talk to you anymore. You're always tuning me out."

"Sorry, what did you just say? I wasn't listening."

She kicked me under the table. "I'm serious. I'm worried that this crazy pizza soup idea is just the tip of the iceberg."

I was about to say something like, "I think pizza soup is a *great* idea, and I'd probably listen more if you weren't always trying to im*prove* me, like making me go see General MacLeary," but realized she *was* right, and not just about how I'd been shutting her out. She'd also been right about MacLeary; I really liked the man. That didn't mean I *wasn't* right, at least partially, but being right isn't always the best solution to an argument.

"I'm sorry, honey," I said. "You're right. It's a process,

though; we need a little time to deepen into our relationship."

"I don't need any time to 'deepen' into it. Why do you?"

"I don't know, because things have changed, I guess. And though part of me is wonderfully happy about it, there's another part that's . . . I don't know, sitting at the top of a roller coaster. And I'm not sure if I'm ready to take the ride down."

"So I'm an amusement park ride to you?"

"Sort of. In a good way, yeah. But mainly it's just the whole prospect of marriage and family. It kind of scares me. Especially when you start acting like you need to improve me."

She looked hurt. "Is that how I've been acting?"

"A little," I said, holding her hand. "Though you were right about the general. I think meeting him was a good idea."

"Well, I'm glad you finally think so."

"I do. So have there been any developments on the case?"

"Not really. Well, one. They found a fingerprint on an empty shell casing that was still inside the pistol."

"What pistol? You mean they found the murder weapon?"

"Oh, that's right, I forgot to tell you. Yes, ballistics matched the slug I found inside the victim's skull to a military issue .22 target pistol from General MacLeary's gun case."

"Ah, no. That doesn't look good. Is it his gun?"

"Yeah. He's had it since World War Two. The good news is it isn't his fingerprint. They're still trying to find a match"

"Well, that's a relief. Is the AG's office still involved?"

"Just observing, or so they say. Plus, we've had a lot of FBI agents and even some army types from the Pentagon skulking around, looking over my shoulder, asking annoying questions."

"What have you told them?"

"I told them to wait for my final autopsy."

"Good girl." I thought of something.

"What are you thinking?"

"I don't know. Otis brought this photographer up to the kennel yesterday." I told her about the strange woman. "She was going on and on about how beautiful Maine is."

"Well, isn't it?"

"Yeah, it is. I just have this uneasy feeling that this case is going to expose some kind of dark, violent secret that's been hidden under that pretty surface for twenty years." I stopped, smiled sadly. "But I guess there's some kind of evil lurking almost anywhere you go. It's part of human nature."

"I'm a medical examiner," she said. "I know."

"So," I said, getting back to the case, "you've got the cause of death nailed, but have you been able to ID the victim?"

"Not yet. All of Katherine MacLeary's dental records were destroyed in a flood twenty years ago."

"That's interesting. This flood, was it before or after she supposedly ran off to Mexico?"

"I don't know. You think there might be a connection?"

I shrugged. "You never know anything until you have all the facts. Since you don't have access to her dental records, can you ID the victim just by looking at the bones?"

"If we could find some X rays, and authenticate them, then yes, they're as good as fingerprints. Meanwhile, there are a few general indications that she may be Katherine MacLeary. First there's the ring the general gave her, then there's the age of the bones, which is a match more or less, and then there's the fact that she'd given birth several times. But I have to run some more tests."

"Like what?"

"Mitochondrial DNA, for one."

"Yeah, but that's not much proof though, is it?"

"No, but if the MtDNA doesn't match her children's MtDNA, we'll know for certain that it *isn't* Mrs. MacLeary."

"Right," I said, "but if it *does* match, you won't know squat, except that it might be her, or it might be someone else who just happens to be related to her on her mother's side, right?"

"Yes, I guess you remember that from the Cady Clark case."

"Yep. That's one case I'll never forget."

"Me neither. And you're right, the trouble with MtDNA is that the genetic link might go back hundreds of years, meaning that the victim and Mrs. MacLeary's offspring might not be mother and daughter, or mother and son, they might be unrelated except for having some very distant maternal link."

I mulled a bit. "What about that thing where they stick Play-Doh to the skull and re-create the victim's face?"

"You mean modeling clay. Yes, we could have a forensic sculptor model a face on top of the skull, though that's usually only done in cases where there isn't any other ID. And it's no-where near as viable as the TV shows would have you believe. You can't get the exact shape of a person's nose or lips based on the characteristics of her skull. That's just impossible."

Out of the corner of my eye I noticed a woman at the next table staring intently at Jamie. I looked directly at her.

Caught, she said to Jamie, "You're Dr. Cutter, aren't you?"

Jamie admitted it.

The woman said, "I'm sorry I was eavesdropping, but I love this kind of thing. I just love all those forensics shows on TV. So they really can't create a person's face like they do on TV?"

"Not exactly, no," Jamie explained. "The most they can do is give you a general idea of their appearance."

"Because I love when they do that." She scooted her chair around to face us better. "How about the way they can re-create the person's whole face on a computer? Is that real?"

Jamie shot me an angry look, like it was my fault she had to talk to this person, then said, "Yes, computers can do the same thing the sculptor does with clay, but it's still only a guess, not an actual reproduction. And unfortunately, the ME's office doesn't have the kind of software that will allow us to do that."

"You could send it to the FBI, though."

"Send what?" Jamie asked.

"That lady's skull," the woman said, quite loudly. The other customers all turned to stare at us.

"Sorry—" Jamie got up, gave the woman an apologetic face, "we have to go. Sorry. This really isn't the right place to—"

"Hey," the woman said defensively, "you started it!"

"That's true. Our bad. We apologize."

"Don't apologize! Stay and tell me more."

"Sorry, I can't."

I was afraid the woman might follow us, but we made it safely outside, where Jamie took my arm and we began laughing.

It was damp and cold close to the harbor, and it was nice to feel her holding me and leaning into me like that. It also made

me want to take her home as quickly as possible and make up
for what she'd complained about earlier. I liked being her man
and I didn't want her to have any reason to want or need or look
for a replacement.

I put my arm around her, hugged her tight and said, "It seems
like you have a big fan back there."

"Yeah. Unfortunately, she's not the only one."

"Really?"

"Oh, yeah. I get letters and e-mails all the time from women
who want to do what I do, or who want to come watch an autopsy."

"That's kind of creepy, isn't it?"

"Tell me about it."

"Well, that one was *my* fault for not keeping our agreement."

"What agree— Oh, you mean not talking about the case tonight. Yes, it was your fault!" She gave me a love tap to the
kidney, a pretty hard one, then said, "So, since you're going to
be working on listening to me more, what do you think *I* should
be working on?"

I said, "You mean, this is a two-way street?"

"Yes, darling, quid pro quo. Just the way you like it."

She'd parked her car over on Limerock, so I had time to think
this over as we walked a ways through the almost pretty streets
of downtown Rockland. If you squinted, it almost became a
romantic town; it was practically Bangor or Skowhegan.

"Okay," I said finally, "how about you knocking off with hitting me all the time? Now that we're married, it's edging its way
into spousal abuse."

"Oh, it is *not*." She shoved me.

"See what I mean?"

"Like you can't take it?"

"Me? Yeah, I can. I'm just not sure my kidneys and spleen
can, though. So try to ease off a little, okay?"

"Okay, I'll work on it." We turned off Union to Limerock.
"Speaking of internal organs, the hospital's five minutes away."

"Why? You want to take my spleen in for a checkup?"

"No. I was thinking about General MacLeary."

I didn't get it. "You want to go visit him now?"

"Not *him*. I checked on his condition before we left for the movie. He's still in a coma."

"That sucks."

"I know. But Reggie and Connie might be there. I'm ready for bed, but maybe we should stop by anyway and say hello."

"I don't think so. I'm not that crazy about Reggie, and you know it. What's your real reason for wanting to . . . ?"

"Well, you're obviously thinking about the case. Maybe we should talk to Reggie and Connie and get some background information on their mother's disappearance."

"You mean her murder."

"We don't know for certain yet that the bones—"

"—belong to Mrs. MacLeary—okay, fine. Still," I said, mulling it over. "I don't know what good it would do to talk to her daughters. Besides, the FBI's involved, and the state's attorney general. You can't fight the wave, honey."

"What wave? This is a murder investigation, not a surfing competition."

"Yeah, one that's going to be taken over by the Feds soon."

"That never stopped you before."

"That was different. I was being framed for murder. Besides, this is a cold case, if it even *is* a case."

"What do you mean if it *is* a case? Whoever the victim was, she was buried in the man's yard with a bullet in her skull!"

"Okay, so someone shot this mystery woman—who's probably exactly who we all think she is—then buried her in the general's yard. I just don't feel comfortable about intruding on their family crisis right now. Couldn't it wait till tomorrow?"

We got to her car, a green Jaguar sedan.

"Tomorrow?" she said, clicking her key chain.

"Sure," I said, then got in my side. "You're tired and you want to go to bed. But you obviously think I should waste my time talking to Reggie and Connie, right?"

"Excellent deduction, Columbo," she said, starting the engine. "Though I don't think it'll be a waste of time. Oh, I almost forgot: there's a Halloween party at the crime lab on Friday night. Do you want us to go?"

"Do you?" I asked as we began the drive home.

"Yes. I think it would be fun."

I thought about it. "Do I have to dress up?"

"Of course," she laughed. "It's a Halloween party."

"All right," I griped. "Though I can never come up with a good costume."

"Just go as Steve Zahn."

"Right. Then how will anyone know who I'm supposed to be?"

"Exactly." She yawned. "And why wait to go to the hospital until tomorrow? Are you as tired as I am?"

"No, just a little tipsy from those beers. The thing is, tomorrow I can drop by after Frankie does his therapy session."

"Oh, right." She thought it over. "But you'd still be intruding then, wouldn't you?"

I shrugged. "Yeah, if I didn't have Frankie with me."

She had a puzzled look as she pulled into traffic, then her face lit up. "Of course. He'll break the ice for you."

"Yeah, now if we could only get him to break the *case* . . ."

6

Frankie was tired, relaxed, and happy as we got on the elevator after our visit to the pediatrics ward. Dogs tend to get like that after they've finished a day's work. Frankie knows that on Mondays his job is to visit the sick kids at Rockland Memorial and try to make them feel better emotionally, if not physically, although there's sometimes a surprising correlation between the two. Emotions carry energy. And in a peds ward, the energy can sometimes hang pretty heavy. Frankie doesn't like the way that feels so he does his level best to turn things around, to repolarize the room emotionally, if you will.

It's inherent in all dogs, in their most natural state, that when met with any new energy—positive or negative—they become more social; that's their hole card, their split-finger fastball, their Mona Lisa. Why else do you think human beings have put up with what some believe are essentially social parasites for tens of thousands of years? It's because dogs are engineered to soak up our negative emotions and turn them into pure, unadulterated happiness. That's their main purpose in life.

That and killing their toys.

So, you might be wondering, why wasn't Hooch with us? He's been a therapy dog almost as long as Frankie.

The thing is, Hooch is such a sweet doggie that it's easy to forget his past history. His original owners trained him with a stick, and I don't mean the kind you throw for him to chase; the kind that leaves a mark, at least on the dog's psyche if nowhere else. In other words, Hooch was abused.

Still, he's been so good and calm and patient for the past couple of years that I was puzzled and upset about his recent behavior: he started growling at the nurses whenever we came to visit the hospital, so I had to stop bringing him. I know this new behavior relates back to his previous abuse somehow but I don't know why it's surfaced now or how to fix it yet.

I was in the middle of my musings when the elevator door opened and Frankie and I got off and walked down the fluorescent-lit hall toward the ICU. As we got closer, more of the hospital smell we'd just left behind in the peds unit wafted our way. Did I ever tell how much I hate hospitals? That was another reason I'd quashed Jamie's idea the night before. If I had to come to Rockland Memorial anyway, why not kill two birds with one stone?

We followed a red line on the floor through a long hallway whose walls were painted a pale green with sea-green bumper guards, gurney high. We came around the corner as two nurses passed by. I heard the skinnier of the two say:

"I'm so in love with him."

"Who?" asked the other nurse.

"Ralph Fiennes." She pronounced it Ralph, not Rafe. "I'm telling you, that man does something to me."

I didn't stop to correct her pronunciation (or ask why she had the hots for Ralph Fiennes, of all people).

I came into the waiting room and saw a tableau of five figures, heads down, shoulders hunched. They were murmuring quietly next to the picture window that overlooks a nice view of the harbor. At least it usually does; today all you could see was a backdrop of silver fog. To the left was a wall with subdued artwork, meant to be relaxing, which it was; you had to wonder how the workmen put the stuff up without falling asleep. To the right was a set of double doors made of frosted glass.

Three of the figures, the ones whose body language exhibited the most distress, were in their fifties and looked to be related to one another. I recognized Reggie Durban and figured that the woman on her left, closer to the window, was her sister Connie.

The third figure was male, looked younger than the women, and except for a reddish-brown beard and longish gray-brown hair that curled over the collar of his shirt and blue Polo windbreaker, he bore a striking resemblance to General MacLeary. If I hadn't known better, I'd've thought him to be the prodigal/radical son, Cord. But since he had no interest in his father's health, maybe this was a cousin.

These three were facing two men I recognized as Camden cops, specifically Detectives Brad Bailey and Carl Staub. Bailey, mid-twenties, with wire-rims and unfortunate orange hair; Staub, early forties, with salt-and-pepper hair like me and what's-his-name, Clooney, the actor (him I could understand the nurse having a crush on). They were dressed casually; both their faces were grave and solemn.

Reggie saw me and Frankie, and her lost/angry green eyes softened, then crinkled in a kind of sad smile.

Bailey and Staub nodded at me as I approached. My first reaction on seeing them was that maybe the general had died or something, but on quick reflection I realized that if that were the case, the family wouldn't be talking to cops, but to doctors.

Reggie gestured toward the other woman, whom I now noticed had soft brown eyes that matched the wilting curves of her face and the crooked line of her weak, trembling mouth. Her pale countenance was framed by a braid of brownish-gold hair, going gray.

Reggie said, "Jack, I'd like you to meet my sister—"

"I can't take this," the sister said. "Excuse me." She reflexively put out her hand for Frankie to sniff, then pushed past us, with a quick pet of his head as she passed. "I have to go to the ladies'."

Reggie shrugged a resigned apology as Connie headed toward the double doors, then said, "Well, anyway, that was Connie."

"Yeah, I figured."

"And this is my brother Cord."

Cord stopped scratching his beard long enough to shake my hand and said, "Sorry about hanging up on you the other day." He looked down at Frankie. "Beautiful field setter."

"That's pretty good," I said, impressed. "Not many people can tell the difference between a field and a bench setter, let alone know what an English setter looks like at all."

He made a facial shrug. "When I was a kid, my father tried to indoctrinate me into the manly art of killing helpless animals for sport. The killing part didn't take but the dog part did. In fact most of us are big dog lovers. All except Reggie."

Bailey and Staub leaned forward, shook my hand and muttered some hellos and good-to-see-yous and the like.

"What's going on?" I asked once that was over. "I thought you would've been replaced by the feebs or the state cops."

"Not yet. So we've got to keep on top of things."

Reggie shot me a look and said, "They think my father killed my mother." She looked at the cops. "It's not possible."

"We don't know for sure yet that the victim *is* your mother."

"If course it's my mother. Who else would it be?"

"Okay, fine. The point is, we need to find out how you knew that the bullet found in the victim matches your father's gun."

I said, "Wait, the ballistics information was leaked?"

Bailey nodded. "It must've been," he said, then looked at Reggie. "How did you find out about it?"

She paused, then said, "Connie told me."

Bailey said, "Mrs. Coster knew about the ballistics report?"

"Yes," Reggie said defensively.

I asked, "How?"

"I don't know. She's married to the governor's son. You do the math."

"Ex-governor," Bailey said.

"Yes, fine, her husband's father is the ex-governor, but Ed Junior is also the current deputy state's attorney general."

"At any rate," Bailey said, "we're not arresting anybody at this point. We couldn't even if we wanted to. Not until he—"

Another nice touch: he stopped himself before mentioning the possibility of the general coming out of his coma so they could come grill him and maybe haul his ass off to jail.

"Can't you do something, Jack?" Reggie said.

"Me? Look, if the evidence is there . . ."

"But you have to help us prove that our father couldn't have done it."

Carl Staub said, "We haven't made any determination about that one way or the other, Mrs. Durban. We're just trying to get to the bottom of the situation."

Cord put a hand on her arm. "Reggie, let it be for now. There's nothing we can do anyway."

"What do you care?" She pulled away. "You don't care about Dad. You never did. Your only concern now is in how Mom's estate will be divided."

He shook his head sadly. "Your first statement is partly true, the second is totally ridiculous. If anyone cares more about how Mom and Dad's holdings are to be divided, it's you."

"Oh, hah!" she said, like a child.

"I mean, Christ, Reg, you could at least let the old man die first before you try to get your claws on—"

She lunged at him.

I had an urge to step in and take control, but there were two cops there already; let them do the work. I looked down at Frankie. He was wagging his tail, a normal nervous reaction in dogs. (Tail-wagging doesn't indicate friendliness—as is commonly thought—but is usually a way of offloading nervous tension.)

While Bailey and Carl Staub were settling the dispute between Reggie and her brother, my mind went to something that had been niggling at it.

I said to Reggie, "When we met in Baja, you said that your mother had left your father to move to Mexico. But if she's dead, then she never made it there, did she?"

"I guess not."

"So what made you think she had?"

"She wrote to me."

"Me too," said Cord.

Reggie explained, "Connie, my father, we all got letters."

"They came from Mexico?" I asked.

A light dawned in her eyes. "Oh . . ."

"Yeah, *oh*. Someone had to've written those letters, and if it wasn't your mother, then who was it?"

Bailey said, "We're going to need to see them."

"Of course," said Reggie.

Cord said, "I didn't keep mine."

"They were in her handwriting?" I asked.

"No," Reggie said. "Mine were typewritten. Though she did sign them at the bottom."

I looked at Cord.

He said, "I don't remember any of the details. Just that they came from Mexico."

I glanced at Bailey and Carl Staub.

"We'll need some handwriting samples to make a comparison," Bailey said to Reggie.

I said, "I'd like to see your father, if you don't mind."

Reggie twitched her shoulder slightly, a minor shrug. "Why? You can't talk to him in his condition."

"Yeah," I smiled, "but if I can get Frankie to nuzzle his hand or something . . ."

"You think that'll help him come out of his coma?"

"It couldn't hurt," I said. "Dogs *do* lower your blood pressure, you know. Besides, he may not be able to talk to *me*, but he can still listen. And I have a few things to tell him."

"What things?"

I said nothing.

She looked toward the double doors. "And where's Connie?"

Cord said, "She went to the ladies' room, remember?"

"There's no ladies' room in there."

Cord said, "That's Connie. She'll figure it out eventually." He turned to me. "I want to speak to the detectives in private. My sister can show you to Dad's room."

Reggie said, "What do you want to speak to them about?"

Cord said, "Never mind."

"Probably to make trouble for Edward." She said to me, "I still don't think you should bring the dog in with you."

Cord said, "My sister is not a big dog lover."

"Who's Edward?" I asked. "And why would Cord want to make trouble for him?"

"He's Connie's husband," Reggie said. "And Cord is always

looking to make trouble for anyone in the government." She led me toward the double doors. "And I'm only saying Dad's already got medicine for his blood pressure. He doesn't need a dog for that. Besides, dogs aren't allowed in the ICU, are they?"

"Frankie is. He's been here a lot. If you don't believe me, just ask Maureen."

"Who's she?"

"The head nurse. And as for your father not needing Frankie, I disagree," I said, as I held one door open for her. "If you ask me, dogs are the best medicine in the world."

"Well, nobody asked you, did they?"

7

While Cord talked to the cops, Reggie took me and Frankie into the ICU. There was a square nurse's station, decorated with paper pumpkins and mock-scary witches and ghosts and such; it sat in the middle of the space and was surrounded on all sides by serious-scary hospital rooms. She took me to the only room with its door closed, which I thought was a little strange—I mean that the door was closed. When she opened it and we went inside, I found something even stranger. Connie was standing next to her father's bed, holding a pillow firmly over the man's face.

"Connie!" Reggie said, flat-footed. "What are you doing?"

The situation called for action, not Q&A. I dropped Frankie's leash, sprang toward the bed and pulled Connie away.

She didn't resist. Almost tonelessly she said, "No, don't stop me. He's still breathing."

Reggie came over to check on her father. "God, Connie," she turned to her sister, "you could have killed him."

"I think that was the idea," I said.

"But he wouldn't stop breathing," Connie said, nodding.

"That's because he's got an oxygen tube in his nose," I told her. "Next time, try taking it out first."

"That's not funny," said Reggie.

"Sorry. Look, I think you'd better go get the detectives."

"Why?"

"Why? Your sister's obviously unstable, and she just committed a crime."

"What crime? She didn't do anything." She pointed to the heart monitor, which showed a normal, yet subdued, sinus pattern.

"Yeah, because I stopped her. Anyway, it doesn't matter; it's still attempted murder."

"Oh, baloney. She didn't really mean to kill him."

"Yes I *did*. I certainly *did*."

"Shut up, Connie. Let me handle this."

"But he murdered Mama, Reggie."

"Connie, you don't believe that."

"Yes I do. I have to. That's why I have to kill him."

"Connie, for god's sake—do you want to go to prison?"

"No," she whispered, her eyes wide. "That's why I have to kill him, Reggie. He's the one who should pay, not me."

"Then don't say another word. I mean it!"

I'd had enough of their routine. I would've gone to get the two detectives myself but didn't feel like leaving the general in the care of his two "loving" daughters, so I went to the bed and pulled the pulse-oximeter cup off the man's finger. Then, for good measure, I pulled a couple of the electrodes from his chest.

The monitor flat-lined and an alarm sounded.

"What'd you do that for?" asked Reggie.

"To get some people in the room. Preferably, sane people."

"Is he dead now?" asked Connie hopefully.

Just then a tall slender nurse came rushing in.

"False alarm," I told her. "I pulled his electrodes out."

"What the hell for?" she snapped, going immediately to hook the general back up to his monitors.

"No reason," I said. "His daughter just tried to suffocate him and I wanted to alert somebody without—"

"She did no such thing," said Reggie.

The nurse looked Connie over. She was still holding the pillow with both hands, as if ready to try it again. The nurse looked at me. "You couldn't press the emergency call button?"

"Like that would've worked."

"In an ICU, yes, someone would've come immediately."

"If you say so. But pulling the electrodes worked too, didn't it? And it's not like doing it put him in any danger."

"Well no, but—" Before she could say anything further, a doctor and two more nurses crowded up the room some more.

"Everyone out! Now!" the doctor said, racing toward the defibrillator paddles. "And what's that dog doing in here?"

"He's a therapy dog."

The first nurse said, "It's a false alarm, Doctor. The patient's electrodes just came loose." She got everything hooked back up, and the alarm went silent and the steady blip-blip of the general's sinus rhythm returned to the monitor screen.

The doctor said, "They just came loose?" then looked down disdainfully at Frankie, who wagged his tail.

"Don't blame *him*," I said. "I'm the one who did it."

The first nurse said, "I'm getting the police.

While she did that, I briefly explained the situation to the doctor. The room quickly became even more crowded. In short order there were three nurses, two doctors, the three MacLeary siblings, the two detectives, plus a dog trainer and his dog.

There were a few "She tried to kill the old man"s followed by "No, she didn't"s, "Yes, she did"s, and "She couldn't have"s, which were interrupted by a few "I certainly did too"s, followed by "Connie, shut up!"s, and the like, until Bailey finally said:

"Okay, that's enough!"

Everybody shut up and the room got still (though the doctor looked down at his watch).

"Obviously something happened here," Bailey went on. "What exactly, I don't know. However, we're not going to take Mrs. Coster into custody. Not yet. But we're going to have to have a word with her doctor, her husband, and her attorney. And we're going to have to investigate the charges made by Mr. Field."

All objections were shouted down and the room quickly emptied except for me, Frankie, and the slender nurse.

"No more funny business," she warned.

"Fine," I said. "And it's Rafe."

"What?"

"The actor you're so hot for? His name is pronounced Rafe, not Ralph."

"Really?" She thought it over. "Well, that's just stupid."

"Ain't it? And don't worry about me and Frankie. He's a therapy dog, and I'm a pussycat once you get to know me."

"That's not what *I* heard. And I'm leaving the door open."

"Fine with me. But could you do me a favor before you go?"

She gave me a look. "What?"

"Could you pull down one of the guardrails so Frankie can kind of nuzzle the general's hand a little?"

She gave me another look—this one had the hint of a warm smile attached—then she did as I'd asked. "Rafe, huh?" she said as she went to the door. "Where the heck does he get *that* from?"

I led Frankie to the bed, gently lifted the general's hand, and put it just as gently on top of the dog's head. He pressed against the old man's hand, then stood there, comforting him.

I pulled a chair up and said softly, "I just wanted to let you know that the other day, after you passed out? I came back, right at sunset, and took your flag down for you. So it wouldn't be flying in the dark. My wife helped me fold it. We tried to put it back in the cabinet, but it was locked, so we—"

"Funny," a voice said from behind me, "you didn't strike me as the Boy Scout type."

I turned to find Cord MacLeary standing in the doorway.

"Well, I *was* a Boy Scout," I said. "Though you're right in a way. It was a long time ago."

He came in, pulled up another chair and sat down. "So, you took down the old man's flag. How true-blue American of you."

"Screw you," I said. "It's important to him."

"That's true. So that makes it important to you, how?"

I nearly told him that he wouldn't understand, but realized I couldn't say that for sure. Maybe he *would* understand. So I said, "Let's just say that he and I share similar ideas on proper flag etiquette, and leave it at that. Besides, from what little I know about your father, I admire him for his courage."

"What courage?" He almost laughed.

"It took courage to stand up to Patton, didn't it?"

"Oh, that." He nodded. "Yeah, I used to admire him for

that. It wasn't until Vietnam that he began selling his soul, and his family, to the highest bidder." He laughed a sour laugh. "I hate to disillusion you, Mr. Field, but if you ask *me*, my father ended up being a traitor to what this country really stands for."

"Well," I said, "to quote your sister, 'Nobody asked you.'"

He shrugged, though he did it a little too casually for my taste. "Too bad, it might have a bearing on my mother's murder."

I scratched my ear. "You know who killed her?"

He shook his head. "I know it wasn't my father. He . . . he loved her far too much to even think of hurting her. I mean, he was totally devastated when she ran off." He stopped a moment. "Though I guess she didn't really run off after all, did she?"

"No, that seems pretty well established by now. And how do you know he wasn't just *acting* devastated?"

He laughed in surprise. "Dad?" He scoffed. "Another thing he could never do is hide his feelings about anything. He's like a dog that way. And it's one of the few qualities I still value in the old bastard. Why? Do you think he's guilty?"

"I don't think anything. It doesn't look good, though, that she was killed with his weapon. If I were still a cop, I would look at him for it. Was the gun case kept locked?"

"I assume so. My father has keys for almost everything."

I nodded, remembering how MacLeary had kept his flag in a locked cabinet. "Would anyone else have had a key to it?"

"That's doubtful. Dad might've given one to Jervis, but Jervis would have had no reason to kill Mom. Plus, he would've had to have been sober to aim and shoot a gun."

I nodded in agreement. "Why does your father . . . ?" I let the question go. It was none of my business.

"Why does he keep Jervis around?"

"Yeah. Why does he?"

"It goes back to an incident in Korea. Jervis was a British commando. The upshot is Jervis saved his life."

"I see. And your father is an extremely loyal kind of guy."

"To his own detriment sometimes, if you ask me."

"So, how loyal is Jervis? I would've thought he'd be here."

He tilted his head. "He's actually been here a lot. Or so Reggie tells me. I have no idea where he is now."

"Uh-huh," I said, wondering how far it was to the nearest tavern. "So, about your sister, what kind of meds is she on?"

He shrugged. "I don't know. It changes constantly. They can't seem to find the right combination." He stopped. "I assume you mean Connie?" I said I did. "Because if you ask me, Reggie should be on medication too . . . but who am I to talk?"

I nodded. "You mean because you like the herb?"

He gave me a sharp look. "Beg pardon?"

"Grass, marijuana, weed?"

"Yes, I caught the reference the first time. I was just wondering why the hell you'd make that assumption. You think I'm a liberal so therefore I must automatically smoke grass?"

"Relax."

"Because I'm not a liberal. Or a communist. Or—"

"Relax. I wasn't making any assumptions about you, or anyone else in your family—though it's a little hard not to."

"Then why did you ask about—"

"Farrell Woods works for me."

"Oh." He calmed down, then said bitterly, "He ought to know how to keep his mouth shut."

"Don't worry, he didn't say anything to me directly; I just inferred it. So, who do *you* think killed her?"

"My mother?" He sighed. "I couldn't say exactly. I'm still kind of in shock to find out she was murdered, and not still living in Mexico." He looked over at the general. "I do know that Dad was involved with some pretty powerful and potentially dangerous people around the time of her supposed disappearance. At the time, since we'd all been assuming she'd run off, it didn't occur to me that there might be a connection between—"

"What was he involved in?"

"Politics, business, a combination. The highlight of his career, after he left Washington, was his eight years as lieutenant governor under Ed Coster, Sr."

"Your sister Connie's father-in-law?"

"Yes. He was a navy pilot in World War Two, but unlike Dad, he left the military afterward. He served in the state senate for twelve years, ran for Congress and served there for another ten, and had his fingers in a number of pies after that. He headed the NRC for a while, worked with NASA, and was the deputy director of the CIA. Then he got involved with nuclear power in Maine, New Hampshire, and Massachusetts before he became governor. He was on a track to run for president until his administration was rocked by a sex scandal his last year in office."

"He must've been a little old for that kind of thing."

"It involved allegations of a love child he'd fathered years before. Nothing was ever proven, the woman he'd supposedly had the affair with ran off, but the damage had been done."

"He doesn't sound that powerful or dangerous."

"You'd be surprised." He gave me a sharp look. "What do you know about the Moose and Eagle Society?"

"Never heard of it. I've heard of the Moose and Squirrel Society, but I think they're just fans of Rocky and Bullwinkle."

"Cute." He looked me over. "I've heard about you, Field, and not just from Reggie. You've solved a couple of high profile cases in the past couple of years. Are you planning to get involved in the investigation into my mother's death?"

I looked at General MacLeary. Frankie was standing there, still nuzzling his hand. I made a careful examination of the old man's face; I thought that maybe, by seeing him in repose, I might catch some hidden clue as to his persona, his inner life, his secrets. All I saw was the face of a tired old man, a face marked with age spots, wrinkles, and the pallor of a coma.

"I never plan on being involved in *any* case," I grumped. "So, what can you tell me about your mother?"

A puzzled look: "Why not ask Reggie? My area is politics. She'd probably have more to tell you about Mom."

"Yeah, but she's a liar," I said simply, "and you're not."

"That's true," he laughed. "Although I'm surprised that you would've already figured that out."

"Yeah, I'm full of surprises."

"All right," he said, "I'll tell you anything I can. How much time do you have?"

8

I had three training sessions scheduled, but if I took Frankie along I could afford to spend a little more time picking Cord's brain. Besides, it would give the general more Frankie-time too, and from the looks of things, he could use it.

So I told Cord I had about half an hour, and he told me about his mother and father, their relationship and finances.

Katherine Chase MacLeary came from a family steeped in old money, political power, and the shady side of American history. She was, in fact, a great-great-grandniece (by marriage) of Rutherford B. Hayes, the only president in American history (unless you count recent events as "history") to lose the general election yet still win office via the electoral college. And Cord was named after FDR's secretary of state, Cordell Hull, who had married Rose Francis Whitney, another distant cousin.

Katherine's parents, Ernest Chase and Lavinia Proux. . .

"Okay," I interrupted, "I don't need to know *every*thing."

"Sorry."

At any rate, he went on, her parents were both educated at boarding schools in Europe in the early 1900s—her father in England, her mother in Switzerland—and would've raised Katherine in the same tradition were it not for two impediments: the Great Depression and the war clouds hanging over Europe in the 1930s. So they sent her to a girl's boarding school on the Vermont–New Hampshire border, which is where she met her future husband.

I said, "Don't tell me your father used to be a girl."

No, he told me, Lamar MacLeary had been a "townie," a local high school kid, often in trouble with the law.

"I'm starting to like your old man more and more."

"You're an ex-cop and you like the fact that he started life out as a hooligan?"

"Like I said, I'm full of surprises. Go on."

Well, from the moment he first laid eyes on Katherine Chase, the young Lamar MacLeary was totally smitten.

"How did he first lay eyes on her?"

Cord hesitated. "That was never spelled out very clearly when our parents told us their story. My theory? He and his buddies had probably been up to some sort of mischief on the boarding school grounds one evening and caught some of the girls by surprise. I remember my mother saying more than once that the first time she saw Dad she'd been 'terribly frightened of him.' That was one of the phrases she always used. The other was that she had 'screamed in terror at the very sight of him.'"

"And did your father have a favorite phrase?"

"He did. He used to say he'd never seen anything more beautiful in his life."

"This is beginning to sound like an old movie I saw once."

"Can I finish before you start with the sarcasm?"

"Look, I get the picture. They fell in love and got married despite her parents' objections and his lack of prospects."

"That's exactly what *didn't* happen," he said.

Lamar MacLeary and Katherine Chase didn't in fact get married over her parents' objections. She married someone else, a much older boy named Sam McCullough, whom her parents approved of, and whom she didn't love. The newlyweds settled near her parents' home in Camden, but it was a loveless, childless marriage. Then, when Hitler invaded Poland, Sam McCullough joined the Canadian Air Force, went to war, and was promptly killed in battle.

Young MacLeary didn't know any of this. He'd cleaned up his act, applied for admission at West Point, and was accepted. Pearl Harbor came during his junior year. "And the rest," Cord told me, "you already know."

"You mean about the thing with Patton?"

He told me that's what he'd meant.

After Hitler and Hiroshima came the cold war. MacLeary stayed in Germany and made a name for himself as a good officer and an up-and-comer. Even Ike knew him by name. A year or so passed, and in the late 1940s he was assigned to the embassy in Paris. And by a strange twist of fate, Katherine Chase McCullough happened to be visiting a cousin there.

"Don't tell me," I laughed. "They met at an embassy party?"

He nodded, his eyes twinkling. "At a masked ball, in fact."

"God, this has got MGM written all over it."

"Doesn't it?" Cord agreed. "My mother was masked, of course, though Dad wasn't. He was in uniform."

"Ah-hah. And she flirted and played coquettish games with him from behind her mask?"

"That she did. Or so the story goes."

"And he," I said, waxing poetic, "not knowing anything about how his rival Sam McCullough had died in battle years earlier, thought he'd lost her forever only to rediscover her that night as she flashed her eyes at him, riding high on champagne, dancing in his arms beneath the spinning chandeliers." I smiled. "You know, your parents' story really *would* make a great movie."

By the end of the night Lamar MacLeary knew he'd found her again, knew how she felt about him, and they fell truly, deeply, madly in love. They spent the next day sightseeing, taking a boat ride along the Seine, drinking wine at a sidewalk café, everything but the Eiffel Tower.

Why didn't they climb the—

It was closed for repairs.

Sadly, she had to return home the next day. By now, though, if there was ever any doubt in either of their minds that they belonged together, it was gone. They wrote to each other constantly over the next two years, he finagled some stateside passes to see her (they met in Maine, Washington, and New York). He was determined now to rise in status, to make good; and he did. He quickly doubled his lieutenant's bars to become captain, then traded those for a pair of gold oak-leaf clusters.

I asked, "Are their letters still around somewhere?"

"They might be. My father went through a few of the Kubler-Ross phases when my mother left. Or was killed, I should say. First he was in denial, then he got depressed, then he was violently angry. He might've thrown them out."

"It doesn't matter. I'm sure we'll find something in her handwriting to compare to those letters from Mexico." I thought about something. "If I remember correctly, Reggie made it sound as if she'd talked to your mother before her disappearance. She gave me the impression that your mother was unhappy at the time. And, if I recall correctly, she even said that your mother wanted to get as far away from your father as possible."

Cord nodded sadly. "I can't say for sure why my mother was unhappy with Dad back then—I have my theories about it—but it's true that she was thinking of leaving him."

"What are your theories?"

He mentioned his father's business and political associates again. "You have no idea how powerful these people are, Field. Or how dangerous they can be when crossed. She didn't like them. She and Dad had some knock-down, drag-out fights over it."

"There was actual violence?"

"No, of course not. Just a lot of yelling. She really wanted him to divorce himself from the society."

"Who, the moose and squirrel? They're just a couple of badly drawn though well-voiced cartoon characters, if you ask me."

"Sure, you can laugh now—"

"Look, if you're right about this secret society, I just don't see your mother's murder being their handiwork. Think about it: her bones are found in the side yard of your father's house? Buried, what, three feet deep at most? If these people had wanted her dead, her body would've never been found."

"Unless they wanted to frame Dad for it."

I laughed. "Twenty years in advance? Based on the very iffy proposition that your father would one day own a fox terrier who would dig a hole in the side yard? I don't think so."

I must've raised my voice because Frankie gave me a look and started wagging his tail.

Cord said, "So who do *you* think did it?"

"We had this discussion already." I went back to using my hospital voice. "I don't think *any*thing yet. I just know that this isn't the work of some powerful cabal of international mystery men intent on world domination."

"How can you be so sure?"

"Because this was a very sloppy murder. Shooting her in the back of the head with a .22, that may have been planned. But very little thought went into disposing the body. I think she was buried in your father's yard simply because it was the closest and most convenient spot to where she was killed."

He nodded and got a far-off look. "You may be right. There was a drainage problem on Dad's property at one time. I remember a fairly deep ditch running from the street to the harbor. I don't remember if it was there at the time Mom disappeared."

"Good, I'll have the police check into that. Now that's something that's really helpful, not this conspiracy crap."

He shook his head. "These people are manipulating world events! They have various factions all over the planet doing things designed to control the American people by making them angry, terrified, and ready to follow anyone who lies to them!"

I laughed. "And the moose and squirrel society are in on it? From right here, in little old Maine? Come on."

Frankie wagged his tail again.

"It's called the Moose and Eagle. And I have the proof."

"Yeah, I'm sure you do."

"Look, I have copies of the plans they made to blow up a hydroelectric dam back in the mid–1980s. I don't know if you remember, but there was a strong antinuke movement at the time. The society's theory was that if one of these old dams failed, more people would support nuclear power plants."

"I don't remember hearing about any dams failing."

"Obviously, they never went through with it."

"That's convenient."

"But just think of the mentality that would even think up such a thing, let alone come up with a detailed plan!"

"Yes, but even if what you're saying is true, I'm not interested, okay? And the reason, frankly, is that it doesn't help solve your mother's murder. Not unless you can show me a direct correlation between her death and this secret society."

"I'll see what I can find out for you." He stopped. "By the way, I think I know why you pegged Reggie as a liar; she *is*."

"I know. She even told me that your father hadn't spoken to you since the Reagan administration. It's obvious that you and your father don't see eye-to-eye, but I think you've been speaking to each other all these years."

"It's true, but how did you figure it out?"

"That's easy. How else would you have known about the problems with the drainage ditch, or your father's business dealings, or the Kubler-Rossian thing he went through?"

"That's true."

"You were keeping tabs on the old man. In fact, I think you care more about him than Reggie and Connie put together."

He looked surprised. "I hadn't thought about it that way, but you may be right. I feel like we're always at odds, Dad and I, but at least I try to engage him. Reggie runs away to Mexico or Bar Harbor. Connie just tried to kill him, for god's sakes."

"Yeah, that was odd. So, how would you describe the relationship each of you had with your mother?"

"You think one of us might've killed her?" I gave him a look. "I forgot. You don't think anything at this point." He thought a moment. "Well, Mom was always on Dad's side whenever I'd try to point out the inequities and injustices of America's terrorist activities. Like Nicaragua, that was U.S., state-sponsored terrorism if I've ever seen it."

"Okay, easy. We're talking about your relationship with—"

"—my mother. Yes, sorry. We loved each other, I guess. But she loved Dad more. With Connie, she was very protective. Too protective if you ask me. And nobody in the family, except Dad, could tolerate Reggie for very long."

"I know the feeling."

He explained a little further, and as he did I got a clearer picture of the MacLeary family dynamic. Connie, who was the oldest, was also the weakest. She made an easy target for Reggie's needs and desires. I had a picture in my mind of two dogs eating dinner. Reggie would be the one who always wolfed down her kibble first and then came racing over to her sister's bowl, intimidated her away from it, and finished what was left while Connie stood hungry and helpless, feebly wagging her tail. Cord was the younger male who had better things to do than get involved in their squabbles, but he was always bringing you his ball right when you wanted to take a nap or watch TV.

I said, "So what's all the dispute about your father's estate that got you and Connie going earlier?"

He shook his head. "Technically, my father hasn't much of an estate. My mother had. Quite a pile of millions, in fact. My father hasn't pressed any legal action over it."

"Like having her declared legally dead?"

"Exactly, since no one has heard from her, he could have easily done that. And Reggie has been bugging him about it relentlessly. But Dad was convinced that she was still alive and so he wouldn't touch her money."

We both looked over at the comatose man.

"I'm *really* starting to like your dad."

"It isn't as noble and romantic and self-sacrificing as it sounds. It's her family's money. And Dad hates her family. In fact, he hates them *because* of their money."

"That only makes me like him even more." I thought of something. "When your mother disappeared, was that out of character?"

"Yes, though Reggie thought she was having an affair."

"Based on what?"

"Her imagination. But she loved Mexico, Mom did. So when we all got those letters postmarked from there, well . . ."

"Did your *father* think she was having an affair?"

Cord nodded toward the general. "You'd have to ask him." He got up and went to the door. He turned. "I have another question: what did you mean by spinning chandeliers?"

"Huh? Oh, that. I was just thinking of the way a woman might waltz with her lover, her head on his shoulder, looking up at the ceiling, where from her viewpoint the chandeliers would seem to be spinning, especially if she were a little tipsy on love and champagne."

"I see. Very lyrical." He thought a moment, then said, "Last question: how did you know I wouldn't lie to you?"

"I just had a feeling. And you've proven me right; if you were capable of lying you'd have kept your mouth shut about these crazy conspiracy theories of yours."

"They're not crazy."

"See what I mean?"

He shook his head. "I'm telling you, if these people find me poking around, I could very well be their next victim."

That was his exit line, and it was a pretty good one. At least it *sounded* good. But he was wrong.

The next victim was someone totally unexpected.

9

The fog had lifted, replaced by ghost sunshine, that kind of semitransparent light you get while the atmosphere is still airing itself out. I got Frankie into the woody and we drove toward the exit of the hospital parking lot. As I did, a black Town Car nosed out of a nearby space and followed us.

I got to the exit, flipped on my right-turn signal, and waited for the traffic in the lane closest to me to thin out. I looked in the rearview and saw that the Lincoln had federal plates. It came too close behind too fast for me to get the number. Then I saw its right-turn indicator start to blink.

There was a lull in the traffic, but I waited until a few more cars were headed in my direction. As I did, the Town Car's horn got tapped, twice. I waited for the right moment then zipped in front of the approaching cars, straight to the other side of the street, and made a hard left, ignoring the horns dopplering behind me.

Frankie was thrown against the door and struggled to retain his balance. He righted himself and gave me a questioning look.

"Sorry, buddy," I said. "But like I told Farrell, you can't be too careful." I shook my head. "Or maybe Cord MacLeary spooked me with all that Moose and Eagle crap."

I looked in the rearview mirror and saw the Town Car, still idling at the exit, unable to follow me because of the traffic.

I quickly made the next right, and lost them, not knowing if they'd actually been following me in the first place.

* * *

Training sessions usually take my mind off thoughts of murder and being tailed, and that's mostly how the afternoon passed, though I did have the occasional question as to whether Mac-Leary had shot his wife, what exactly the Moose and Eagle Society was, and why Cord thought they might've been involved (and if they were the ones who'd sent the Town Car after me).

My first session was with Kimber, a rescued terrier mix, who had a mild case of separation anxiety—some light barking and a little destructive chewing. I gave her owner some exercises designed more to change her own neediness than Kimber's. I also taught her how to use fetch to teach Kimber to stay, particularly the "peekaboo stay," where the dog has to stay while you hide. When you release her, she gets to chase the ball.

The next session was with Dougie, a miniature black poodle who'd been to puppy class but hadn't retained much of anything; it's quite common for a pup who was the star of his puppy class to have a complete drop-off in learning by six months.

When I was finished with Dougie, I headed back toward Rockport to work with Buster, a chocolate Lab with aggression issues. We passed a dog park, and I was reminded that Buster's aggression started when another dog attacked him there one day. His owner, Abby Butler, was distraught. She couldn't take him there anymore, and she had to be vigilant when walking him because she could never tell which dog would trigger his aggression, though intact males were a good bet. To top it all off, she said, Buster seemed depressed. He wouldn't play anywhere except at home, and then only in spurts.

I was a little nervous about it, although it had nothing to do with Buster's propensity for attacking unneutered males. Abby is an attorney and had been assigned to defend a former Lewiston cop named Randall Corliss, who'd recently been put in jail on a blackmail and felony murder rap. I'd been partly responsible for his arrest and felt a little awkward about working with his attorney's dog.

Another thing is that Abby had hired a previous trainer, a young woman who'd apparently "studied dog training" at a strip mall in Belfast. She'd been unable to resolve Buster's issues, but Abby wanted her to attend our sessions anyway. I agreed, reluctantly, though now that I'd decided to bring Frankie along, I thought it might not be a bad idea to have this other trainer there to handle Frankie while I took control of Buster.

While I was thinking about this, a shiny black Town Car pulled past me on the left, then zipped by and sped off.

Government plates again, and this time I could read the number. I pulled off to the shoulder and wrote it down, then used my cell phone to call Sheriff Flynn.

"Got it," Flynn said, after he'd written it down. "You really think they were tailin' you?"

"Who knows?" I said. "But I want to find out who they are."

"Okay, I'll check into it."

I thanked him, then drove to Buster's house and got there a few minutes early, which made it a little before four. I pulled under a gorgeous oak that was still tantalizing the sky with its crimson leaves. Frankie lifted his head and looked around.

Just then a familiar-looking car—a Honda Civic with faded red paint—pulled up across the street, and a tall slender young woman with hair and eyes the color of wet sand got out. She reminded me of Sloan, a former kennel employee of mine. She finished locking her car, turned and crossed the street, and I realized it *was* Sloan.

She saw me looking at her and gave a half wave.

I left Frankie in the car and joined her on the front walk.

"So you're a dog trainer now?" I asked as we walked toward the house.

She shrugged. "Mostly I'm a dog *walker*," she said, "but I'm trying." There was a shy pause, then she asked, "How's Leon?"

Like you care? I wanted to ask. I just said, "Fine. And if you wanted to become a dog trainer, why not come study with me?"

"I don't know . . ." She sped ahead of me.

I caught up with her on the front steps. "What do you mean you don't know?"

"I don't know. I didn't think I could work with you."

"Why not? Because of what you did to Leon?"

She turned her head away from me and then said sadly, softly, almost imperceptibly, "I didn't do anything to him."

"You led him on, then you disappeared."

She had her hand out to ring the bell; it was trembling. "This was a mistake; I should go." She turned away. "Tell Ab—"

"Sure, run away," I said. "That's what you always—"

She turned on me, her face livid. She pointed a finger at me. It was steady as Lady Macbeth's dagger. "I'm smarter than you," she said with a kind of vindicating triumph.

I almost laughed, but stopped, not out of politeness, but because of the conviction in her voice.

"You're smarter than me? What does that—"

"I see things. I notice things."

"Okay . . ."

"Don't patronize me."

"Was I patronizing you?"

"Yes." She stepped back, looked down at her shoes. "You're always patronizing me." She looked back up, her eyes harder now.

"Sorry."

"The fact is—" She came at me again. "—I al*ready* studied dog training with you. I don't need to drive all the way up to—"

"How?"

"I have a perfect memory." Her eyes dared me to contradict her. I didn't. She nodded, taking this in, then went on. "I remember everything I ever heard you say about dogs, whether you were talking to me or I overheard you talking to someone else. I also remember everything I saw you do when you worked with a dog. I could tell you mistakes you made you're not even aware of."

"Like?" I was intrigued.

"Like Saki, the Akita. You were always letting her get away with all the stuff she pulled because you were in love with her. If you'd been working with the client, instead of the dog, you would have been all over them for letting her pull that stuff. I'm serious."

"No, I know." She had me pegged on that. "You're right. It took me a lot longer to train her than it would have if I'd—"

The front door opened and there stood Buster and Abby. Buster, a sturdy Lab, with a body that favored the English standard more than the American variety, looked up happily at Sloan with his gold-green eyes and wagged his tail. Sloan leaned over him, scruffed his ear, and he gave her a big kiss.

Abby, tallish, with curly red hair and searching brown eyes, beamed and said, brightly, "I thought I heard voices."

There was a quick introduction and handshake, etc. Then Sloan stood upright, straightened her coat and said, "I was just telling Jack I think you'll be better off if I don't partici—"

"Um," I interrupted, "we were just discussing strategy."

"Well, don't stand out *there* and do it, come on in!"

"I'd like to get started out here first," I said, "if you don't mind, while Buster is still excited about seeing Sloan."

"Okay," Abby said, curious. "What do you want to do?"

I explained that I'd brought Frankie along, that he was still inside the car, that he was unneutered, and that I'd like to take the two dogs for a walk together.

"No," Abby said nervously. "Buster *hates* intact males."

"I know. That's why I brought Frankie."

Abby protested some more, very worried about what might happen. I calmed her fears, then asked Sloan to leash Buster for me, which she did. I took his leash, then we all went out to the street. I stayed back a fair distance as Sloan opened the door to the woody, got Frankie leashed up, and let him jump out. Buster tensed up but he didn't growl or lunge.

Abby said something about how handsome Frankie was, though I barely heard her. I was on alert, plus I was praising Buster.

Frankie shook himself easily, very relaxed, then looked at Buster. The instant he made eye contact, Buster went nuts and lunged for Frankie with all eighty pounds of his Lab strength. I held him back—though it wasn't easy—and praised him some more. I was about to tell Sloan to do the same but she beat me to it.

"Why are you praising him?" Abby said, confused.

"You should always praise a dog who's feeling aggressive."

Abby said, "That doesn't make any sense."

"Yes, it does," said Sloan. "Good boy, Buster! The only reason praise works as a reward for good behavior is because it changes the dog's emotional state. It makes him feel happy."

"That's right," I said. "And since all behavior comes from emotion, when you change a dog's emotional state—"

"—you automatically change his behavior," Sloan said, finishing my little slogan for me.

I smiled at her. "You *have* been listening to me."

She gave me a "Well, duh!" look.

We continued walking the dogs together. Buster kept trying to "kill" Frankie. Frankie was a little on guard himself, but not enough to start barking or growling back; he just made sure not to make eye contact with Buster, and to keep what distance he could. Buster didn't care. He kept barking and trying to lunge.

Abby was tense, worried. She said, "I think you should stop praising him. It doesn't seem to be working."

"It doesn't matter," I said.

"It takes a little time," said Sloan.

Abby still looked worried.

We got to the end of the block, then crossed the street. Once we got to the other side, Buster's behavior slowly changed. He became less interested in Frankie and more interested in sniffing around and looking for a place to pee.

"See?" said Sloan. "It's already working!"

I said, "Well, it's not just the praise, it's the fact that we're walking them together. I can't explain why it works exactly, but it always eventually defuses the aggression, at least temporarily. I think it has something to do with the way wolves travel together, moving in synch, side by side, when they set out on a hunting expedition. It's a natural mechanism for creating pack harmony, which is essential for group hunting."

Abby said she thought that pack social behavior was all about a struggle for dominance, so I explained that dominant behavior is actually rare in real wolf packs. Sloan chimed in with some of her own thoughts, most of them borrowed from me.

Buster found a good spot to pee, and we stopped and waited.

Abby said, "It sounds like you two know each other."

"Yeah. Sloan used to work for me," I said.

Sloan tensed up, perhaps worried that I'd tell Abby about the night Jamie and I caught her making out with Leon (with her top off) in the front of the kennel when she should've been keeping an eye on the dogs in the back.

"She was a good employee," I said. "I hated losing her."

"Yeah," she lied, "I had a heavy classload that semester."

Buster finished peeing and we started walking again. When we did, Frankie was a little bit ahead and Buster pulled to catch up. Then, when he got close enough, he sniffed Frankie's butt.

Frankie turned his head and gave Buster a casual look.

Buster looked away and stared at something across the street. The critical thing, though, is that he didn't growl or get tense.

Frankie looked away too, studying some distant bushes. Then Buster looked back at Frankie and stuck his nose where it had just been. Frankie let him do it and just kept walking.

I said, "He's making his first social gesture."

Frankie kept walking. Buster finished sniffing Frankie's butt and moved forward so he was walking parallel to Frankie. They were now just inches apart, their gaits in synch.

"This is just amazing," said Abby.

"I should've thought of this," said Sloan.

"Well, it's only a start," I said. "We can go back now and move on to the next step. Does Buster act up when dogs he knows come over to his house? Does he get possessive about his food?"

She said he didn't, so we went back to the house, where I took the dogs into the kitchen, had them both sit, then took turns feeding them bits of cheese. Each dog waited politely while the other one gulped his treat. It was like a tea party.

Abby said, "This is so amazing."

"Yeah, but the next time Frankie comes over, *if* he does, Buster will probably try to attack him again."

"I don't understand. Then why did we even *do* this?"

"To show Buster that he can get along with another dog he initially felt aggressive toward. The next step is to try something outside. Is your backyard totally fenced off?"

She said it was, so we went through a sliding glass door and out to a stone patio with a wooden picnic table and a well-used gas grill. The dogs were on lead and ignoring each other again, sniffing the stones or looking around. Frankie pulled Sloan over to the grill and began sniffing like mad. He likes BBQ.

Sloan stood, holding him, and gave me a smile.

"What?" I said.

"Nothing. I've just never seen you use these tricks before. They're really cool . . ."

"Yeah? Well, if you thought those were cool, wait'll you see the next one."

10

The next trick was to let the dogs loose to see if they'd play together. And like I said, it turned out to be pretty cool.

Normally I wouldn't put Frankie (or any dog) in a situation where he was almost forced to interact with an aggressor. But (a) Frankie has a way of handling any tense situation, of knowing exactly how to act and react in order to either get the other dog to leave him alone or get him to play, and (b) I could tell from the softening of Buster's face that he was now open to a friendly, and possibly playful, encounter with Frankie.

Sure enough, after we unhooked their leashes the two dogs ignored each other for a bit, then Frankie came trotting over to Buster, his carriage upright, but not in a tense way. Abby was about to give her dog a stern warning but I held my hand up.

"Just watch," I whispered.

"I'm not paying the vet bill," she whispered back.

"There won't be one," I said, hoping that was true.

Buster let Frankie approach, but barked at him, jumping back a half step with each bark. And with each bark his eyes broke contact with Frankie's, though he kept a watch on him out of the corners of his eyes. Then Frankie, instead of continuing straight toward Buster, tried a sideways tack. Buster twisted around and tried a hip check, which Frankie quickly dodged. Then Frankie went into a play bow. Buster mirrored him. They each feigned a quick lunge at the other, Frankie first, then Buster.

They did a few more, then finally Buster jumped up, tore off, and began zooming around the yard with a huge smile on his face. Frankie followed.

"Amazing," said Abby.

"It's dogs," I said. "You have to trust their nature."

The boys did a dozen laps or so, then gradually tightened their circles, until they wound down into a soft-mouthed wrestling match, which ended up with the two of them lying on the grass side by side, breathing heavily and smiling.

Sloan said, "This is very cool."

"I'm amazed," said Abby. "Is that all there is to it?"

"Probably not," I said. "Sometimes just bringing the dog's prey drive to the surface like this can make a systemic change, but we'll probably need to do some more sessions."

Sloan excused herself to use the bathroom. Once she was out of earshot I said to Abby, "It's funny, but I wasn't looking forward to this."

"Why?"

"Well, I'm at least partially responsible for putting Randy Corliss in jail. I mean, you must know that, right?"

She sighed. "Yes, well, I was a little concerned about that myself, but Sloan says you're the best trainer in the state. And it certainly looks like she was right!"

"Thanks." I took a moment. "Do you just do criminal law? Because I lost my attorney a while back . . ."

"Jill. Yes, that was so sad."

"So, I don't know, maybe it's just because we went walking together, like the dogs, that I now feel connected to you, but—"

"Oh, I don't think I could represent you. Not until Randall's case is decided. Though maybe you could help me with his case?"

"Help that creep?"

"No, I just mean, I'm trying to get the DA to agree to a deal. Randall has a lot of dirt on this drug dealer Eddie Cole."

"No kidding. He used to be on his payroll."

"Allegedly. At any rate, I was hoping to broker a deal for a lighter sentence. My client is willing to agree to a plea and provide all the details he has on Cole, but the DA won't even talk to me about it."

"Well, don't look at me," I said. "Regis is one of the last people I'd make a deal with."

"Regis?"

"Sorry. That's my pet name for the bastard. Besides, I don't have any clout with the DA." I thought it was interesting, though, that the DA was showing no interest in obtaining information about Eddie Cole. It reinforced what I'd told Farrell Woods about Cole having some pull inside the justice system. "And why is Regis still in custody?" I asked. "I thought he would've made bail."

"He did. But unfortunately he was caught shortly afterward trying to leave the country using a fake passport. That's why his first attorney quit and I ended up representing him."

"That sounds like him."

"Well," she said with a worried look, "I just thought I'd ask." She laughed. "You know I'm just trying to get the best deal I can for my client, even if he is a macho slimeball."

"So he's tried hitting on you, huh?"

"Hitting on me? He actually tried to squeeze my . . . !"

Sloan came back, we worked out a training timetable, to be geared around Sloan's walking schedule with Buster, then I hooked Frankie up and we left.

As I walked toward the street, I looked back and saw Buster standing in the front door, wagging his tail, as if wishing Frankie could've stayed a little longer. Abby had a similar look in her eyes as well, though she wasn't wagging her tail.

"I think you should talk to Leon," I told Sloan as we got to her car. Afternoon shadows had started to creep across the streets. School kids with backpacks were chattering and chasing each other around the street, kicking up leaves on the lawns.

"Me too," she said softly. "But I can't. I just—"

"Because you're shy."

"Yes."

"You're painfully shy."

"Yes. About some things, yes."

I stood a moment. "Don't you think you owe it to him?"

"No. Why do I owe him anything?"

"Because he thinks he did something wrong, that something's the matter with him. Now *he's* shy around girls."

She smiled a little, shook her head. "He was always shy, he just bulled his way through it with his tough-guy act."

I could tell she still liked Leon. A gust disturbed her long, lank hair. She pulled a strand behind one ear. She almost looked pretty doing it, and I saw now why Leon had liked her.

"Maybe so," I said, "but his tough-guy act is out the window now. He's forgotten how to act confident."

"But there's nothing wrong with him. He's really sweet."

"Like I don't know that? You think I haven't tried to tell him that? But you're the only one who can make him believe it."

She put her hand to her mouth. "I can't."

"Of course you can, as long as you want to bad enough."

She just stood there, with the fear welling in her eyes. She's just like a scared puppy, I thought.

So, Jack, I took the idea further, *how do you get a scared puppy to warm up to you? Come down to her level and offer a treat?* That wouldn't work with Sloan, though. Or would it?

I came around and parked my hip on her fender, putting my eye level below hers. I smiled and said, "Look, you know you're going to feel better if you get it out in the open, talk to him."

She shook her head, looked down, looked at me, said nothing.

I smiled. "You know, you may be smarter than I am . . . how smart *are* you, by the way?"

"You mean my IQ?"

I told her that's what I'd meant, so she told me and I gave her a surprised look.

"Well," I said, "you *are* a lot smarter than me."

"I already knew that. And it's smarter than *I*, not *me*."

"Okay, fine, the point is . . . but wait a second, with an IQ like that, why aren't you at Harvard or Stanford instead of—"

"Don't start trying to be my guidance counselor, okay?"

"But it doesn't make any sense."

"It does if you know the reasons for it, and you don't."

"What are they?"

She shook her head. "What were you about to say before?"

"Huh? Oh, even though you're smarter than I am, I'm a lot

older than you, and I've been in a lot more relationships than you have, and I know that one way to get rid of the bad feelings you have right now is to talk to Leon."

"But—" Her face shrank again. "—isn't he still mad at me?"

"Maybe. But he'll get over it. And I don't think *you'll* ever get over being mad at your*self* until you explain things."

"How do you know that?"

"Because your feelings won't go away just because you ignore them or try to run away." She tensed up again, so I said, "Look, you feel better after clearing the air with me, don't you? And we had fun with Buster."

"That's true." She took a deep breath. "Okay. I don't know how you conned me into it, but I'll talk to him. Okay?"

"You promise?"

"Yes, I'll call him tonight."

"Well, don't just call him on the phone, unless it's to figure out a time to talk to him in person."

"That's what I *meant*," she said, shaking her head at me. "You're still patronizing me."

"Sorry." I shrugged. "It's what I do."

She put her hands in her coat, got out her keys, turned and started to open the car door. She turned back and said, "Do you think Buster is going to be all right?"

"Sure he is," I said. "As soon as he gets over his fear."

She gave me a knowing smile.

"What?" I said, smiling back.

"You think I don't know that that last comment was directed at me? At least partially?"

"What do you mean, 'partially'?"

She got in her car. "I'll see you later, Jack."

I hope so, I thought as I watched her drive off.

I drove into Camden to pick up a few things, then grabbed a lobster roll at Sharp's Wharf, took it to a picnic bench, and had a nosh while the afternoon breeze kicked up its heels, making the mostly bare-boned sailboats rock and bump into each other. There was a gang of leaf lookers in sweaters and parkas, up from New York or Philadelphia or Washington, waiting in line to go on a sunset cruise on one of the sloops. Frankie ignored them. He sat at my side, drooling and watching me eat.

When I finished, I let him gobble the leftover bits of bun, then called Lou Kelso in New York and caught him up on the case.

After I was done, he said, "The Moose and Eagle Society? I've heard of the Moose and Squir—"

"Yeah, I already used that one. See what kind of background you can get for me on the MacLeary clan, the whole lot of them. And the deeper you can dig, the better."

A pause. "You gonna pay me for all this grunt work?"

I chuckled. "Why? You're a millionaire now."

"Yeah. For that matter, so are you, Jack."

"I am?" This was news to me.

"Your wife is, anyway."

"Crap," I said. "I'd forgotten about that. That's going to make my life complicated."

"What is?" Kelso asked. "Being rich?"

"Well, it complicated *yours*, didn't it?"

Another pause. "I may have been a little too drunk during the incipient stages to remember. Meanwhile, my first question is, why does this seem to be coming as a surprise to you?"

"Jamie's trust fund? Because she and I haven't talked about it since last summer, when we first set the wedding date."

"I see."

I asked, "And what's your second question?"

"Oh. How much does she get?"

I explained about the structured payout: one million for getting remarried, and the rest of the ten mil when she turns thirty-five.

He gave a low whistle. "Her old man must be filthy rich."

"Yeah. Jonas invented a few gizmos for neurosurgery that are used in hospitals all over the world every day. He likes to tell people he's one of the thirteen richest doctors in America."

He laughed. "He has a funny way of counting things. And anyway, you're still married to a millionaire."

"It looks like it."

"Buck up, Jack. There are worse things in life than having a rich wife. And remember: money can't buy you happiness, but the truth is, happiness can't buy you money."

I laughed. "Very clever."

"Thanks. Just indulging in a little paronomasia."

My brain slipped a cog or two. "What? What do you have to be paranoid about?"

"I didn't say I was paranoid. I said I'd just entertained myself with a little paronomasia. It means a play on words."

"Then why not just say that?"

"Because it's more fun to say paronomasia. For instance, and this is just for the sake of argument, what if there were no such thing as a hypothetical question?"

I laughed.

"Oh, and before you go, what's another word for synonym?"

"Good-bye, Lou," I said, laughing.

"Wait! I've got more!"

I hung up on him, but laughed all the way home.

11

It was close to sundown when I got back to the kennel so I expected to see my Suburban parked in the gravel drive, but it wasn't there; Farrell Woods's pickup was. That meant he was still out doing the drop-offs for the day, which was odd. He's usually finished and on his way home by five-thirty.

I let Frankie run off and do some dog-type stuff while I went into the kennel to see if I could talk to Mrs. Murtaugh. As soon as I came in the door, Farrell's beagles began their symphony of yips and howls from their kennels in the back.

"You had to wake them up!" Mrs. Murtaugh shouted. Her watery blue eyes twinkled at me. She had her coffee-colored car coat on and was closing the door to the grooming "salon," a small room past the front counter. We said our hellos and whatnot, or tried to over the din, while she looked around for her hat, found it—a greenish, knit thing—then put it on top of her silver hair and pulled it down over her ears, though it wasn't that cold out.

I said, "Did Farrell's truck break down again?"

"What?"

"Never mind," I shouted. "Let's go outside!"

She nodded and I followed her past the rawhide bins and the bags of dog food. (I sell Merrick and Prairie.)

"At last," she said as I closed the front door behind us. "I can hear again!"

I agreed, then made my usual offer to walk her up the hill

and across the road, which is where she lives, but she likes to feel independent, so she declined.

"So," I said with a nod toward the blue Bronco, "did Farrell's truck break down again?"

"No," she said. "Not that I know of. Why?"

"He's running late. And he hasn't called in?"

She said no, then told me how much we'd made on grooming for the day, which was negligible, just Ginger the Airedale, her niece Audrey Stafford's dog, and a couple of Persian cats: Mr. Willowkins, and Princess Piraboo. (Don't get me wrong, I like cats, but if I had one, I wouldn't give him a name like that.)

"Oh, by the way," I said as we walked a little ways together, "I ran into Sloan today."

"Really? How is she?"

I told her about my session with Buster, then lied and said that Sloan had asked me to say hello to everybody.

"That's nice," she said. "Though I doubt she meant to say hi to D'Linda. Those two never got along." I was expecting her to launch into her usual long discussion about the personality conflicts between the two girls—D'Linda, her assistant, was always fighting with Sloan—but she asked me what I was making for dinner.

"Pizza soup," I told her.

She laughed. "Well, I don't know what it is exactly, but from the sound of it I'm sure Leon will like it."

"I think he will. And listen: I may have to do the pickups in the morning. Can you come in early?"

She agreed to do that, we said good-night, and I watched her trudge slowly up the driveway, then I whistled Frankie over and we went up to the house, where I was greeted (i.e., got slobbered on) by Hooch. I put down their evening's provender, then called Woods's cell phone, but it went directly to his voice mail.

Jamie got home while I was putting the finishing touches on the pizza soup, some steamed broccoli florets with slivered almonds, and some garlic bread. She and Leon loved the soup, though I thought it could've used a little something-

something, I wasn't sure what. A little less oregano? A little more salt?

"Oh, I know what it is!" I finally said.

"What?" Jamie asked.

"For the base. I should have added some tomato paste, not just the tomato sauce and the canned tomatoes."

"Really? I thought it was really good."

"Yeah," Leon said. "I wish you'd make this every night."

"Yeah, I'm not going to make it every night. Pepperoni is okay once in a while, but—"

"Yes, but you could do all kinds of pizza soup," said Jamie. "You could do plain, you could do mushrooms and olives . . ."

"Yeah," said Leon. "And is there any more garlic bread?"

I said there was some keeping warm in the oven, and watched him go grab a couple of slices, and hoped Sloan would call.

Then while Jamie did the dishes and Leon took Magee out to the carriage house, I tried calling Farrell again on the kitchen wall phone, but got the same recording.

"I'm getting worried about him, honey."

"Who, Leon?"

"No, Farrell. Though I ran into Sloan today and she promised she'd call Leon tonight."

"Why?"

"I asked her to." I told her about the conversation, then said, "It was tough not spilling the beans to Leon, but I didn't want to build his hopes up in case she doesn't call."

"Well, let's hope she does. I think that was very sweet of you to ask her to talk to him. I hadn't noticed how shy he was around girls."

"Well, I guess I noticed because I was a teenage boy myself once, and I know how he feels."

"You were shy around girls when you were Leon's age? I find that hard to believe."

"Why do you think I spent so much time surfing? And I've got this knot in my stomach over Farrell's disappearance."

"He's done this before, you know. What did he call it?"

"Staying under the radar. Yeah, but he only did that because he thought his life was in danger, remember?"

"All right." She dried her hands on a towel. "Do you want me to call Uncle Horace and maybe the state police, and ask them be on the lookout for him and your car?"

I nodded slowly, deliberately. "At this point, yeah. Something must've happened to him."

"Still, it could just be a traffic accident, couldn't it?"

"Maybe. If it is, there'll be a report on it and we can at least find out what hospital he's in. Meanwhile, I've gotta feed Molly and the super group and give them some exercise."

"The super group?"

I explained, but she still didn't get it. "Never mind," I said. "You're too young for the reference."

"If you say so. I'll make those calls."

I whistled at Frankie and Hooch, who were asleep in the living room. They jumped up, shook themselves and came running—more food? We went out onto the side porch, where the light from the kitchen window cast a soft yellow glow across the blue shadows of evening.

I let Molly and the beagles out of their pens, and we all went down to the play yard. It was great to see Molly play, that is once one of the other dogs was able to josh her out of her digging habit. It was still her favorite means of downloading tension. But once she got pestered enough, it was lovely to see how adaptable and happy she was, the way she'd play with each of the beagles in a way that was perfectly suited for that dog, though her favorite was Townes Van Zandt. Mine too. He was a little shyer than the others, which reminded me of Leon.

Around the time I was thinking about him, Leon and Magee came down and joined us. I asked him if he'd finished his homework and he said no, but couldn't resist a chance to let Magee in on some of the action, so I opened the gate and let him race inside.

After watching the wheaten play for a bit, he said, "Yo, Pops, I know I'm grounded and all, but would it be okay if Sloan came up to see me some night? It wouldn't be a date or nothin'."

"Sloan?"

"Yeah, she just called me. She said she saw you today and thought about me, you know, wondered how I was doin' and shit. She was wonderin' if she could come up and talk to me and shit."

I put my hand on his shoulder. "That'd be fine."

He grinned. "A'ight."

"And it's a good thing you asked me first, instead of just letting her come over."

He nodded. "I'm serious about doing my time, yo."

"That's good, Leon. I appreciate your attitude."

After playtime was over, I got the dogs resituated in their kennels. But before I came back up to the house, I grabbed the small Maglite from the woody then went through Farrell's truck.

I searched the glove box, the various slips of paper on the dashboard, even the trash under the seats, to see if there was anything that might tell me where he'd disappeared to.

I didn't find much except a photo of Tulips, tucked under the visor in such a way that if he flipped it down slightly he could look at her while he drove. Behind the photo I found what appeared to be a phone number written on the back of a sales receipt from Taco Bell. It said, "BXP—439–0009."

I had no idea if it meant anything or not, but I took it with me up to the house anyway.

Jamie was in the living room and had some music playing—a female R&B singer, whose name I can never remember, was asking some guy to unbreak her heart. It was sad, seductive.

We sat on the couch and she filled me on what had gone on from her end: nothing. There were no accident reports involving Woods or my car. And while Flynn and the state police were friendly toward me to a certain extent, and Jamie was the chief medical examiner, and they were in business with her so to speak, it was a no go. A twelve-year-old boy had gone missing, and that's what most of their manpower was focused on.

"I might have something," I said, showing her the phone number. I picked up the receiver on the phone next to the couch and dialed. While it was ringing I told her what had happened with Leon and Sloan, and she expressed her happiness with the results. After a few rings a recorded voice said:

"It's Brent. Leave a message, all right? Okay . . ."

I almost hung up, but pulled a bluff, "Hey, Brent, Farrell Woods gave me your number." Jamie looked at me. I shrugged. "Anyway, we were supposed to hook up tonight but I can't locate him. If you know where he is, let me know." I left my number.

· Jamie wanted to know who it was. I told her his name was Brent, which she already knew from hearing me leave the message. But beyond that, I told her, I had no idea, though I now had a feeling it might be Brent Pfleger; I didn't mention that.

"What else can we do?" she asked.

"You got me. Maybe he'll call back. Until then . . ."

She was tired and had a staff meeting in the morning. She had to prepare for it too. I wasn't in the mood to read or listen to music. She wasn't in the mood to pace the floor, so we sat for a while, switched on the TV and clicked around, just talking about Leon and Sloan and what we thought might happen, until we found a W. C. Fields movie. He always makes me laugh.

We watched it for a while, but I still couldn't get my mind off Farrell, not even during my favorite scene where Fields is trying to take a nap in a hammock outside his apartment building but is interrupted by a loud, well-meaning insurance salesman looking for someone named Carl LaFong. Fields and the salesman traded the name back and forth, spelling it and respelling it, until Jamie said:

"You really must be worried. You always laugh at this scene. Though I can never figure out why you think it's funny."

"Me neither."

"You don't know why it's funny?"

"I have no idea. It just always makes me laugh."

"Yes, except tonight."

I was about to agree with her when the phone rang. I picked it up. It was the same voice I'd heard on the answering machine.

"This is Brent. You called me?"

"Yeah, I'm looking for Farrell Woods." I motioned for Jamie to turn down the TV.

He asked, "Why are you looking for him?"

"He's got my car and I haven't been able to track him down."

"So? Why call me?"

"He said he might hook up with you later."

"Bastard," he said. "He told *me* he didn't want anybody else to know about it."

"It's okay; I'm cool. So you're going to meet him?"

"Yeah, at his place in about twenty minutes."

"Good. Let him know I'm trying to reach him."

"Sure, okay. What's your name?"

I hesitated. "What's yours?"

He paused. "Hey, pal, I thought he gave you my number."

"Yeah, but he just told me your first name."

"Yeah, well, I don't know either of your names."

I should've just told him it was Jack Field, but for some reason I didn't. I said, "It's Carl LaFong."

"Carl La what?"

"LaFong. Big *L* small *A* big *F* small *O* small *N* small *G*." Jamie was doubled up with laughter, though she was trying hard not to be heard. "LaFong," I finished. "Carl LaFong."

"Okay, I got it. I'll tell him that some asshole named Carl LaFong's lookin' for him."

"And your name again?" I asked, but he'd hung up on me.

Jamie came up for air and hit me repeatedly, still laughing. "Now," she gasped, "I get it! Now I see why it's so funny!"

"Yeah? Why?" I asked, dialing Woods's home number.

She stopped short. "Well, that's the thing," she said. "I still have no idea." She started laughing again.

I got no answer from either Farrell's cell phone or the one at his house. I was getting frustrated at being unable to do anything. "I'm gonna go up there," I told Jamie.

She stopped giggling. "All right. I'll get my shoes on."

"No, you stay here. You have to be up early."

"It's just a little after nine."

"Yeah, and by the time we go out there and talk to him and find out what's up, then come back, it'll be midnight. Besides, there may be some things going on you don't want to know about."

"Like what?"

"Like stuff related to his former life as a drug dealer. Something may have come up from his past."

"Okay," she said. "Oh, that reminds me. I think I figured out why I like hitting you so much."

"Why?"

"I think it has to do with Spencer. He was always picking on me when we were kids, and I developed an automatic reflex of hitting him before he could do something to me. I think it kind of turned into an unconscious way of relating to the men I love."

"That makes sense, sort of." I stood up. "Now that you know the cause of it, maybe you can work on not doing it so much."

She shook her head. "You're such a wimp about it."

"I am not—you want to see the bruises?"

"See what I mean? Call me when you get there, okay?"

"I will," I said, and I meant it. But things happened

12

I took 131, which runs in a fairly straight line from Union to Searsmont—I wanted a good piece of road to stretch out behind me so I could keep a sharp eye in my rearview mirror to see if anyone was tailing me. No one was.

Just past Searsmont came Windsor Corners, where I got on State 3 and took that straight to Belfast.

When I wasn't looking in my rearview mirror, or thinking about Farrell Woods, or jamming my foot down hard on the gas, I was hearing Jamie's laughter in my head. So I ping-ponged back and forth between smiling and relaxing in my seat, to sitting forward and banging one palm hard on the steering wheel for no reason.

I got to Belfast around ten, regardless.

The downtown area was dark except for a few cars, some ghost-green streetlights, and the brightly colored neon signs and warm yellow glow emanating from the bars. Halloween was a week away. It's been my observation that around the time the clocks change every year, certain types of people—normally quiet, young, industrious, nine-to-fivers—tend to come out of the woodwork and turn into raucous nighthawks. They have a brief, jaunty explosion of, what?—joy? desperation? a frantic combination of the two? It always lasts through mid-November, then slowly dies and is resurrected for one last jarring bright flash in that dark space between Christmas and New Year's.

I got stuck at a light, next to the bridge turnoff, and watched a gang of five or six such revelers dancing their way up the sidewalk, out the door of one bar and on to the next, moving in time to some music I couldn't hear and didn't want to. I wanted other things. To lie quietly with Jamie. To get good news about Farrell Woods. To see Leon resolve things with Sloan. To have my old police siren back—*damnit!*—so I could *move*.

None of those things happened. The light just turned green, and I drove out of town and on into the night.

13

If you travel north of Belfast, up Oak Hill Road, just past Hurd's Pond, Farrell Woods once told me, you'll find a black mailbox attached to a wooden post, with the name "Woods" written in reflective silver letters, though the top thingie on the *d* has been worn away, so it looks like it says "Wooos," which, for a man with ten beagles, is just as fitting as his real name.

My headlights found the mailbox, and I turned onto the long, winding, dirt road, past some semi-marshland on both sides, the left side bounded by a barbed-wire fence, and came up slowly to Woods's cabin, a single story affair with a wraparound, mosquito-screened front porch, a dead lawn, and two droopy willows, one on either side. There were some pines and alders scattered behind the structure, along with a ramshackle shed to the right.

I saw two vehicles on the property. One was a '75 red Ford pickup that Woods uses for spare parts. It was parked with the hood up. The other was a red 1956 Nash Rambler, with no doors or tires. It was up on cinder blocks by the shed. And except for the lack of hanging kudzu vines, the initial impression you got when first seeing the place was that you were no longer in Maine, that you'd been transported somehow into the Deep South.

It had last rained on Saturday morning, just before Jamie and I visited the general, so there were no tire impressions visible in the dirt, at least not from my vantage point.

I switched off the lights and the engine, opened the glove box, grabbed a Maglite, the big one, then got out of the car and walked up to the house. I didn't bring my gun with me; I don't own one anymore, though I halfway wished I did.

The door to the screened-in porch was unlocked so I went in to the smell of beagles. The porch was dusty and had probably been painted white at some point. I danced the light around and saw some ratty lawn furniture, a wooden spool made to hold industrial cable, now acting as an end table, with a citronella candle sitting on top of it. Maine mosquitoes, I thought, they'll even find a way to get inside your screened-in porch. There weren't any clues: no bloody footprints, no cast-off knives, guns, or bottles of poison, just a coating of dust mixed with beagle hair.

I went farther in, to the front door, which had also been painted white at some point in time. I pressed the bell thingie but nothing happened; no sound came from inside the house. So I knocked on the door. As I did, it creaked open.

I caught my breath, stepped back. Woods had said, "I'm always careful, Jackie boy," but leaving the front door of your house unlocked? That wouldn't qualify. I wished I had that gun.

I wondered whether I should go inside or go back out to the car, drive to where some people were and call for backup.

As I was going over my options, I heard a woman's voice moaning softly, not the pleasant kind I hoped to be hearing from Jamie later. It was soft yet had an urgent, pleading undertone. It wasn't coming from far away, probably just across the living room—if Farrell had one—yet it felt like it was floating across a distant lake or sifting through the sands of a far-off desert.

I swung the door wide and stabbed the darkness with my flash while feeling around for the light switch. I found it. A weak, yellow glow from a bare overhead bulb gave just enough light to chase the shadows back. I heard a shuffling sound, footfalls, then a soft yet substantial thud, like a sack of potatoes being dropped on a loading dock. I moved quickly through the living room—where a threadbare carpet with a tattered gap almost tripped me—then I blundered through a wide arched opening into the kitchen/dining room, where I found two bodies spread across the cracked linoleum.

One of the bodies belonged to a woman, lying facedown, close to the doorway. She was still moaning, flailing her arms; she was trying to push herself up off the floor.

The other body wouldn't be getting up again. He was lying faceup with the back of his head resting quietly in a pool of blood. At first I had a horrible feeling that I'd finally found Farrell Woods, but quickly realized the dead guy wasn't as tall. I flashed the beam over his face. He was young, college age, blondish with sneering, puckered lips, and a pair of thick glasses with one of the lenses missing; he wouldn't need it now.

I found the light switch for that room, then quickly knelt next to the woman and helped her up on her side, asking if she was all right, saying some vaguely soothing words. As I lifted her torso off the floor I saw who it was: Tulips.

She sat back on one hip and weakly tried to brush the long black hair out of her face, revealing a deep, savage looking cut over her left eye, with a peculiar, crescent-shaped indentation. She also had a thin red trail of blood leading down from a vein in the crook of her right arm—the vein most junkies favor.

Her eyes were closed and she was mumbling something that sounded like "we open," though she kept choking on the *p* sound, making it sound like "we oaken."

"Tulips," I said, shaking her shoulders. "It's me, Jack."

"Whaaa?"

"It's Jack Field. Are you all right?"

She shook her head. "OD," she said. That came out clear.

"You're OD'ing on heroin?" Her eyes were still closed so I slapped her in the face a little to get them to open.

"Ow!" She opened her eyes and looked at me. "Jack?"

"Yes, it's me," I said slapping her again, harder this time.

"Ow! Stop . . ." That was good. She'd felt the pain. If she really had taken too much of the drug, at least I now knew I might be able to get her to a hospital in time for the doctors to give her some epinephrine and activated charcoal.

"When did you shoot up?" I asked.

She closed her eyes and shook her head. "I didn't."

"Tulips!" I shook her hard. "When did you shoot up?"

She opened her eyes. "I didn't. I'm clean," she said simply. "Still clean." She closed her eyes again.

"Someone did this to you?"

She nodded, her eyes still closed.

It might have been true. "Are you right-handed or left-handed?"

"Whaaa?"

I slapped her again. "Right-handed or left?"

"I'm right-handed," she said, her eyes fluttering.

"Okay, so someone shot you up. Who was it?"

"We oaken."

"We oaken?" She was nodding off, which didn't mean she was dying. Junkies nod off all the time right after a hit. I crouched down, lifted her up in my arms and started to carry her toward the living room, when a pair of very bright headlights swept across the front window, sending crazy shadows everywhere. I took Tulips quickly to the right wall and edged along it, still moving toward the window, but giving whoever was out there a smaller target. It might be the same person who'd just killed her "friend" and had just as recently shot her full of dope.

I heard a car door close, then a vaguely familiar female voice called out, "Jack?" A pause. "Hey, Jack! You in there?"

I got to the window, looked out and saw Peggy Doyle. She looked over at the woody, then back toward the house. She kind of stood for a moment, with one hand on her hip.

I yelled, "Peggy! I'm coming out. Call an ambulance!"

"Are you hurt?"

"No," I yelled, carrying Tulips's now unconscious body toward the front door. "But I need you to get on the phone right away."

When I got outside, she was on her cell, doing as I'd asked. "My twenty is Oak Hill Road," she said, "about a mile past—"

"Don't have them come here," I said, "it'll take too long." I took Tulips over to Doyle's sheriff's department Jeep. "Tell dispatch you'll meet the ambulance on your way to Belfast."

She repeated what I'd said into the phone then came over to

open the door for me. "Why am *I* taking her? What's going on?"

"You have to hurry or she might die of an overdose."

She helped me get Tulips's floppy personage into the passenger seat, and we secured her body with the seat belt.

"Ah, Jesus," she said. "An overdose of what?"

"Heroin," I told her, then pointed her toward the driver's side door.

"She's a junkie?"

"She used to be. Someone was trying to kill her, and wanted to make it look like she OD'd. Now get going!"

She went to her car door. "And that's all I get?"

"For now. If you want an explanation, call me on my cell once you're on the road. But go now, quick! Okay? And don't tell anyone who she is or where you found her."

She had the door half open, stopped and said, "Okay, what did you just tell me to do?"

"Look, just go. I don't want anyone knowing her identity. I'll explain later, trust me." I started to go back inside, turned and said, "And how the hell did you end up here tonight, anyway?"

She gave me a shrug. "Jamie was worried," she said, then got in the car. "She called and asked me to keep an eye on you."

"Well, it's a good thing she did." I said, though Doyle had already closed the door and started her siren.

I watched her scatter dust clouds down the drive, then hurried back inside to have another look at the body.

The pool of blood, I now noticed, had come from a precision knife wound in the throat, cut straight through the jugular vein. I got down on one knee and took a closer look (which wasn't fun), and saw that the killer had cut through *both* jugulars, straight from the left ear all the way to the right.

My mind went still for a moment.

I'd been cursing my lack of knowledge about the armed forces since meeting MacLeary, but I knew one thing: certain military units, in certain countries of the world (the U.S. being decidedly one of them), teach their soldiers how to make exactly that kind of precision cut. It's always done while restraining the victim from behind, it takes less than two seconds to complete, and the killer is out the door before the victim's body hits the ground.

Well, I thought, Farrell Woods had military training, yes, but in the K–9 Corps, not one of those secret commando outfits, so it was unlikely that he'd killed this guy. Or was it? Maybe he *had* been a commando and had used the K–9 Corps as a cover. If that were the case, it would've been easy enough to have kept it a secret; that's what those units are all about.

But why would he kill this guy? And why would he give Tulips an overdose? I mean, he was in love with her, though I'd gotten the feeling lately that he was jealous. Was this dead guy with the broken glasses the professor Woods was jealous of?

Too much conjecture, I thought, and not enough fact.

I stifled an urge to run to my car and drive straight to one of those bars in Belfast. Instead I forced myself to go through the victim's pockets and found his wallet. The name on his driver's license made things look worse for Woods: Brent Pfleger.

Just then I heard a door open behind me. I don't remember what happened next.

You never do.

14

I woke up to the sound of Peggy Doyle's voice.

She had me by the shoulders, and besides yelling in my ear, she was shaking me. Hard.

"Strong hands," I said, coming to a little more.

"What? Thank god, you're all right?"

"You have strong hands."

"Thank you. What the hell happened?"

"I don't know." I sat up, looked around. "Where's the body?" I asked, and immediately knew I'd said too much, though it was true: Brent Pfleger, or the former corpse thereof, was gone.

"What body? Jack, what's going on?"

"Uh, what do you mean?" It was all I could think of.

"You just asked me where the body was."

"Did I?" I sat there. "I must've been dreaming. I guess I got sapped when I came back inside. How's Tulips?"

She said nothing for a moment. "I don't know. I got her transferred into the ambulance down the road a piece, then tried you on your cell phone. When you didn't answer, I came back here. They took her to EMCC."

I got up. Slowly. "God, my head hurts."

"I can believe it. When I came and saw all the blood, I thought that you'd been murdered."

"Nah, it just feels like it."

"So where did the blood come from?"

"Uh, I'm not sure."

I went to the kitchen sink and looked underneath it. No bleach, just a lot of grime and dust, a can of Drano, some lighter fluid, and a box of mousetraps.

"What are you looking for?"

"Bleach and some old towels."

"What are you planning to do?"

"Clean the floor."

"Okay, stop right where you are."

I didn't stop. I went to a utility closet, to the right of the refrigerator. I found a couple of brooms, a wilted rag mop, an empty plastic bucket, and various brands of cleaning products, all the boxes, tins, and bottles coated with dust.

"Jack, I'm serious."

I went past her to a door on the far left side of the kitchen. It led to a laundry room, which had a dryer with a box of Tide on top and a washer with a bottle of Clorox on its lid. There was also a wicker hamper, coming unwickered at the edges. I opened it and found dirty laundry, including some big towels.

"The mother lode," I said, coming into the kitchen with the bleach in one hand and the towels in the other. "Grab that blue bucket from the utility closet, would you?"

"No." She had one hand on her shoulder radio.

"Okay," I said, and stood there.

"You're going to tell me what's going on."

"I don't *know* what's going on." I stopped. "Here's what I *do* know. There was a body here." I let her take that in. "Yeah. His neck had been slit from ear to ear, commando-style. I also know that someone shot Tulips full of dope, and Farrell Woods has been missing since this afternoon."

"Is that all?"

"No. I was going through the victim's pockets when I heard a noise. The next thing I remember is you shaking me awake."

"So why clean up the blood?"

I took a beat. "Because either Farrell did this, which I don't think he did, or someone's trying to frame him for it."

"Who'd want to frame him?"

I told her about the roach in my ashtray, my discussion with Farrell, and his offer to find out where Eddie Cole was hiding.

"Okay, that makes sense, I guess. But what you're doing is insane. You can't tamper with evidence at a crime scene."

"Except when I'm done, there won't *be* any evidence. And if no one but me knows about the body, it won't be a crime scene."

"You're forgetting that I know."

"Do you?"

"Jack, you just told me there was."

I shook my head. "That's hearsay."

She laughed. "In a courtroom, yes. In a police investigation it's called an eyewitness account."

I shrugged. "Sometimes witnesses change their stories."

"And look at you. You're soaked in the victim's blood."

I looked down at my clothes then back at her. "I'll get rid of them. Farrell's a little taller than I am, but—"

"And skinnier. But this kind of thing never turns out—"

"Don't worry; I'm sure I'll find something to wear."

She stood her ground. "You're still forgetting one thing."

"I know," I said.

"Do you?"

"Yeah." I liked Doyle. She was smart; she knew all the angles. "Whoever took Brent Pfleger's body has to be the same person that knocked me out. Right?" She nodded. "And why would someone who was trying to frame Farrell for murder come back to get rid of the body? Why not leave it here?"

"He wouldn't."

"And why wouldn't he have killed me too?"

"Right. Which points the finger straight at Woods."

"Maybe. Then again, maybe it means someone else took the body. But don't worry," I said, going to the utility closet. "If Farrell did this, I'll still nail him for it. Especially what he tried to do to Tulips, if nothing else. That's another thing, see—"

I was interrupted by some tinny disco music. Doyle reached down to her belt and unholstered her cell phone.

"Doyle here." She listened, her face got happy (or a little happi*er*), and she said, "Thanks. That's good to know." She listened a bit more, then said, "Yeah, I'll be there in a half hour or so to fill in the details." A brief pause. "Okay, thanks again."

She holstered the phone. "That was the hospital. Your friend is going to be okay, though she'll be a little out of it for a few days."

I expressed my relief, then said, "Disco?"

"What?"

"Your ring tone? You chose a disco tune?"

"I like Abba. Now, here's the thing," she began. "Let me finish. If I don't actually witness someone tampering with evidence, I guess there's not much I can do about it, is there?"

I smiled. "I could really use your help here, but—"

"No, I've got to file my report. Though you have to promise me that if you start feeling woozy, you'll give me a call."

"I'll be all right. I've just got a splitting—"

"I'm not leaving unless you promise to call me."

"Okay, I promise. What are you going to say?"

"About what?"

"In your report. About where you found Tulips?"

She nodded. "I guess I'll have to be as vague as possible—"

"—without being *so* vague that it gets red-flagged?"

"Yeah. That oughta work, at least until Tulips comes 'round and tells her version."

"She won't remember that you were here. She was already out by the time you arrived. She *will* remember who shot her up, though. She was trying to tell me that before the drug took her away. Which is one reason I don't think Farrell did this."

She nodded. "You think she would've told you if he had?"

"I'm pretty sure. She kept trying to give me the killer's name, but all she could say was 'we oaken.'"

"'We oaken'? Are you sure?"

"Something like that. Why?"

"I don't know. It sounds vaguely familiar. And have you figured out what you're going to do when this missing body is found somewhere and eventually ends up on Jamie's autopsy table?"

I said nothing.

"I didn't think so." She gave me a harsh laugh. "Okay, I'll let you play this your way, Jack. Just one thing: what are you going to tell Jamie?"

I took a deep breath. "I don't know that yet either. But I'll have plenty of time to think up something."

She shook her head. "Now you're really playing with fire."

"Don't I know it."

After she left I took off my jacket and jeans so I wouldn't get blood on my car seats, then went outside and moved the woody behind the shed so it couldn't be seen from the road. There was a stone-rimmed fire pit back there, for burning leaves and trash.

I should have called Jamie, but I was in a rush. Besides, I thought, it's past midnight and she's fast asleep. Just to make sure she couldn't call *me*, though, I turned off my cell phone.

I came back inside and started the cleanup, diluting the bleach with water first. It took more work than I'd thought, and I ended up not only using Farrell's dirty towels to wipe the floor clean with, but most of his dirty clothes as well.

I put everything, including my own clothes, into the washer.

My plan was to burn everything, but wet fabric won't ignite. Plus when a blood-soaked piece of cloth *does* burn, it stinks like hell. How do I know? Every NYPD officer, from the lowest beat cop to the biggest brass, is expected, at some point, to attend a controlled burn of evidence that's no longer needed. It's done at an incinerator on Staten Island. You don't volunteer, you don't do it as part of your regular rotation; a perverse computer at One Police Plaza spits out your name whenever it feels the urge, usually in midsummer, and you have to stop what you're doing, suit up, sign vouchers, and witness the conflagration. And like I said, if there's blood involved, it stinks like hell.

I checked the time. It was still too late to call Jamie, but I wouldn't have called her even if it weren't. By this point I felt that anything I might tell her about what I'd been doing would only put her in an awkward position, professionally.

Once the wash was done, I put it in the dryer, on high, then ran the washing machine again to make sure any residual trace evidence went down the drain. Then, while the clothes and towels were spinning around, I took a quick hot shower, followed by a rather unsavory search of Farrell's closet; it was the first time I'd gone through another man's clothes since I was a kid going through my dad's pockets for spare change to buy comic books.

I'm a 32 waist, and despite the fact that he's taller than I am, Farrell wears a 30, so that was a problem. But I managed to pull on a pair of jeans that stretched enough for me to walk around in but not enough for me to bend over and put cuffs in them. So I had to take them off, then cuff them, and then put them back on again. Then I found an oversize T-shirt and an old hooded sweatshirt and put them on, wondering where he'd hidden the matching sweatpants, if there were any. They would've ridden a lot easier on my crotch than his damn beanpole jeans.

When everything was dry, I put it all in a big garbage bag, then took it to the kitchen, grabbed the can of lighter fluid from under the sink, found a box of matches in a drawer, picked up the garbage bag and took it to the door. When I got there, I turned, stood a moment, and looked back at the room.

I couldn't see any blood evidence, but that didn't mean a CSU team wouldn't. If they used luminal or amido black, or any number of other forensic tools, they'd know. But at least the bleach would have degraded the DNA so it wouldn't be admissible in court. While I was checking the scene, I finally saw the baseball bat, the one I'd been clipped with. It had rolled under the table. I went over and picked it up. It had blood on the sweet spot, my blood, so I took it along with the rest of the stuff.

I went outside and was shocked for a moment to see a big fat October moon, a few days shy of full, coming over a far-off row of poplar trees, intersecting the horizon. It felt like I was suddenly under a spotlight, that I'd been caught in the act.

"Too late now," I said, then went behind the shed, emptied the garbage bag into the fire pit, doused the clothes and towels and the baseball bat with lighter fluid, and set them on fire.

It's a little early for Guy Fawkes Day, I thought, taking a few steps back as the flames flared up and licked at the sky.

When I was sixteen, I'd spent my fall semester in England. Guy Fawkes Day was in early November, and I now recalled the scene along the road outside Hailsham, of men and women in wool coats, rustic types for the most part, warming their hands over bonfires made of tree limbs, unused lumber, and broken fence posts, their children scampering and squealing as the sparks flew into the air.

I hoped like hell that anyone passing by my fire on this cold October night in Maine would think it was just some night owl burning a pile of leaves, not evidence of a murder.

I stood there watching the flames die down, waiting till everything had burned to ash, thinking about my brief life in Sussex, my current one with Jamie, and feeling guilty as hell.

I poked the ashes with a stick and laughed sourly to think of how I'd spent a good deal of my professional life learning various tricks for getting inside the mind of a criminal. "Well," I said out loud, "you've really got the hang of it now, Jack."

I got in the car, unzipping Farrell's jeans first so I could get my legs bent enough to drive. There were no sirens and no black Town Cars tailing me. At one point I passed a turnoff to a lake named Nichols Pond and saw, off in the distance, what looked like another bonfire. That was it, no other signs of life until Belfast. Come to think of it, there were damn few signs of life there either, just a guy filling up at a self-serve on the outskirts. Sure, I thought, as our eyes met in slow motion, nothing memorable about seeing a '38 Ford station wagon drive by at 2:00 A.M. He'd have no reason to mention *that* to the cops.

I made it home safe. The only problem was a nagging feeling that I'd forgotten something; that I'd left some evidence behind. Now I knew why criminals return to the scene of the crime. I nearly turned back a dozen times myself, and even sat outside my house for a few minutes before I finally went in.

I tiptoed up the stairs, hoping Jamie would still be asleep so I wouldn't have to explain everything, but when I opened the door, I found it didn't matter; she wasn't there.

Frankie woke up and thumped his tail on the down comforter.

"Hey, good boy," I said casually. He thumped some more and did his smiley-face (mistakenly called a "submissive grin"). "Where's Mommy?" I asked him.

He just wagged and smiled.

I saw that the lamp on the nightstand was lit and there was a scrap of Jamie's notepaper propped up next to the phone.

I sat on the bed. Frankie stayed lying down but wiggled his body in my direction. When he reached my side, he rolled over on his back. I scratched his tummy and picked up the note:

Jack where are you!? Your cell phone's been turned off. I hope you're OK. I had to go out—car fire, north of Belfast, two bodies. Call me! I love you! Are you okay!? CALL ME!!

I love that woman so much. And I wanted desperately to talk to her about everything. I really did, even though I couldn't, as much for her sake as for mine. But I had to talk to somebody.

I picked up the phone, dialed, and waited. After five or six rings a sleepy male voice answered.

"Hey, Kelso," I said. "Sorry to call so late, but I have to talk to you. And you should know that what I'm about to say will be told to you in your capacity as my attorney."

"Oh, Christ," he muttered. "Who'd you kill?"

15

I explained the situation, and he assured me that anything I told Jamie was covered by spousal privilege, and that even if she blabbed to the cops I'd be in no danger of being prosecuted.

"But she would *have* to tell them, wouldn't she?"

I could hear him thinking. "Technically, she'd be obligated to inform them of what she knew about what happened, particularly if the body was eventually found somewhere and she had to perform an autopsy. But if the police investigated and found evidence at your friend Farrell's house that you'd tampered with the scene, they still couldn't prosecute you because anything they found would be inadmissible as 'fruit of the poisonous tree.'"

"I'm not worried about that."

"You should be. If they find a way around it, you could go to jail. So, you're worried about putting her job in jeopardy?"

"Yeah."

"Well then, don't tell her."

"But what happens if the body *is* found? What do I do?"

"I don't know!" He sounded petulant, peeved. "It's the middle of the night! Call me when all my brain cells are working and maybe I'll have an answer for you. Meanwhile, you'll just have to cross that bridge when you've burned it."

"Hah," I said. "You're not too sleepy to engage in a little parono-what's-it, though, are you?"

"Paronomasia. And no, I'm never too tired for that, or rarely.

By the way, I'm going to have to bill you for this call. Three hundred dollars ought to cover it."

"Okay . . ."

"Don't get pissy, Jack. I have to have a record in case there's a need, pursuant to any future legal proceeding."

"Lawyers," I said, with a tone.

"Yeah, lawyers. How many dog trainers get called at three in the morning because their goddamn clients just committed a crime and they don't know what to do about it?"

"Touché," I said.

After we hung up I called Jamie. She answered with a quick, "Are you okay?" but she was in the middle of an examination of the two bodies in the car she'd mentioned in her note. I told her I was fine, that Farrell hadn't been home, that Tulips was in the hospital, and that I was dead tired and going to bed.

She said she was worried about Tulips, even more worried about Farrell, but glad to know I was okay. Then she asked, "Why was your cell phone turned off?"

"Oh," I lied, "I was just being cautious. I didn't want to go inside the house and have my phone go off in case he was in some kind of trouble. That's when I found Tulips—"

"You could have turned it back on when you realized Farrell wasn't there, though, couldn't you?"

"Yeah, if I'd thought about it. But by that time I was only thinking about getting Tulips to the hospital."

"How did you call the ambulance?"

"I didn't. Doyle showed up and she called them. Look, I'm sorry, honey, but I'm zonked. I'll talk to you in the morning. Okay?"

"Okay," she said unhappily.

We missed each other the next morning, though. She didn't come home because it took so long to examine the bodies at the lake. Then she had to go straight to Augusta for her staff meeting. By the time that was over, I was out on the road doing the morning pickups for day care (which Farrell normally does). She called me while I was coming home, but I didn't answer.

When I got back to the kennel, it was sunny with a brisk

breeze, and I found Peggy Doyle's Jeep in the driveway, and Peggy herself standing in the door of the kennel, waiting for me. She was wearing her sheriff's parka and had her hat in one hand. Mrs. Murtaugh stood behind her, wearing her white groomer's coat.

The dogs I had that day all knew the drill, so I didn't need to leash them up. I just opened the tailgate and they jumped out and ran straight to the play yard. I followed them, motioning for Peggy to join us, which she did.

As we walked down the hill I heard Mrs. Murtaugh yell: "Jack, you've got about a million phone messages!"

I could hear the sound of ten beagles howling behind her.

"Okay!" I shouted back. "I'll be up in a little while."

"What about these beagles? And Molly? Do you want me to bring them down there too?"

"No. Just let them out and stand back. They'll all come down on their own!"

"Okay!" she shouted. "And I need to talk to you!"

"Okay, I'll be up in a little bit."

Doyle and I got to the gate. I opened it to let the dogs in, we followed them, and I held the gate, ready for the onslaught of hounds, while she told me she had two important bits of information: Tulips was stable, though still unconscious, and the Portland police had found my Suburban. It was in the lot at the Portland airport.

"Huh. Why didn't they tell *me* about it?"

She grinned, shook her head. "I think they've been trying to reach you all morning. And not just them, the state police and the Rockland County Sheriff's Office. You apparently don't answer your phone, except when you feel like it."

I nodded absentmindedly, then said, "Good girl, Minnie!" to a red dachshund who was barking at a Westie named Muskoka, who was doing her best to get Minnie to play by doing play bow after play bow. "Good girl!" Minnie looked at me, wagged her tail slightly, then gave Muskoka the cold shoulder and raced off to find her friend Cassie, a silver miniature schnauzer.

Good, I thought: another fight averted by praising the aggressor before she gets too wound up.

The hills rang with the baying harmony of ten beagles, the deep, resonant bark of Hooch, and the excited yips of one wire-haired fox terrier. They all raced toward us. All except Hooch. He stopped to bark at Mrs. Murtaugh. She scolded him, causing him to bark even louder. Damn; there was that aggression again. This time it was aimed at Mrs. Murtaugh instead of the nurses.

"Hooch!" I yelled, using a high silly voice. "Good boy!"

He stopped barking and came running.

"Is this a bad time?" Doyle asked with a hint of sarcasm.

"No, but I have to keep an eye on the dogs whilst we talk." I opened the gate as Molly and the beagles, and finally Hooch, arrived. Much madness ensued, mostly of a playful nature, though Molly was still gravitating toward one of the sand pits.

After watching the dogs to make sure things went smoothly, I said, "So the police think Farrell might've left town?"

"That's what it looks like. It kind of puts a crimp in your theory that he's not the phantom killer, doesn't it?"

I shrugged. "It depends on when he left the car there."

"The parking lot ticket shows that the vehicle entered the lot a little after three A.M. last night."

"Okay," I said slowly. "Still, once Tulips comes out of it, she'll be able to tell us whether . . ." I stopped.

"What?" she asked.

"What did you put in your report about her?"

"Nothing. I just said that I found her unconscious body in the vicinity of Oak Hill Road."

"Good. It's totally vague but entirely truthful."

"Thanks. And I didn't say anything about seeing you there. When she comes out of it, though, that could be a problem." She looked at me long and hard. "What did you tell Jamie?"

"Nothing yet."

She shook her head and went to the gate. "You usually know what you're doing, so I'm not going to question you this time. Not yet. Besides," she shrugged, "I'm just a deputy till a week from Tuesday. Even then, homicide won't be my responsibility. But hopefully you'll have the whole case solved by that time."

"Yeah," I laughed. "It depends on which case you mean."

"I'm sorry?"

"Well, there's also the twenty-year-old case of old bones to consider."

She got a funny look on her face.

"What?" I asked.

"I don't know. You seem sure this is only related to Farrell asking questions about Eddie Cole, right?"

"That's what it looks like."

She shrugged. "Well, you're the expert, but it seems to me like an exaggerated response on Cole's part."

I hadn't thought of that but she was right. "Meaning?"

"Meaning maybe it's related to something else." She looked at the dogs for a moment. "When did Woods start asking questions about Cole, before or after Mrs. MacLeary's bones were found?"

"After," I said. "But that's a stretch. I don't see Cole having any connection with that case."

"It's possible there's a connection, though, right?"

"I guess, but it seems awfully unlikely. Oh, and listen, can you do something for me?"

"Sure. What?"

"Well, I'm going to be pretty busy with dogs all day. Can you find out what flights left Portland after Farrell parked my car there?"

"Oh, yeah," she said, digging into her pocket. "I nearly forgot." She held out a slip of paper.

"What is it?" I came over and took it.

"Nothing. Just a list of all the flights out of Portland this morning, starting with a five A.M. flight to L.A."

"You're going to make a great sheriff."

"True that."

16

I'd gotten the dogs situated in their pens—each dog with its own bone—and had taken Hooch up to the house to hang out with Frankie, when Jamie called again. This time I answered.

"Hi, honey," I said. "I was just about to call you."

"Jack! What is going on?"

"What do you mean?"

"I've been calling you and calling you, all morning!"

"I know, but I've been busy, sweetheart. Without Farrell to pick up the dogs, I've been running around like a crazy—"

She took a breath. "So, how are you?"

I told her I was fine, then relayed what Doyle had told me, including the location of my car.

"I'm glad they found it, but why would Farrell just run off like that without telling you?"

"You got me. It might have something to do with—hang on." I heard a beep and looked at the caller ID. It indicated a call was coming from the 213 area code: L.A. "Can I call you back?"

"Honey! I need to tell you something."

"I know. I'll call you right back." I clicked the phone over to the incoming call. "Dog Hill Kennels."

"How's the super group?" said a familiar voice.

"Where the hell are you?"

"LAX," said Woods. "I'm between planes. Sorry to run out on you again, but it couldn't be helped."

"Oh, yeah? Well, we really need to talk."

"I know, but not now. I just wanted to let you know I'm okay, and I'm following a lead on Eddie Cole. It's gonna blow your mind. I'll call you around midnight on Thursday and explain."

"Why not explain it now?"

"Because my flight is boarding soon, and I don't want to say anything on the phone. Not on any of your phones, anyway."

I lowered my voice so Mrs. Murtaugh couldn't listen in, even though I noticed now that she was pretending very hard not to listen. "Are you saying my lines are bugged?"

"Let's just say you were right about Eddie Cole having a connection inside the judicial system. Do you remember that diner? The one where Dennis Seabow got a rufie the night he was framed for Marti MacKenzie's death?"

I had to think a minute. "Oh. Yeah, I remember."

"Okay, there's a pay phone by the men's room. I'll call you Thursday night and explain what's going on. At least what I know so far. Don't tell anybody else about it. Not even Jamie."

"Okay," I lied. "But listen, Tulips is in the hospital."

"For what?"

"Someone gave her a hot shot."

"Oh, no. Oh, Jesus. Is she okay?"

"She will be. I think I found her in time."

There was an intake of breath. I could picture him at a pay phone at the airport, standing there in his jeans and fatigues, his duffel bag at his feet, fighting the urge to come back home to see Tulips. I wondered if I should tell him about Brent Pfleger's body, then thought maybe the phone really was tapped.

"She should have come with me, damn it! I was afraid something like this would happen."

"One question, did you ask Brent Pfleger to come over to your place last night?"

"No. Hell, no. Why?"

"Never mind. I'll tell you Thursday night."

"Okay, I gotta go; they just called my flight. And be on the lookout for a Korean guy, about six-four, built like a Humvee. His name is Ryoken and he's very dangerous."

"Did you say Ryoken?"

"Yeah. Why?"

"No reason. I'll talk to you later."

The phone beeped, and I clicked over to Jamie again.

"Jack!"

"Sorry, honey, I have to make another call." I hung up, then dialed Kelso. "Hey, Lou. How long would it take for you and your pal Dr. Lunch to get up here?"

"Hello, yourself."

"I don't have time to discuss it. How long?"

"Christ, Jack. Let me think." He thought. "I'll find out. He's teaching chemistry classes all day, but if he thinks the money's right, we could be there by seven or eight. Why?"

"I need to have him check my phones for bugs."

He cracked up.

"What's so funny?"

He kept laughing. "Jesus, Lunch can do that without leaving town. He could probably do it from the teacher's lounge."

"Including my cell phone and Jamie's?"

There was a pause. "No. A cell phone can be bugged just by tapping into the wireless frequency, as long as the person listening in has the decryption software, which isn't easy to get unless you're with the government. As far as I know, there's no way, electronically speaking, to find out if someone's tapping your cell phone, which is one reason I rarely use them."

"Okay, thanks for the info. Can you have him check my home phone, the kennel, and Jamie's phones at the ME's office?"

"Will do. I'm still working on that other thing."

"What other thing?"

"What do you mean, what other thing? The MacLearys, the Moose and Eagle Society?"

"Oh, right. Thanks. Oh, and see if you can find the name Ryoken in any of your databases."

"Ryoken? How do you spell it?"

"I don't know. He's a Korean goon, very dangerous."

I hung up just as Jamie called me back again. I felt bad about dodging her calls, but things were really starting to pop.

"Sorry, honey," I said. "I just had to take two very important calls in a row. One was from Farrell."

"He called you? Where is he?"

"He's in L.A. But the main thing is he's okay. I think some-one is after him again."

"That's terrible."

"Well, it sounded pretty bad. How was your staff meeting?"

"Fine," she said, and I got her to talk about her day, while I mulled things over and pretended to listen to her.

I snapped to attention when I heard the name Kurt Pfleger come buzzing through the handset. Then she said, "The thing that puzzles me, though, is the way the second victim was killed."

"Wait a minute, what? What second victim?"

"Weren't you listening? The bodies from the car fire last night. That's why I called you. One of them was Leon's friend from the dance. The one who smoked grass in your—"

"I know, Kurt Pfleger. That was the part I heard. What were you saying about a second body?"

"Okay, I'll repeat it. It seems like I've been doing that a lot late—"

"I know, I know. I'm sorry. I've had a lot on my mind with Farrell's disappearance and—"

"Anyway, what I said was Kurt Pfleger was in the driver's seat and he burned to death. He was alive at the time the fire started. In fact he called 911 from inside the car. The car was parked on the dock at a lake north of Belfast. The fire burned through the dock, so it was a real mess getting to the bodies."

I wanted to ask if it was Nichols Pond. That was where I'd seen the bonfire while driving home last night.

"At any rate, there was smoke damage to his lungs, so we know he died in the fire. The other victim was already dead."

"How did *he* die?" I asked, though I knew the answer.

"He exsanguinated due to a slit throat."

My heart stopped. "Slit?" My mouth got dry. "How slit?"

"From ear to ear. It was pretty gruesome. It looks like Kurt might've killed him. They haven't found the murder weapon."

Mrs. Murtaugh was staring at me.

"What?" I whispered.

"You're as white as a ghost."

"Thanks. Could you find something to do besides listen in on other people's—"

"Fine!" She got up and went into the grooming room.

"And call D'Linda!" I shouted after her. "And have her come in, would you? I need to go down to Portland later to get my car."

"You call her!"

"Jack, who are you talking to?"

"Mrs. Murtaugh. Have they ID'd the second body yet?"

"No. He didn't have any identification on him. They took his prints, but they haven't found him in the system."

I had an idea. "Have Kurt's parents come to ID the body?"

"Not yet. They're on their way."

"Okay," I said, hating myself for what I was about to suggest, "you might want to have them take a look at the other body."

"Why?"

"Maybe they can identify him too."

There was a pause and then she said, "That's brilliant. You're right; Kurt's parents would probably know who his friends are, so they might know him. What made you think of it?"

"It just came to me," I said, trying to keep my voice from giving me away. "Anyway, it's worth a shot."

Those poor Pflegers.

Once I was off the phone I went to apologize to Mrs. Murtaugh, though I didn't think I had any reason to. She did, though. Her face was set, her chin clenched, her arms held tight across her chest. I apologized, but her expression didn't change much.

"Okay, what is it? What's wrong?" I asked.

"Nothing."

"Alice . . ."

She uncrossed her arms. "I want a raise."

"Okay, but I don't . . . I don't pay you a salary, you know." She gets paid per dog or cat she grooms; I get ten percent. "Do you want me to raise our prices?"

"No, but you should pay me just to be here. I do more than clip and shampoo, you know. I'm here all day long."

That was true enough, except that I'd never asked her to

spend the day at the kennel. I always thought she did it to keep from being bored and lonely. Her husband died before I bought the place and all she has now are her cats. Her grandkids rarely visit. She likes hanging out with the doggies and making coffee and cupcakes in my kitchen, which is open to all my clients.

"Okay. I'll pay you for your time from now on. But then we'll have to split the grooming fees fifty-fifty."

She made a mean face. "Then never mind."

"Alice, do you need money?"

She shook her head, shrugged. Then gave me a pleading look. "What about health insurance? Shouldn't your employees get—"

"First of all, you're not an employee, and second, you already have health insurance. It's called Medicare."

Her face contorted. "But I don't understand the new benefits. I was supposed to sign a bunch of papers and I only got confused, so I signed up for the wrong plan. Now all my medicines cost twice as much, and I don't know what to . . ." She began to cry.

I went to the front desk, grabbed my chair, rolled it next to her, sat down and let her do it on my shoulder.

"It's all right." I put my arm around her. "I'll make sure you can afford your meds this month. Okay?"

"I don't know what I'm going to do."

"It's okay. I'll help you take care of it. And you're not just my employee, Alice. You're like family to me and Jamie."

"Really?"

"Yes. You know you are. Now, how much do you need?"

Her face was like a child's. "Two hundred dollars?"

I didn't even think about it; I just opened my wallet.

She hugged me and thanked me and cried and cried, then said, "I'll call D'Linda." She wiped away her tears. "And if she says she can't come in, I'll make damn sure she does anyway."

"Thank you. And I'm going to need to look over all your Medicare paperwork and your pharmacy bills so we can fix this."

"I'll bring them over tomorrow," she said, smiling.

17

It was a little after one. The dogs were all asleep: the beagles and company in the kennel, Frankie and Hooch in the living room. D'Linda was on her way. I was on the side porch, having a tuna fish sandwich. A cold wind was scattering the leaves across the lawn; storm clouds darkened the horizon. The phone rang and I went inside to get it.

It was Kelso. He told me that Dr. Lunch had done the scan on my home and business phones. They were clear. The three lines in Jamie's office, however, were being tapped.

I was surprised to hear it. "By who?"

"By whom. And it's funny you should ask, because I thought Lunch wouldn't be able to get that kind of information, but he did, sort of. By the way, you owe him five grand."

"Five thousand dollars? For what?"

"It's a thousand per line; you've got two, Jamie has three."

"Fine. I'll send him a check."

"Send it to me. He likes cash."

"Okay, all right. So, who's bugging Jamie's tele—"

"All I know is the device has a signal that's consistent with technology used by the military or the CIA."

"Jesus. Any idea where the bugs were planted?"

"Probably on the main line, not the phone itself, but Lunch said that was a guess on his part."

"Thanks, Lou. Nice work."

"I'm not done yet. He says he's never heard of the Moose and Squirrel Society, which—"

"Moose and Eagle."

"Whatever. Which means that either it means nothing, or it's more secretive than anything he's ever come across."

I thought it over. "Well then, I vote for the first."

"That's what Lunch thinks too. As for the MacLeary family, there's not much I could dig up that isn't in the public record. The general served at the Pentagon through 'eighty-two, then retired suddenly to Maine. He became a fixture in state politics for a while, serving in the Coster administration as lieutenant governor from 'eighty-three to 'eighty-nine. It was mainly a PR position."

"And his daughter Connie is married to the governor's son."

"Right. Do you remember the rumors about the Reagan team's secret meeting with Bani Sadr during the 'eighty election?"

"No. Who's Bonnie Sauter?"

"He was second-in-command in Iran at the time."

"Oh, yeah. Bani Sadr. What about him?"

"Well, supposedly, there was a meeting in Paris, in which an agreement was made to ensure that the American hostages in Tehran would be held captive until after Reagan took office."

"Are you kidding me?"

"No, it's common knowledge. At least the rumor about it is. And if you remember, the hostages were released right after Reagan took the oath of office. Down to the millisecond."

"Yeah, so what does that have to do with General MacLeary?"

"His travel log shows that he was in Paris at the time this meeting supposedly took place."

I laughed. "Well, that explains Cord's obsession."

"Who? Oh, the son. Yeah, part of the information I just gave you can be followed directly back to a website he's set up."

I laughed again. "Well, I wouldn't put much stock in what he says." I explained my theory that most of Cord's life has been spent trying to get his father's attention. "Besides," I told Kelso, "he believes the U.S. government is deliberately controlling world events to terrify the American voters."

"Yeah well, so does Lunch. And if you've got six hours of your life you don't mind wasting, he'll explain to you exactly how it's done and why."

I laughed again. "He and Cord ought to have dinner sometime." I was still chuckling, but this new information troubled me a little. "Listen, if Lunch is off the deep end about politics, how reliable is his information about the bugs?"

"It's only about ninety-nine-point-nine percent accurate."

"Because I don't want to be handing out five grand to some crackpot and then find out—"

"Trust me—when it comes to this stuff, he's never wrong."

"So, what do *you* think about these conspiracy theories?"

There was a pause. "To me they're valid and they're not. It depends on where you're standing inside the Zen hologram."

I smiled. "I forgot about you and your Zen hologram idea. Still, I don't know how it's going to help me with the case."

"Neither do I. But what is it you always tell people about finding out what's important to their dogs?"

I knew what he was referring to. One of the best ways to train a dog is to find out what's important to him, then act as if it's important to you too, even if it's completely ridiculous.

"Yeah," I said, "but this conspiracy stuff is only important to Cord, and I don't see him as a suspect."

"That may be, but it could also be important to somebody else and you just don't know who yet. Maybe Cord got the victim riled up about it, and that's why she was killed, who knows? I do know one thing: for you the dogs are always the key to any puzzle. Think about the dogs and you'll figure it out."

"If you say so."

"Have you talked to Jamie yet?"

"Yes and no." I explained about the discovery of the two bodies, one of whom had his throat slit.

"Oh, man. I do not envy you."

"Me neither."

After Kelso hung up I started to worry. Not about explaining things to Jamie, or where I was standing in the Zen hologram, or the veracity of Cord's theories, only about the wiretaps. I had to tell Jamie about them, but not over the phone, obviously.

And why was Molly at the center of the case, or was she?

This reminded me of something I'd forgotten to take care of. I called Reggie's cell phone. We discussed the general's condition a little—he was stable but the doctors weren't optimistic that he'd come out of the coma anytime soon—then I said:

"You know, I have your father's dog here at the kennel."

"So?"

"Well, it was a bit of an emergency when I brought her here; the general had just keeled over. But now that it looks like it's going to be some time before he's able to take care of her, I was wondering if someone in the family would want to keep her."

"I certainly wouldn't. I'm flying back to Mexico tonight."

I expressed my surprise.

"Why shouldn't I go? There's nothing I can do here. And don't ask Connie. She hates that dog worse than I do."

Connie would've been the last person I'd've asked, though I didn't tell Reggie that. "What's she got against Molly?"

"How should I know? All I know is she's terrified of her. She's been afraid to go near Dad's house since he got the dog."

"Huh. Well, anyway, I don't mind taking care of the little scamp, if you want me to. I just thought I should get some kind of official permission from someone in the family is all."

"Well, you've got it," she said, and hung up.

Just then I heard tires crunching on gravel and went out the side door, thinking it might be D'Linda, but it was an unmarked police car. I could tell by the blue bubble light on the dash.

I came down to the lawn. The car pulled to a stop and two men in jackets and ties got out. The driver was slim, young, blond, shorter than his partner. The partner was a bit chunky, with reddish-brown hair. He seemed to be having trouble getting his joints working after having been in the car for a while. (It's an hour's drive from Augusta.) They stood there for a moment, with their doors open, and looked around.

The stocky one stared through me with dead, uninterested eyes and said, "Are you Jack Field?"

"Yeah?" I walked a little closer to their car.

He twisted his spine a little, popped his neck. "I'm Mike

Dorris," he said, not giving me his official title. He looked me over some more. "You don't return your phone messages."

"Sure I do, when I have time."

"Anyway," he nodded his head toward the backseat of his car, "the attorney general wants to have a little chat with you."

This was an odd yet interesting development.

"Okay," I said, mustering up a winning smile, "I'll be sure to call him and set up a time to do that."

"Yeah. He'd kind of rather do it this afternoon."

"Oh, I can't," I said with a facial shrug. "I'm busy."

He looked at the other one. They closed their doors and came toward me. The stocky one pulled out a set of handcuffs. The metal caught a ray of sunlight. It glared at me as if the cuffs were brand new, as if they'd never been used before.

"Okay, before you get too fancy," I said, backing up a little, "where's the warrant?"

He stopped. His lip twitched. He twirled the cuffs around his short, fat fingers. "We don't need a warrant," he said.

The other one said, "We're not cops."

That froze me. "Then who are you?"

"Like I said, the attorney general wants to have a chat."

Now I knew what was going on. Connie's husband, Ed Coster, Jr. had probably sent two of his department's own investigators to bring me in, even if it meant I'd be able to file a false arrest complaint later on.

I said, "Well, I don't mean to be difficult, you guys are just doing your jobs, but I *am* going to need to see some ID."

They got out their wallets.

I came up to take a closer look. They didn't have badges, just photo IDs from the AG's office, as I'd suspected.

"Okay," I said with my hands up. "I'll come peacefully."

As they marched me to the vehicle I was a little worried that I wouldn't be able to get back in time to take home the dogs I had in day care, but luckily D'Linda—a plump, florid-cheeked, girl with overworked straw hair—arrived just as I was about to be *pushed* into the cop car. (The blond kid tried putting his hand on top of my head the way they do, but I backed him off with a hard look.)

I asked D'Linda if she'd take care of the dogs for me if I didn't get back in time, and she said she would.

Once I got in the backseat—sans cuffs, mind you—I reached into the side pocket of my cargo pants and pulled out my cell phone. I held it down, a tad below the level of the backseat, waited till the car's starter motor kicked on, then hit the speed-dial number for Otis Barnes. Then, when I heard the tinny, far-away sound of him answering his phone, I said loudly, "So, you guys are investigators for the attorney general's office?"

"That's right."

"And you don't mind putting me under false arrest?"

I could hear Otis squawking at the other end. I hoped he'd catch on before Dorris and his partner heard him squawking too.

Dorris was saying something about it not being false arrest, that I wasn't in custody, and why was I making such a big deal.

I said, "If I'm not under arrest, then why did you threaten to handcuff me when I refused to come with you?"

Now I could hear steady silence coming from the other end of the line. I looked down at the phone to make sure it was still connected, that Otis hadn't simply hung up. He hadn't.

"We're just following orders," said Dorris.

"Whose orders? From Allan Forbert or from his political appointment flunky?"

"His *what*, now?"

"You know: Junior? The ex-governor's son? He's the one who told you guys to come pick me up, isn't he?"

Dorris looked over at his partner. They shook their heads.

"No comment," Dorris said.

"No comment?" I repeated loudly, for Otis's benefit. "Ed Coster, Jr., the deputy AG, is trying to intimidate me because I saw his wife try to murder her father, and you've got no comment?"

There was a heavy silence coming from the cell phone, *and* from the two gents up front, though the blond kid was now giving me some strained looks through the rearview.

I said, "So, where are you guys planning on taking me?"

More silence.

"To Junior's office in Augusta?"

"Do you know how to shut up?" Dorris asked wearily.

Some autumn scenery passed in silence, then Dorris said to me, "You know, you got some kind of wild imagination."

"Nobody told us to intimidate anybody," said Blondie. "Coster just told us to pick you up, and if you was give us any trouble, he said he didn't mind if we got a little physical. Which we didn't!"

Dorris hit the younger man on the arm. "Shut up, Todd."

Todd shut up. So did I. Everything was silent now except for the sound of tires on gravel, though I was practically certain I could also hear the sounds of Otis Barnes scooting his chair back from his desk, grabbing his keys, and running out the door.

But then, I have some kind of wild imagination.

18

They stuck me in a room with old plaster and new furniture—
two black and chrome chairs, a coffee table, and a bare overhead bulb—and left me for nearly an hour, with no secretary to
dodge questions from and no old magazines to read. The only
things of passing interest were a newspaper and a paperback
mystery someone had left on the coffee table. The novel was
one in a series written by a New York dog trainer I admire: not
as a novelist, but as someone who knows his way around dogs.
So I picked it up and tried a few pages. It didn't grab me, but
then I don't like mysteries, though I *did* like the dog training
angle.

I had tried calling Otis again, just as soon as they left me
alone, but I couldn't get a signal inside the building. I had to
hope that he was on his way. There was no way I was going
to call Jamie, even if I could have. Not if her phones were
bugged.

After I gave up on *To Collar a Murderer*, or whatever the
silly thing was called, I paced a little, pissed off at being kept
waiting. Coster probably designed it that way, felt that by making me wait, I'd lose my cool, and then he'd be able to use that
against me.

Good, I thought, then stopped pacing and sat down. Now
I was *two* steps ahead of him. I could have worried about the
pickle I might be in—bozos like Junior can make your life mis-
erable if nothing else—but I didn't. Instead I worried about the

bugs on Jamie's office phone, Farrell Woods's disappearance, Tulips and the general, the impending conversation between Leon and Sloan, and whether I could rehabilitate Buster and turn him back into what he was meant to be, a good doggie, a purely social animal.

Okay, fine, Jack. But you're locked in a room in Augusta, and there's nothing you can do about any of that. Not right now.

So what can you do?

Well, I told myself, *I like to solve mental puzzles, so I could do that. Maybe work on the case, or both of them.*

I let my mind go blank and tried that Zen thing Kelso talks about. I also thought about the players in the drama, and what was most important to each of them. I also thought about Molly, and how she was the center of the case. And when I did, I knew who'd killed Katherine MacLeary; it was as clear as day.

I didn't know it with enough certainty to go to the DA and have him swear out an arrest warrant (I wasn't about to take this to the attorney general), but I could steer the police in the right direction, as long as they were cops I could trust. All I'd have to get them to do was check a certain party's fingerprints against the ones on the empty shell casing in General MacLeary's .22.

Satisfied with myself, I picked up the paper and glanced at the article on the MacLeary murder. It featured an old photo of Mrs. MacLeary, and I remembered the name of the old movie star she reminded me of: she looked just like Olivia de Havilland in her prime. I thumbed to the local news and found an item about a ground-breaking ceremony for a nuclear power plant to be held the next morning in Owl's Head, with Ed Coster, Sr. presiding.

Just then the door opened and Jeffrey Compton appeared, wearing a dark blue pinstripe suit and a chagrined expression.

"Sorry to keep you waiting," he said.

Like hell, I thought, but smiled and said, "That's okay."

"My office is just a few doors down."

He led me into a marble-floored hall with arched ceilings. His wing-tips sent echoes rippling past the clumps of men and women in business suits who huddled over legal briefs, or strode purposefully toward doorways, or paced while speaking too loudly into their cell phones. One figure stood alone. He held a cup of coffee loosely in one hand, but the way he stood on the balls of his feet, his muscles relaxed yet ready, made you wonder if he was wearing track shorts under his sharkskin suit, and just where the starting line was supposed to be. I had a good idea where the finish tape was; it was pasted across my chest.

Our eyes locked for a moment in slow motion, then he looked away and took a deliberate sip of coffee.

I knew he wasn't a feeb; they always come in twos.

Compton said, "Here we are," and held a door open for me.

Before I stepped across the threshold I looked back down the hall, but the man with the coffee cup was gone.

Compton led me past a middle-aged secretary in a white blouse and a head of orange hair with white roots, ensconced behind a desk. She had a mystery novel open in front of her. It was by the same author as the one I'd tried to read. Compton said nothing; he just led me to another door. She glanced up briefly; her eyes darted over to me, then went back to her book.

We went through another door and came into a room a bit larger than the one I'd wasted an hour of my life in. It had the same basic décor with a few additions: a black-and-chrome desk, black-and-chrome filing cabinets, and a lot of black bookshelves, filled with thick, heavy legal tomes, mostly brown and green. He had a framed photo of a brown Portuguese water dog on his desk.

There was a tubby little guy in a white long-sleeve shirt and crimson tie. He sat waiting for us in a chair that he'd pulled away from the desk and then shoved into a corner, where he could watch both me and Compton without straining his neck. I had a pretty good idea who he was but said nothing.

He was in his late fifties, medium height, with fat cheeks, fat arms, fat thighs, and fat fingers. He wore a lukewarm smile of mild interest that didn't spill into overfriendliness. He gave a nod then looked away to show there'd be no further interaction.

I sat facing Compton's desk, picked up the photo and said, "Nice looking Portagee."

He sat, said, "Kiki? He's a *Spanish* water dog, actually."

"Oh, I didn't know they had them. He looks like a cool doggie." I looked at the guy in the corner. "Some people are scared of dogs. Your wife, for instance; she's terrified of 'em."

He scowled. "What gave you that idea?"

"Huh? Oh, I think Reggie told me."

"Reggie's full of shit. My wife loves dogs." He looked at Compton. "Too much, if you ask me. We've got this little red Pomeranian that barks whenever I come near Connie. I guess he thinks he needs to protect her from me or something."

"No," I said. "He's not feeling protective of her. He's feeling possessive."

"Say what?"

"It's quite common in little dogs who get too much attention. It unnaturally overstimulates their social needs."

"No kidding. Because Connie *does* fawn over him too much." He looked up at Compton. "At least I always thought so."

"The thing is," I said, "a dog's social behaviors are directly related to his need to hunt; dogs are group predators. So while they enjoy physical affection, they need more playtime than cuddle time. But that's not why you dragged me up here, is it?"

"Me? I just happened to be passing by."

"Oh sure, I believe you."

"Okay, enough." Compton turned on a tape recorder. "I've just been given a police report about an incident you supposedly witnessed at Rockland Memorial yesterday afternoon, and I wanted to go over it with you." He opened a scarlet leather notebook, which held a yellow legal pad, then took a pen from his shirt.

"Fine," I said. "Just so I know, why is Tubby here?"

There was an exhalation of breath from Junior, followed by him shifting his weight around.

"Never mind," said Compton. "He's merely . . . um, observing. Now, can we go over the incident?"

"Why not?" I told him what had happened, he made a few notes on the legal pad in his leather holder, and when I was done he closed it, stood up and put his hand out for me to shake.

"That's it? That's what you dragged me up here for?"

"Sorry. I'm just following procedure."

"Yeah, right."

I stood up but didn't shake his hand; I just turned to go. I was halfway to the door when Junior said, "Where were you last night, Mr. Field? From around ten o'clock on?"

I turned to look at him. "Who are you again?"

"Never mind that. Just answer the question."

"No."

His neck went back. "You said what?"

"You heard me. You haven't told me who you are. I obviously have a pretty good idea, but say I don't. Why should I talk to you?"

"Maybe because you want to go on living—"

"Shut up. That was rhetorical; I'm talking. If you want to know my whereabouts last night, or any day of any week, tough. I don't have to tell you a damn thing."

He twisted in his chair, reached in his back pocket and pulled out a legal document, folded in three and wrapped in blue stock paper. "You ever heard of a material witness warrant?"

I'd not only heard of them, I'd used them. They're a handy way to lock someone up for a few days if you can find a judge who'll let you get away with it.

I said, "You ever heard of habeas corpus?"

Compton said, "Just answer his questions, Jack."

"No. Better yet, fine. I don't remember anything about last night. I got a bad bump on the head—I don't know how or when—and it seems to have erased all my short-term memory."

A look passed between Compton and Tubby. I'd answered the question. They had nothing to hold me on except pure meanness.

"Did you go to a hospital to get it looked at?" asked Tubby.

"Gee, that's another thing I don't remember."

The buzzer on Compton's desk buzzed. He hit a button and said, "Yes, Darlene?"

"There's a very insistent reporter out here to see you."

"Send him in!" I said, then turned to open the door.

"No, Darlene, do not send him in."

Too late; the door was open. I said, "Come on in!" to Otis, then stepped out of his way.

He sprang into the inner office (he was pretty spry for an old guy) and pointed a voice recorder at Tubby. "Mr. Coster, is it true that you're attempting to intimidate a witness in your wife's attempted murder of General MacLeary?"

"That's ridiculous. My wife did no such thing."

"You didn't answer the question. Are you attempting to use the power of your office to intimidate a witness?"

"Of course not."

Compton was on the intercom. "Darlene, call Security."

"I've already called them, sir."

"Good."

I told Otis, "They just now threatened me with a material witness order." I nodded at the document in Coster's hand.

"That's patently untrue," said Coster.

"Fine," said Otis. "Show me that document in your hand."

He put it in his pocket. "Get out of here now, or I'll— This is a state office; you can't come barging in here like—"

"I didn't barge in. I was invited."

"Not by me, you weren't."

Otis said, "I can find the judge who signed that order. Plus, two AG investigators say you sent them to this man's kennel with orders to handcuff him and rough him up if necessary."

"What investigators?" asked Junior.

Otis looked at me.

I said, "Mike Dorris. His partner's name was Todd."

"Those two incompetent . . . !" Coster sputtered.

Otis said, "The public is also going to wonder why your wife just fled the jurisdiction with this attempted murder charge still hanging over her."

"Get out of here now!"

"Connie flew the coop?" I asked Otis.

"Yeah. She and Reggie just boarded a flight to Mexico."

"Interesting."

Coster said, "My wife has been under a great deal of stress and needs a vacation. That's all."

"So you admit that she's fled the jurisdiction?"

"I admit no such thing. There are no charges against her, just the word of this friggin' dog trainer, so she isn't fleeing from anything but his big fat mouth."

"Do I have a big fat mouth?" I asked Otis.

He looked me over. "Not especially."

I said, "I'll tell you who *does* have a big fat mouth, and a big fat ass . . ." I looked pointedly at Junior.

"Get out of here, now!"

Otis and I looked at each other, shrugged, and left.

Once we were safely in the hall, we saw two security guards rushing toward Compton's office.

"It's the short, tubby one that's causing all the trouble," I said as they passed, hoping they'd never met Junior before.

"Well, that was fun," Otis said as we hurried toward the main lobby. "But it doesn't do either one of us any good."

"Sure it does. It kept me from going to jail." I looked around for the coffee cup guy but didn't see him.

"I'm happy for you," Otis said, "But what good does it do me? Without corroboration for what allegedly happened at the hospital, this is a nonstory. I've got a deadline in two days."

"Fine, I'll tell you who'll corroborate it for you, though it probably won't do you much good . . ."

"Who?"

"Connie Coster."

"You're kidding."

"Nope. If you can talk to her, she'll be happy to confess."

"Great," he said as we went through the main door into the late afternoon sun. "How do I talk to her if she's in Mexico?"

"That's a problem, I guess."

"Then again," he said as we walked toward the parking lot on Western, "she may not be."

"What do you mean? She may not be what?"

"In Mexico. Ed Jr. and his dad could be hiding her at the Moose and Eagle Lodge."

I started to laugh. "The what?"

"The Moose and Eagle. It's her father-in-law's private hunting lodge, north of Skowhegan."

Between bouts of helpless laughter I explained about Cord's conspiracy theory version of the Moose and Eagle Society.

"Well," Otis said, "I suppose they could be intent on world domination, but from what I know, it's mostly about drinking expensive scotch and killing things with guns."

"So this lodge is owned by Ed Coster, Sr.?"

"That's right," he said as we got to his car, a boxy Volvo, bronze, I think. "Do you need a ride back to Camden?"

"Yeah, thanks."

"Hop in."

I remembered my Suburban. "Well, no, actually. I need to go down to Portland. My Suburban is in the airport parking lot."

He stood there thinking. "The thing is, I should probably go to the airport myself. I'd like to find out if Connie Coster really went to Mexico or up to Somerset County."

"How can you find that out in Portland?"

"I'm not just an editor, I'm a reporter, that's how. I've got the flight number. If we get there before the shift change, I can talk to the boarding personnel to see if it was really her on that flight. On top of that, I know the pilot who flies Coster's guests upstate."

"Well, it looks like you got yourself a hitchhiker."

19

It was getting close to four o'clock—the rush hour was rev-
ving up to slow everything down. The roads between Augusta
and Portland would soon be bumper-to-bumper. Not like the
L.I.E. or the West Side Highway, but close enough for Maine.
One good thing about such traffic—it's hard to tail somebody
without being seen. I didn't see anyone behind us the whole
way down.

We took I–95 south, and I asked Otis about the two Ed
Costers. Junior I had a good sense of from meeting him face-
to-face. As for Senior, he was close to ninety years old, had
homes in Augusta, Old Orchard Beach, and of course the hunting lodge upstate. Senior had pretty much been the kind of man
Cord had described to me. The one piece of information I got
that I hadn't learned from Cord was the name of the mystery
woman he'd supposedly had the affair with back in the early
1950s.

She was a Mexican housemaid named Margarita Ortíz.

"What's that look mean, Jack?"

"Nothing."

"It's not nothing. Her name means something to you."

"Keep your eyes on the road."

"Who is she?"

"Look, Otis, seriously—I have no idea. I just know of a very
dangerous drug lord from San Diego named *Miguel* Ortíz. He
was marginally involved in the Gordon Beeson case."

He thought back to the case, remembered something. "He was the one buying the forged artwork from Ian Maxwell?"

"That's right. But it's doubtful that there's any connection between him and Ed Coster Sr.'s mistress."

"Yeah, it's a fairly common last name for a Hispanic."

"That's right."

We inched along for a while.

I said, "You *could* research it, though. Right?"

"What? To see if they're related?"

"Yeah. Where is she now, by the way?"

"No one knows."

"Interesting. Do you know where she was *from* in Mexico?"

"A little town in Baja, as I recall."

"There's another coincidence; Miguel was also from Baja."

"So are a lot of people."

"That's true," I said. "So are a lot of people."

Otis dropped me off next to my car. I found the key where Farrell had left it (though I had a spare set of my own), and then just for fun, before I got in and started 'er up, I popped the hood and checked for any mechanical devices that shouldn't be there—like a bomb, for instance. I didn't see anything. Just for good measure, though, I got down on my hands and knees, rolled over on my back, and scooted underneath to check the undercarriage.

It was clean.

I got home a little after seven to find that Jamie was, as they say, hoppin' mad. She and Doyle were ensconced on the big leather sofa in the living room. On the coffee table were some cups and saucers and assorted coffee things.

Frankie and Hooch came up to me and circled around for a bit till I took them into the kitchen and put down their evening meal.

While they were eating I came back into the living room to a lot of angry conversation, mostly about me not answering my phone, pointed questions about how the hell I knew the second body on Jamie's autopsy table was Kurt Pfleger's brother: she'd remembered he was the one I mentioned on Sunday night. This went on for a while, with no chance for me to do anything but say I was sorry.

It became clear that Doyle hadn't squealed about what transpired the night before. That was a relief.

"Sweetheart," I assured Jamie, "this isn't a continuation of what we talked about the other night. The reason I haven't returned your phone calls is that your office phones are bugged."

She gave me a smile of disbelief, the kind where your mouth is smiling but your eyes look shocked. "What?" She searched my face, and when she saw I wasn't making it up, her eyes got angry. "Who the hell is tapping my phones?"

"I don't know for sure, but I think—"

"And you still could have called me on my cell phone."

"No, it's probably bugged too."

She asked me how the hell I knew all this, and I told her. Now she was really mad. "But who? Who's doing this?"

I said I thought it might be Ed Coster, Jr.

"Why?"

"Why would he *do* it? Because—"

"No," she said, "why do you think it's *him*?"

I explained about the type of electronic device that was being used. "So it probably isn't the state police or the FBI; it has to be someone from the CIA or the military."

"But Ed Jr. doesn't have any connection to either."

"Sure he does." I told her about his father's ties to the CIA, then said, "Plus, when I was in his office this afternoon—"

Another explosion: "You were in Augusta? When?"

I told her.

"And you didn't come see me?"

"I didn't have time." I explained my itinerary, then said, "Plus, if they've tapped your phones, who knows if your office has been bugged? I had to wait till we were both home."

"This is unbelievable!"

"And listen to this . . ." I told her about Junior's question as to where I'd been last night. "Why would he ask me that? He had to have heard our telephone conversation this morning."

She got up, started pacing. "I'm going to put an end to this.

I'm the state medical examiner, for god's sakes! They can't get away with this kind of crap."

"Now, honey . . ." I said to her, then glanced at Peggy.

"Don't look at me, Romeo."

"Well, not to be rude or anything," I said, "but is there a reason you're here?"

Jamie said, "That's *very* rude."

I said, "Sorry, but—"

"I had something I wanted to discuss," said Doyle. "And since you weren't here, I thought I'd catch up with Jamie."

"So what did you want to discuss?"

"Trust me, this wiretapping thing takes precedence."

"Anyway," I said to James, "I think the best thing for now is to let Ed Jr. think he's got us fooled. That way we can plant false information in future conversations and lead him in the wrong direction. Then, maybe we can find out what he knows."

"Knows about what?"

I shrugged. "I haven't got the faintest idea."

"Great." She sat down, tried to pour herself another cup, but the warmer was empty.

I went to grab it, but Doyle beat me to it.

"I'll get it," she said, then scooted into the kitchen.

Jamie said, "What would Peggy want to discuss with you?"

"I don't know,"

Frankie and Hooch finished their chow, came back and pestered me for attention. I petted them for a second then said, "Okay! Find a toy!" and they ran off together to the toy basket.

"By the way," Jamie said, "Mrs. Murtaugh told me to tell you that the refrigerator repairman came by while you were out and fixed the problem."

"What problem?" I asked.

"How should I know? That's what she told me."

Perplexed, I said, "There's nothing wrong with the refrigerator."

"Anybody want some real cream this time?" Doyle asked from the kitchen.

"Wait!" I shouted, jumping to my feet. "Don't open—"

There was a fractured moment in time, almost before I heard

the explosion, when I saw Doyle's body and the door to the refrigerator flying, sailing, being flung across the kitchen.

Doyle's body went straight back toward the big round oak kitchen table, where it landed. Her arms were twisting around, her head bobbing up and down as she hit hard, then slid across the smooth tabletop. The big white refrigerator door chased her, end over end, twisting from tip to tip, but flew past, toward some glass-doored cabinets. This horrifying ballet had a color backdrop: a single, near blinding flash of white, followed by a billion yellow-orange flames. All the kitchen windows exploded in a burst of glass. My eardrums popped, I went deaf, yet I thought I heard three screams sounding in chorus. I think one of them was mine. The screams were followed by a lot of frantic barking and a toneless, incessant ringing in my ears.

My chest, my arms, my face, my feet, my brain went numb.

There was a moment of utter silence; yet it wasn't silence at all, really, just a sudden stillness. The dogs were barking, you could even hear the beagles and Molly from the kennel. But there was an almost vibrationless hum hanging in the air.

Then Jamie and I ran as hard and as fast as we could to see if Doyle had survived, and if so, what kind of shape she was in.

She was moaning, which told us she was still alive. Good.

I stood there asking stupid questions about how she was while Jamie went into action, holding her hand and telling her, "Don't try to move. Just lie still. Tell me where it hurts."

Doyle moaned some more and said, "My head and my back."

"Is anything broken? Jack, don't just stand there, call the police!" Then to Doyle, "Can you feel your fingers and toes?"

"I don't know. All I can feel is this pain when I breathe."

I went to the phone. Leon appeared in the doorway. He was in sweats and bare feet. Magee stood trembling next to him.

"What happened?" he asked.

"The refrigerator blew up," I said as I heard the phone ringing on the other end. "We're all right. Go put your shoes on. There's broken glass in here. And don't bring Magee back with—"

"Nine-one-one, what is your emergency?"

While I explained the situation, Leon turned around and went back outside. Magee followed him. Frankie and Hooch poked their noses into the kitchen. They were trembling like Magee.

"Hang on," I said to the 911 operator, then to the dogs, "Go lie down! Go!"

They didn't want to.

"Go! Go to place!"

They finally turned and trotted back to the hearth. They were so stressed they cuddled up together on Hooch's bed.

I finished the 911 call, said, "They're on their way."

Jamie—still with Doyle, still holding her hand—said, "The pain was too much; she passed out." She gave me Doyle's medical breakdown; a broken collarbone, possible concussion, but no punctured lung and very little, if any, internal bleeding. "Her breathing is good, it's not ataxic or apneustic."

"Should we take her down the mountain to meet the ambulance? That would save time, right?"

She said no, she didn't want to move her for fear there might be a cervical fracture. "Who would do this?"

"I know exactly who did this," I said, then told her who.

"But that's insane." She pulled out a chair and sat down, still holding Doyle's hand.

"Not necessarily. It's just out of proportion to what we think we know about what's going on."

"What does that mean? Where are you going?"

"To get the broom. I'm going to clean up this glass."

"No, leave it till the crime scene unit gets here. We have to leave everything just the way it is as much as possible."

"Oh, right." I pulled out a chair, scraping glass as I moved it back, then sat next to her and looked at the streaks of Doyle's blood staining the table.

She reminded me: "You were saying it's out of proportion . . ."

"Oh, yeah. My brain is still a little numb from . . . the thing is, here I was thinking that Junior was trying to intimidate me so I wouldn't testify against Connie, but that's not why he had two of his investigators drag me up to the capital today."

"Oh. You think he did it to get you out of the house so someone could plant that bomb in the refrigerator?"

"That's right. Which means something a lot more serious is

going on. Something we don't know anything about yet, or if we do, we don't know how it's connected to Ed, Jr."

"He doesn't want us finding out what it is."

"He wants us dead, at least he wants me dead. He even threatened to kill me today." I looked at Doyle. Her chest was heaving slightly, her eyes closed. "This is all my fault."

"How is it your fault?"

"I thought I knew what I was doing." I shook my head, angry at myself. "I thought it was a game, what happened in his office today. I thought I was two steps ahead of him. Now I see that he was playing me, or someone else was using him to do that."

"You couldn't have known he, or *they*, would do this." She looked around at the destruction. "Besides, you distracted her at the right moment. If you hadn't yelled at her she would've taken the full brunt of the blast and might not have survived."

"That's true, I guess."

She sighed. "This is so out of control. I wish we could've stayed in Mexico."

"We may have to go back there at some point." I explained about Reggie and Connie fleeing the jurisdiction. "That reminds me." I went to the phone and called Otis to find out what he'd learned at the airport.

"I was about to call *you*, Jack. I just heard over the scanner that a bomb went off inside your house?"

"Yeah, in my kitchen." I told him what had happened and why I thought Junior was behind it.

"Well," he said, "Connie didn't board that plane for Mexico. And my pilot friend made a trip upstate this afternoon."

"So she's at the lodge?"

"Probably. Do you want me to give this thing about the bomb to the wire services?"

"Yeah. Let them know that Junior may have been behind it. And fax me the location of that lodge. I may have to go up there."

"I'd go up myself but I've got a paper to run."

"I forgot; you're not just a roving reporter, are you? Hey, did you find out anything about the Ortíz connection?"

"Not yet. I hope I get something before Thursday." That's when the *Herald* comes out.

"I'm looking forward to seeing Molly's picture on the front page." I got off the phone, explained things to Jamie, then said, "It's a shame we can't link this to Junior directly."

She disagreed. "The police can reconstruct the type of bomb used. They'll check their database for bombers who—"

"I know. They might find the guy who planted it, but that'll take days or weeks, and even longer to establish a connection to Junior. We don't have that kind of time."

I got up and went back to the phone.

"Who are you calling?"

"Kelso."

"Why call him now?"

"Because I need him on our side of the battle."

"I guess your policy of not fighting the wave is out, huh?"

"This isn't a wave, honey, this is war. And I need him and anyone else I can find for a small army I'm putting together."

She got out her BlackBerry. "Good idea. I'll call Flynn."

"Now we're cooking. When you're done, I want a word with him too. And anyway," I said to her while dialing Kelso, "you can't ride a wave until you get on top of it."

20

The morning was cool, though the sun shone brightly on the ribbon-cutting ceremony at Owl's Head Bay. I stood among a crowd of about fifty people, most of them paid, I suspected, to show up for the cameras, though a coterie of placard-toting protesters claimed their share of lens time; the power plant had been okayed by a secret vote of the legislature, which left a lot of people angry.

A few TV crews were there to cover the story, though only one had an on-scene reporter—Donna Devon, from the station in Portland where I do my dog-training tips on Saturday mornings. I'd told her to have the newsroom ready to break into regular programming in case of a surprising, one-of-a-kind event.

"Why, what's going to happen?" she'd asked.

"If I told you it wouldn't be a surprise."

"You have to give me something . . ."

"Fine. It has to do with the bombing of my kitchen."

Last night I'd had to stick around for the police to arrive while Jamie rode with Doyle in the ambulance. Then, once the investigators finished processing the scene, which took till at least four in the morning, I had to clean up the mess: the broken eggs, splattered milk, catsup, mayonnaise, pasta sauce, orange juice, salsa, pickle fragments, and, of course, all the glass. (Don't ever let your refrigerator explode; the cleanup's a bitch.)

After Jamie and Doyle left, Sloan came over to see Leon, and I enlisted her help to keep an eye on the dogs and take care of their needs while I was dealing with the cops. She'd spent the night in the downstairs guest room. I'd also called my contractor, Doriane Elliot, and she sent a crew over first thing in the morning to fix the windows. She promised to have a new refrigerator in place by the end of the day. She even asked me for a grocery list so she could stock the fridge, god bless her.

I wasn't alone in the crowd at the ribbon-cutting ceremony. A state police detective named Greg Sinclair was on one side of me, Otis Barnes on the other. Sheriff Flynn and two of his deputies, big ones, stood next to Sinclair. To their right were Brad Bailey and Carl Staub, who'd finally been taken off the MacLeary case. It was now being handled by the state police.

Ed Coster Jr. was on the viewing stand, sitting on a folding chair, along with several dignitaries of one type or another. His father, the former governor, stood trembling in front of the big red ribbon. The huge ceremonial scissors shook in his palsied hands. Two lovely young women in satiny gowns were posed next to him. A brisk ocean breeze was blowing and they seemed ready to keep him steady, or from falling over, if necessary.

Coster's frail condition caused a bit of tension in the crowd. Would he cut the ribbon? Would he fall down?

He put his arms forward, the ribbon fluttered in the breeze. Uh-oh, I thought, he's not going to be able to cut it! But then it caught on the lip of one of the blades. Chop! He was an old hand. The ribbon floated to the ground in two sinuous pieces.

There were cheers, mixed with boos from the protesters.

It was at that moment that Sheriff Horace Flynn, along with his two very large deputies, took the stand and approached the contingent seated behind the action. All cameras and all eyes swerved away from Coster Sr. to this new piece of action.

Flynn asked Junior to stand up, then informed him that he was under arrest for conspiracy to commit murder and for sponsoring an act of terrorism on U.S. soil. The deputies pulled Junior's arms behind his back and handcuffed him.

Flynn then did a perp-walk right past Coster Sr., who stood frozen, stunned, unable to speak.

"Dad!" Junior cried. "Do something! Stop them!" His voice had a high-pitched, childish, whining quality; a tone that most microphones pick up readily.

Coster Sr. waved his arms feebly, trying to stop Flynn, but didn't realize he still held the scissors. The point of the shears stabbed one of the two lovelies right in the arm.

She squeaked, put her hand up to the wound, drew it back, saw the blood, then shot him a hurt, open-mouthed look.

By now Flynn had marched Junior past Coster and up to the TV crews. He stopped to tell Donna Devon, "This man used terrorist tactics to cover up his wife's attempted murder of General Lamar MacLeary, an American hero who served this country for over fifty years. Add to that the attempted murder of Deputy Peggy Doyle, who was selected by the people of Rockland County to be their next sheriff. And just like General MacLeary, Deputy Doyle lies in the hospital today, close to death, and all thanks to the crimes of Ed Coster, Jr."

The crowd started booing Junior. (No one likes him.)

"Quiet!" shouted Coster Sr. "You're not being paid to boo!"

Donna Devon asked Flynn, "Sir, you're only a county sheriff. You don't have the legal right to arrest him, do you?"

"Yes I do, Donna. This cowardly act of terrorism was committed in my county."

Junior shouted, "I didn't do anything! I'm innocent! Dad!" He turned toward the stand. "Dad! Call my lawyer! No, better yet, call *your* lawyer!"

"But he's not really a terrorist, is he?"

"What do you call someone who plants a bomb in a public place in order to intimidate or kill a witness? In this case, it nearly killed Sheriff-elect Doyle. To me, that's an act aimed at the heart of all human decency, and it needs to be punished."

My kitchen is well-known as a place for my clients to come, have coffee, and schmooze if they like, so technically it's a public place, but Flynn was stretching the truth quite a bit.

Otis turned to me. "Aren't you worried this'll backfire?"

"I don't care. I just want him tied up for a while."

"And aren't there usually state troopers at these events?"

Sinclair said, "Yeah, I think they got sidetracked today. Lucky thing too; if they'd been here, they might've felt it necessary to stop Flynn."

"That is lucky," said Otis. "Where are you going, Jack?"

"To the hospital."

Now that Junior was taken care of, my next order of business was to check in on Doyle. I got sidetracked, though, when Cord MacLeary, who'd been there protesting the event, caught up with me along the side of the road where I'd parked my Suburban.

"Hey," he said, out of breath. "I found something that could be important." He shoved an old envelope toward me.

"What is it?"

"Remember you wanted evidence of a direct connection between my mother's death and the Moose and Eagle?"

"Which is a hunting lodge, it turns out."

He shook his head as though he'd heard the same lie a million times. "That's just a cover," he said, then pushed the envelope at me again. "But this isn't about the dam conspiracy."

"What's it about?" I took the envelope.

"The Coster sex scandal. Read my mother's words."

I did. They were beautifully handwritten on translucent notepaper with green and pink trim: spring roses on a trellis.

August 13, 1988

My Dear Lamar,

Now that Margaret has given us all the facts, you have to realize this wasn't just a youthful indiscretion; it's a sick, perverted crime. Imagine if it had been Reggie or Connie! You must resign immediately as Lt. Governor. If you don't go public with this, I will!

Katherine

"This is your mother's handwriting?"

He said it was.

"What makes you think she's referring to the sex scandal?"

"The date! That was right at the peak of the press coverage. And it was written two days before she disappeared."

"Okay. Where did you get it?"

"I looked through some of Dad's old things."

"The police already searched the place, didn't they?"

"Sort of." He shook his head in disdain. "But I knew all of my father's secret places for hiding things; they don't."

That fit. I could just imagine young Cord combing the house, looking for his father's secrets.

I said, "Do you know who this Margaret is?"

"I assume she's the mother of Ed Coster's love child."

"That's a different name than I heard, though she could have changed it. And why did *your* mother think it was a crime?"

"I think it's obvious. Especially the line urging my father to think about if the victim had been one of his daughters. Ed Coster obviously raped the woman."

"Maybe." I pocketed the envelope. "I'm going to hang onto this, if you don't mind."

"I don't mind. So this is the connection you wanted. If Ed Coster knew my mother was going to blow the whistle on rape, that would be a good motive to kill her, right?"

"Yeah. That would be a good motive."

Doyle, who was in fine spirits—probably too fine for her own good—had a bed in the ICU. Her left eye was swollen, purple and red, her left arm dangled from a metal brace, and the top of her head was bandaged. She was lucky; the blast had just broken her collarbone and a few ribs, and given her a slight concussion.

There were the usual "How are you?"s and "How do think?"s, which ended with: "You've gotta help me get out of here, Jack."

"I don't think so," I said, smiling and taking a seat. "You're in no condition to leave yet."

She said, "Who cares? I've gotta get that bastard."

"Who?"

"You know who."

"Junior's in jail. I had Flynn arrest him."

"No, I'm not talking about Junior. Arrest him on what?"

"Attempted murder, promoting an act of terrorism."

"Ow, ow," she said. "It still hurts to laugh." She settled and said, "But Junior had nothing to do with planting that bomb."

I told her I thought she was wrong and why.

She shook her head. "It was Ryoken. He's a Korean—"

"I know who he is, sort of. How do *you* know about him?"

"That's what I came by to tell you last night. Remember the other night, the name you said Tulips kept trying to give you?"

"She kept saying 'we oaken,' I remember."

"Well, that sounded familiar, though I couldn't place it at the time. I kept thinking about it, and yesterday I remembered where I'd heard it. When I was with the Lewiston PD, we knew that Eddie Cole had a Korean-American enforcer named Henry Chu. He was an ex-marine who got booted from the service because he was too violent, too crazy. He landed in Lewiston, where he got hooked on crack; he loved to break bones. They sometimes called him Ryoken."

"I know. Farrell Woods told me some of this already."

"Well, I spoke to Tulips yesterday, and she told me—"

"Really? How is she? I should drop by and see her."

"She's coming along. Anyway, she told me it was Henry Chu who killed Brent Pfleger, then shot her full of heroin."

"I kind of figured. Did she tell you how it happened?"

"He snatched her from the Bates parking lot, tied her up, took her to Woods's place, then forced her to watch him kill Pfleger."

"This guy is seriously twisted," I said. "Does she know how to find him?"

"No. She's terrified of him. She won't even talk to the police about him. But I think Corliss might."

"That's a dead end; he's in prison. And he's not going to talk to you or me since we're the ones who put him there."

"Yeah," she said, "but when he was a detective, he kept files on all of Eddie Cole's people. Ryoken had to be in his files."

"The police probably have them. They went through every—"

"They didn't find them; they weren't in his safe."

I thought a bit and said, "How do you know all this?"

"Because while you and Jamie were basking in the sun, surfing and drinking margaritas, I was working my ass off to make sure the charges against him stick."

"Okay, so do you know where the files are?"

"I'm pretty sure his lawyer had them. And *she* gave—"

"That's a good guess."

"It's not a guess," she said. "Not entirely." She told me that after she'd talked to Tulips, she'd driven up to Lewiston.

"But, Peggy, Eddie Cole wouldn't be stupid enough to go back there. The police have been looking for him for almost two—"

"No, they haven't. The police stopped looking for him shortly after he escaped from custody. Ask your friend Sinclair. All the charges against him were dropped."

I didn't express any surprise to learn this.

"What I hear," she went on, "is that the DA is following orders from the attorney general's office. And come to think of it, if you ask Sinclair, he won't tell you anything, because it's supposed to be top secret."

"When did you learn all this?"

"Yesterday afternoon. That's why I came over to see you right afterward. I saw Eddie Cole come out of his building early this morning. He met with Corliss's lawyer. She gave him a CD."

This was meaningless to me. "So they like the same music."

"Jack! CDs are used to store computer files nowadays."

"They are? I thought people used floppy discs."

"You really need to update yourself on how all this computer stuff works, you know that? Anyway, I happened to have a parabolic microphone and I overheard their conversation. Cole asked if there were any more copies of what was on the CD, and the lawyer said no, that she'd gotten rid of Regis's computer."

Abby seemed like a straight-shooter to me. She had probably lied to Cole to protect Corliss. I said, "If Cole's got the files, just go to the Lewiston PD with what you overheard."

"No. My surveillance took place outside the bounds of the Fourth Amendment. Besides, the Lewiston PD has tried to get a search warrant before. It's been knocked down by someone higher up every single time."

"So what did you think you were going to do? Break into his drug den on your own, in your condition, and make off with this CD that may or may not have information about this goon Ryoken?"

She thought it over. "I'm on drugs myself here, okay?"

I thought of something, but didn't speak.

"What?" she said. "You just had an idea."

My cell phone did its thing.

"What is that? Some kind of lame hip-hop riff?"

"It came with the phone." I clicked it on. "Yeah?" A pause. "Where are you?" Pause. "No, I'm in Rockland. Grab a cab and meet me at the diner near Jamie's office. Bring Lunch with you." Pause. "Okay. Meet you there in an hour."

I got off the phone and said to Doyle, "Look, I know Corliss's lawyer. She's a dog-training client."

She smiled. "You're going to frisk her office, aren't you?"

"No. Not unless it's absolutely necessary."

"But that's the idea you had. That's just brilliant, Jack. Of course the lawyer was lying when she told Eddie Cole she didn't have the computer."

"I certainly hope so. I don't want to have to break into Cole's place to get that CD until I know more about who's going to be there. Flynn and I were damn lucky to get out alive the last time we did it."

"Take me with you." She tried to get out of bed, but her arm and shoulder were being held in place by a triangular brace.

"Stay here. I'm going to talk to her first. If she doesn't come clean with me about this Ryoken character, then I'll go through her office."

"Okay," she grumped, lying back down. Then she smiled. "And say hello to Lou for me, will you?"

"Sure." (They'd danced together at the wedding.)

"And, Jack?" she said as I reached the door. "You can program your cell phone to play any kind of ring tone you like."

"Really?"

"Yep." She smiled and shook her head at my ignorance.

"Even a Townes Van Zandt song?"

She laughed some more. "Yes, even a Townes Van Zandt song. I'll show you how to do it sometime."

"Okay, thanks. I'll see you later."

I left her room and went next door to say hello to MacLeary, even though he was still in a coma. When I came in I saw Jervis, leaning over the old man's bed. He heard me, pulled back, and when he did, I saw a vial in his hand. I also saw a drop of liquid dribbling down the general's chin.

"What the hell are you doing?" I said. "What did you just give him?"

21

Jervis's eyes were clear, his face calm. He said, "You can ask him yourself, sir." He nodded toward MacLeary.

I looked and saw MacLeary's eyes twinkling at me. "I have less than twenty seconds to talk to you before I go back into my coma. I just want you to know that my wife, my wife isn't . . ."

It had been less than twenty seconds all right. He was out.

I looked at Jervis. "What the hell is going on?"

"Perceptive question, sir. It would seem that my old friend, my employer, wishes to remain in bed, as it were, for the time being."

I was stunned. "He's been faking his coma?"

"Oh, no, sir. Well, yes, at least since the police discovered the connection between the bullet found in the skull and the general's gun. For various reasons he'd rather not be incarcerated for any length of time."

"But how? How can he fake a coma?"

"It's a Chinese herb, very potent but completely safe. We discovered its existence while being held prisoner by the Communists in North Korea. It's what enabled us to escape."

"I don't get it. If he's not guilty, why not stand up to the police, help with the investigation? What's he afraid of?"

"As I said, there are various reasons for his decision."

"Okay. And you're not . . . you seem perfectly sober."

"Ah, yes, the drunkard act. That I *can* explain, sir. You see, years ago the general saw a Japanese movie about an emperor who was in a similar situation to his. The emperor's chief samurai very cleverly pretended to be a foolish drunk until the critical moment when his skills were needed to protect his king."

"So you're playing the part of the drunk samurai?"

"I attempt to, sir. Without the actual drinking of course."

"May I ask why?"

"Well, like that Japanese emperor, my employer has many enemies, some coming from within the government itself."

You realize that's insane, I wanted to say, but just said, "So what have you been doing since the bones were found? You haven't been here at the hospital the whole time."

"No, that's true, I've been doing my best to look into things. However, I haven't time to discuss that just now." He took a seat, slouched back in it and said, "The nurse will be here soon."

"Okay. But what was he just trying to tell me?"

"That? Ah yes, he believes his wife is still alive."

"Is she?"

He shook his head. "I rather doubt it, sir, though I'd never contradict the general."

"Then why—?"

"Guilt, sir. He failed her, or so he feels, and thinks he deserves to be abandoned by her to pay for those failures. I've been asked to look for evidence to substantiate his . . . delusion, I suppose you'd call it. And I've found something, but—"

"What did you find?"

"It doesn't amount to much, but I found out that Mrs. Mac-Leary transferred $200,000 from a secret bank account two days before she disappeared."

"What secret bank account? You mean in Switzerland?"

"No, sir. The Grand Cayman Islands."

That was just as good. "And where was it transferred to?"

"A small town in Mexico."

Oh, boy. This was getting close to the bone. "How did you find out about it? Was there some sort of paper trail?"

"In a sense, yes."

"Okay, I need something I can look at, some sort of paperwork proving that this took place."

"I'm afraid the only thing I can provide is the account numbers. I'd tell you more, but—" He closed his eyes, his face went slack. It even seemed to have taken on a jaundiced color.

Two seconds later a fullback of a nurse entered the room.

She looked me over. "Who are you?"

"Jack Field. I'm an investigator with the ME's office."

She looked at the general. "He's not dead yet."

"No. I'm investigating his wife's death."

She looked at me suspiciously, then came over and checked to see that everything was in order with the old man's ventilator, his IV drip, etc. Then wrote something on a chart and left.

"I want to know more about this money transfer," I said to Jervis, "but I have to meet someone now." I waited for him to open his eyes. He didn't. "I'll just give you my cell number."

"Not to worry, sir. I have it."

"Of course you do. Can I ask you something? Reggie told me that Connie is afraid of the general's dog. Is that true?"

"Yes, sir."

"Un-huh. And how long has she been . . . the way she is?"

He opened his eyes. "You mean off her nut?" I nodded. "She had a breakdown when her mother ran off. She's been . . . well, like that ever since." He closed his eyes again.

"Well, keep in touch. I'd really like to talk to the general the next time this Chinese herb wears off."

"I'll contact you, sir, and give you those account numbers."

"That'd be great. And stop calling me sir."

"I'm afraid that's not possible, sir." He had the hint of a smile on his face.

I shook my head and left the room.

I couldn't stop laughing in disbelief on the drive up to Lewiston. Or maybe it wasn't disbelief. I had a sour feeling in the pit of my stomach. Maybe what I was feeling was sadness at what had become of General MacLeary, this great man who'd led his troops into battle with courage and had served his country with clearsightedness. He'd been reduced to a fearful, guilt-ridden shell, playing out this sick, paranoid drama with Jervis, a drama that had been going on for at least twenty years. What kind of man hides behind a fake coma in a hospital bed? A coward, pure and simple; General MacLeary was a coward. And now that I thought about it, he might even be insane, or close to it.

Still, any data is good data, even if it's disturbing. This drunken samurai act of theirs told me that something more was going on than what I knew about.

I wondered if I ought to tell MacLeary's doctors about it. Would that be meddling or would it help jolt the old fool out of his dementia? It couldn't be healthy for him to keep going in and out of coma at will. I mean, how could Jervis know for certain that the herb was safe?

My ruminations were interrupted by a lame hip-hop riff. I pulled to the side of the road. It was Donna Devon. She wanted to know why I thought Junior had been involved in the bombing. I told her about his two AG investigators, then mentioned that Junior had threatened to kill me while I was in Compton's office.

"No kidding. Will Compton confirm that?"

"He should. He's a straight enough guy, I think." I didn't tell her about the tape recording. I wanted to save that for if Compton didn't back up my story or misremembered Junior's words.

"Any idea on where Sheriff Flynn is holding Coster, Jr.?"

"Sorry. I have no idea. Besides—"

"You wouldn't tell me if you did."

"That's right."

I was about to get back on the road when I realized I'd forgotten to call Abby Butler. I punched in her office number, we chatted about Buster's improvement (he had started to play and seemed happier overall), and I said I was glad, then told her what I wanted and what I was offering in return.

"I'll ask him and get back to you," she said. "And thanks, Jack. I know he doesn't deserve anything from you."

"It's quid pro quo, Abby. I need to find this guy. Regis may be a dirtball, but Ryoken is a stone cold killer."

22

Kelso, Dr. Lunch, Jamie, and I met in the coffee shop near the morgue. Lunch, a strange-looking mutt, late fifties, with black hair going white around the temples, pasty skin, and pewter eyes like a rat's, gave me and Jamie a list of code words for us to use when we were having conversations that might be overheard. I told everyone about the note from Katherine MacLeary, and about the general's fake coma and the drunken samurai scenario.

Jamie said, "That's got to be dangerous. I'm not aware of any substance, other than a strong narcotic, that could mimic a coma. And that man shouldn't be on narcotics in his condition."

I agreed. "But we can't tell his doctors about it."

"Why the hell not?"

"Because I promised I wouldn't."

"Well, I didn't make any promises." She was furious.

"Okay. But still, if you can think of a way for his doctors to keep an eye on his condition without giving away your reasons for making the suggestion, I'd feel better about it."

She shook her head. "I'll see what I can come up with. But I'm calling them as soon as I get back to my office." She stopped. "Oh. I forgot about the taps on my phones. Damn it!"

Dr. Lunch had a black nylon bag next to his seat. He opened it up and gave all three of us our own secure cell phones.

"They're preconfigured to hijack your own cellular service

so you won't have to memorize or write down any new numbers."

I tried mine out. I punched in the number for Jamie's cell phone and almost immediately heard her Mozart prelude and a soft but insistent buzzing sound. She answered both phones, then clicked off her old phone..

"Pretty cool, huh?" I said to her over my phone.

She laughed. "You *would* love this. You'll be like a kid with a walkie-talkie."

Lunch said, "The ring tone has a special sonic design that enables you to know when the phone is ringing, but when it's overheard by someone unfamiliar with it, it sounds like background noise."

I said, "That's ingenious."

"Well," Lunch said, "I recommend you only use the phones for calls that might involve sensitive information. And I suggest you spend some time accommodating your ears to the ring tone."

We did that, then got back to the subject of the case.

"It's like one big jumble," Jamie said.

"I know," I said. "There are all these unconnected threads." I didn't bring up the gossamer links from the MacLeary case to Brent Pfleger's murder, via Eddie Cole.

Kelso said, "They only *seem* unconnected because we haven't found the secret yet. It's like a Rubik's cube. It's impossible to see how the pieces fit until you solve the puzzle."

"Jamie can do the Rubik's cube," I said.

"You can?" asked Kelso.

"Yeah," she said with a shy shrug.

"That's pretty cool. So can Lunch."

Lunch smiled and started jabbering something about how all the moves are commutators and how it all related to group theory.

Jamie said, "I don't know about that. I just got all the whites on one side, then went from there. My father can do it much quicker than I can. And he can do it one-handed."

"One-handed?"

"He's a show-off," I said. "Plus he's very dexterous, which comes in handy since he's a neurosurgeon."

"That *is* handy," said Lunch. "He sounds like someone I'd trust to work on my brain!"

None of us made the obvious zinger; it just hung in the air unsaid, along with the smell of coffee and doughnuts.

"Anyway," I said, "this case isn't like a Rubik's cube. It's more like a mystery novel where you have to trust the writer."

"Trust the writer?" asked Lunch.

Jamie shook her head. "Jack thinks we're all characters in a series of mystery novels."

"Cool," said Kelso. "Very Zen."

"I know," I said. "So it's just a matter of trusting the writer to tie everything together in the end."

"Give me a break," muttered Jamie. "Check please!"

After we paid the waitress, Jamie went back to the morgue, while Kelso, Lunch, and I rented a van and some carpet cleaning equipment, then began making the rounds of the capitol building, showing forged work orders explaining the equipment and our coveralls, which Lunch had packed on the flight from New York. He'd also brought a set of phone company coveralls and a pair of cleated boots, although those would come in later on.

We planted bugs on the phones in Junior's, Compton's, and even Attorney General Allan Forbert's office. (I should say Lunch planted the bugs, while Kelso hacked into the computers and I cleaned the damn carpets.) I also listened to the cassette tape in the recorder on Compton's desk to see if Junior's threat to kill me was still on it. It was, so I pocketed the tape.

"You don't have to actually clean the rugs," Kelso said at one point. "Just turn the machine on so it sounds like you are."

"Ah, what the hell," I said. "It takes my mind off things."

When we were done at the capitol, we returned the van and the carpet equipment, changed into phone company coveralls, and made the rounds of all the telephone poles necessary to plant bugs on Junior's home phone, his father's home phone, and Allan Forbert's. (I had to actually climb the poles myself because I was the youngest and in the best shape of the three of us.)

Then we drove to Lewiston, which was a last minute addition of mine, and planted bugs on the lines leading into Eddie Cole's apartment building. After I got the hang of the cleated boots,

I actually kind of enjoyed being a lineman for the county.

During the drive time between locations in our little escapade, I brought up the sick game that Jervis and MacLeary had been playing again.

"These two might not be crazy," Lunch said. "You're not paranoid if someone's really out to get you."

"Okay, maybe he really does have enemies," I said, "but even so, would you spend twenty years of your life going through this kind of elaborate charade?"

"Probably not," he agreed.

When we were finished I gave Kelso the keys so he could drive us back to the kennel and I could call Jamie on my cell phone. Lunch sat in the backseat with a laptop and a set of receivers, all tuned to different frequencies.

I had a fairly lengthy conversation with Jamie, which doesn't bear repeating. We just rehashed some old stuff about the explosion, Doriane's renovation, getting a new refrigerator, maybe a new stove, and the like. The real reason for the call was for Lunch to send a tracking signal from Jamie's office phone to each of the devices we'd planted, to find out just who'd been listening in on her. We got two "echoes," as he called them: one from Junior's office, the other from Allan Forbert's.

I said, "So this goes higher than we'd thought."

"It looks like it," said Lunch.

Kelso said, "We know Junior was appointed by Forbert. Now we need to find out how Forbert's connected to Ed Sr."

I said, "Well, an attorney general has to be elected, meaning he has to spend time and money running for office."

"Right," said Kelso. "Which would require a war chest. So as the saying goes, follow the money."

Dr. Lunch said he'd check on Forbert's financial records to see if he was connected to Ed Coster Sr. He began typing things into his laptop.

"How can you check on his financials from back there?" I asked.

He explained about WiFi.

"You mean you can access the Internet while we're driving? I thought you had to have a phone line or something."

"Modern times," said Kelso. "Catch up."

"Amazing," said I.

I let Kelso drive for a while. I wanted to check in with Flynn, Mrs. Murtaugh and D'Linda, and Leon.

Flynn had assigned some deputies to my property; they were in place at both ends of the county road leading to the kennel, keeping an eye on things. He wasn't the only one. The cops don't like it when a law enforcement official is attacked. Jamie is the chief medical examiner, and she could've been blown to pieces as easily as I could have, so Flynn's deputies had help patrolling the hillside; the state police were there too. Most of their work so far involved keeping unrelenting reporters off my property, and occasionally making rounds, poking the alder bushes with their batons to flush out the pesky photographers.

Meanwhile, Flynn had let it be known to the press by way of a prewritten news release that he felt—owing to the fact that Junior was accused of nearly killing a deputy—that Junior might not be safe if he were to be kept in a holding cell at the sheriff's headquarters in Rockland. As a result, Junior had been taken to an undisclosed location for an indefinite amount of time until he, Flynn, felt it was safe to have Junior arraigned.

"Aren't you a little worried about the legal repercussions?" I asked him.

"Hell no," he snorted. "I'll be out of office by the time anyone can do anything about it."

"Can you give me an idea about where he is?"

"Why?"

"I want to run some disinformation past the enemy."

"Sure, then; what do I care? This is a secure line. He's being kept in a cabin in the woods just north of Wiscasset."

"A cabin in the woods? You couldn't find a quiet motel?"

"I tried that. He kept screaming. I don't like the little turd but I can't conscience keeping his mouth wrapped in duct tape till this is all over."

"You always were an old softie."

"Bull," he snorted. "No matter what kind of crap he may have pulled, I'm not going to stoop to his level."

"Very noble," I agreed.

Next I called Mrs. Murtaugh, and she told me everything was fine with the doggies. Then I called Leon, who told me he and Sloan hadn't had any time for their conversation last night and had set up a date for another talk.

"Okay," I told him. "But only because the kitchen blew up. Your next date has to come after you're through being grounded."

"Whatever," he said with a cocky sound in his voice that told me he'd probably made out with her again. "It's aw' good."

When I was done with my calls, I told Kelso my theory of why Mrs. MacLeary had been killed, and by whom.

"I don't buy it," he said. "Even if she married into the Coster clan, I don't see enough of a motive for her to kill her own mother."

"Never mind the motive. You told me yourself that I should let the dogs tell me which direction to look in, right?"

"Yeah?"

"So this is what the dogs are saying, at least Molly is."

Dr. Lunch guffawkled (a combination guffaw and chuckle), then he said, "And people think *I'm* out to Lunch . . ."

Huh, I thought. I finally knew the reason for his nickname.

"Besides," I said, "Connie knows her way around guns. She won some marksmanship medals when she was a teenager."

"That doesn't mean much," Kelso said.

My cell phones sounded. Both of them. I answered the more annoying of the two. It was Donna Devon. Jeffrey Compton refused to confirm that Junior had threatened to kill me.

"He denied it?"

"He didn't deny it, he told me he couldn't comment on anything relating to an ongoing investigation."

"Did you ask him point-blank if Junior threatened me?"

"Yes. And he clammed up. I'm sorry, Jack. I can't air that part of the story just on your word for what happened."

"That's okay." I clicked the phone off.

Kelso said, "That's a pretty lame ring tone you've got."

"I know," I said, preoccupied.

I thought of something, then pulled out the cassette tape I'd stolen from Compton's office tape recorder and said to Lunch,

"Is there any way to transfer what's on here to your computer and create some kind of file that we could e-mail to the station?"

He took a pocket cassette player and some connecting wires from his pockets. "How much of it do you want transferred?"

We put the tape in and I rewound it, punched Play, rewound it, punched Play until I heard my voice. Then I gave the tape back to Lunch. While he went to work transferring the recording, I opened my glove box and went through my cassettes until I found my favorite Townes Van Zandt tape, then asked him if he could download one of the songs to my cell phone.

"Sure," he said. "I'm almost finished here. What's the e-mail address?"

"Hang on."

I called Donna on my secure phone, told her about the tape and, over her gleeful cries, asked for her e-mail address.

Dr. Lunch e-mailed the digitized recording, then asked me which tune I wanted on my cell phone. I told him, and once all was said and done, Donna Devon had incriminating evidence against Ed Jr., and my old cell phone was programmed to alert me to any incoming call with Townes singing "Mr. Mud and Mr. Gold."

Modern technology, ain't it wonderful?

Abby Butler was the first person to call me with Townes on my phone. I let it play for a bit.

"You're not supposed to listen to it," said Kelso. "You're supposed to answer it."

He was right. In some ways the lame hip-hop riff was better because I always answered the phone as quickly as possible when it was playing. Still, I let Townes go through to the line, "His eyes like bullets burned," before I finally answered the secure phone Lunch had given me.

"Bad news, Jack," said Abby. "My client is perfectly willing to tell the authorities everything he knows about Eddie Cole, but he says he won't even discuss Henry Chu for any reason other than total immunity and witness protection."

I said, "Well, I'm not in a position to promise any—"

"Yes, I know. But on the other hand . . ."

"Go on."

"What if I dig around on my own and get the info *for* you?"

I thought it over. "You have access to his computer files?"

There was a pause. "Something like that."

"I'll be happy to do what I already offered, but I don't know if it's such a good idea. You'll be putting yourself in danger."

"Let me worry about that."

"Okay, but why go out on a limb for Regis of all people?"

"Because he's my client and he deserves the best deal I—"

"No, he doesn't. He deserves whatever he gets and more."

"Even so, he's my client. You could have easily walked away from me and Buster when he tried to kill Frankie."

"No I couldn't have; I like Buster. He's a good boy under all that aggression. And besides, he's a dog. He doesn't know any better. He's just acting on impulse and emotion. Corliss has always acted purely out of horniness, greed, and ego."

"Okay, but he's still my client."

I gave up. "Fine. Let me know what you find out. Just be careful. *Very* careful."

"I will."

Dr. Lunch took his headphones off. "I think I got an echo."

"You mean her phone is being tapped?"

He shrugged. "It could be. Or it might just be the RF signal pinging off the side of the mountain."

"What mountain?"

He pointed out the window.

"Oh, right," I said. "I forgot, in Maine they call these little hills mountains." We were approaching the general store in Perseverance. "Pull over here, I want to pick up some groceries."

We found a covey of news vans clustered around my driveway. As soon as they saw us approaching, the cameramen all dropped their coffee cups, put away their cell phones, and shot into action, hoisting their cameras on their shoulders. The sound technicians handed mics to reporters, and the reporters checked their hair and wardrobe and glanced at their note cards. They were like a pack of wild (though well-coiffed) dogs, ready to spring.

Kelso wanted to run them over.

I said, "No, this'll give me a chance to plant a sound byte for the evening news."

He put on the brakes, I rolled down my window, waved at everyone to calm down, and said, "I have a brief statement."

"Mr. Field! What do you think about Sheriff Flynn taking Ed Coster Jr. prisoner?"

"Mr. Field, over here! Was the bomb an attempt to stop your wife's examination of the body found in General MacLeary's yard?"

"Please, people! I'm not going to answer any questions! I just want to make a brief statement." (I had to repeat that about seven times before everyone shut up.) "Good, thank you. I just have one comment: Yesterday afternoon Ed Coster Jr. threatened to have me killed if I didn't recant my testimony against his wife. I have a tape recording of him making this threat. Wait! Wait! Let me finish! I refused to give in to his threats. As a result, a bomb went off in my kitchen, nearly killing Peggy Doyle. That's how Ed Coster Jr. deals with people. He tries to intimidate them, and when that doesn't work, he has them killed. Please, people! Let me finish my statement! Thank you. I also think it's unfortunate that Sheriff Flynn took matters into his own hands instead of waiting for the judicial process to take its course. Flynn's actions, though legal, may hinder the prosecution's case when Junior goes to trial."

I rolled up my window.

Kelso said, "That was good. You made it sound like an arrest and trial are inevitable."

"Thanks," I said. "I learned that technique from you. Okay, now you can run them over."

He didn't actually do it, though he did gun the engine a few times.

23

We got safely down the driveway. Doriane Elliot's crew had gone for the day. The kitchen was still a mess, but not as bad as it had been. Sheets of plywood now covered the broken windows. It wasn't pretty, but it would help keep the house warm when the temperature dropped (it was supposed to get below freezing overnight). But there was one good thing waiting for me: a brand new, brushed stainless steel refrigerator.

It hummed a quiet welcome as I put the groceries inside.

Once I'd done that, I checked in with Mrs. Murtaugh and D'Linda. Everything was cool with the doggies so I sent them both home. Then, while Kelso checked the cars for transponders and Lunch set up his listening equipment (a ton of it) in the downstairs bedroom, Leon and I spent a little time in the play yard with Frankie, Magee, Hooch, Molly, and the beagles.

"So how are you feeling about what happened last night?" I asked him.

"You mean the bomb and Peggy getting hurt? I'm a'ight."

"You sure?"

"Yeah. Didn't nobody get killed, so yeah." He took a moment, then said, "There's no school till Monday."

"How come?"

"Everybody's freaked out about Kurt Pfleger. The school had a memorial today, then sent us home."

"What was it like?"

He shrugged. "The usual shit. 'Don't do drugs.' It was cool, though. Mr. Van Noy let me say something."

"What'd you say?"

"I told the kids what happened to my moms and pops and my two brothers, you know, how they was killed by drug dealers."

"Were you okay with that?"

"Yeah, it felt all right. I cried a little, but I think it was good; I think some of Kurt's friends are gonna think twice now about the kind of shit they been doing."

"I'm proud of you, Leon."

"Nothin' to be proud of. I just tol' 'em what happened."

"Still, that took courage."

"Nah." He smiled.

I was making dinner—my own version of beef Stroganoff, with farfalle (instead of egg noodles), crumbled ground beef spiced with a little cumin along with sautéed onions and sour cream—when Kelso came in and told me I was on TV; they were running the tape of Junior threatening to kill me.

After the sound byte played, Donna said, "The conversation you just heard was recorded a little after three P.M. yesterday. Approximately four hours later"—a pointed newscaster's pause—"a bomb exploded in Jack Field's kitchen, nearly killing Rockland County Sheriff-elect Peggy Doyle and causing tens of thousands of dollars in damage. State prosecutor Jeffrey Compton, who recorded this conversation in his office in Augusta, confirmed its authenticity. When we tried to reach Mr. Coster's attorney to comment on this new development, he refused to speak with us.

"As of this hour, the location of Ed Coster, Jr. is still unknown. Meanwhile, Attorney General Allan Forbert has filed a writ of habeus corpus, demanding that Ed Coster, Jr. be released into the custody of the state police. A judge will be hearing a motion on that demand in approximately ten minutes. Marty?"

"Thanks, Donna. Coming up after the break, a Halloween experience you and your kids won't want to miss. We take you on a trip through Maine's largest corn maze."

"Right, Marty. It's just north of Waterville. And come to

think of it, maybe that's where they're hiding Ed Coster, Jr."

Laughter. "Could be, Donna. They've probably hidden him in that corn maze." More laughter. "We'll be right back."

Jamie came home while dinner was still warm, and while we ate we went over the day's events.

The MtDNA was a match, which meant that Katherine Mac-Leary hadn't been excluded as the victim, though it didn't prove definitively that she was. They still hadn't found any of her X rays to compare to the bones Molly had dug up. The police were able to match several metal buttons, though, to the ones on a dress in a photograph taken of her.

I told Jamie my theory about who'd killed Mrs. MacLeary and got the same argument I'd gotten from Kelso: there was no motive. I gave her the same argument I'd given him, and she laughed and told me the DA wasn't likely to try for an indictment on my dog-related hunch. I agreed and had a laugh at the way she'd put. Then I asked who was in charge of running the prints on the empty cartridge. She asked why I wanted to know and I told her.

She absorbed what I said, thought it over. "Well, if the prints match those of your suspect, that would generate enough interest for the DA to put it in front of a grand jury."

"Do you trust the people in the fingerprint lab?"

"Of course. Though now that you mention it, with my phones being bugged and all, I'd hate to see that print disappear. I'll be very careful about how I handle it."

"We have to be very careful about how we handle *everything* from now on."

24

Nothing much happened that night, or the next day for that matter, which was Thursday. That's how these cases go sometimes. There's a lot of buildup, a lot of media excitement, then a sudden lull in the action. It rained all day and I spent most of my time with Leon and the dogs.

Jamie called around noon and, using Lunch's code words, told me that she'd put the fingerprint lab to work on my idea that Connie was the shooter. She also told me that she'd picked up some Halloween costumes for the two of us to wear.

I asked her what they were and she said it was going to be a surprise. "You're going to love mine, though," she said. "It's a bit daring and involves a little décolletage . . ."

"Cleavage? Yeah, that's got my interest, all right."

"Well, why shouldn't I dress sexy once in a while?"

"I'm not complaining! So, what about my costume?"

"You will *love* it, trust me. What's your favorite book?"

I thought about it and said, "You mean, they make a Holden Caulfield costume?"

"No, silly. When you were in high school, what did you tell me was your favorite novel?" I drew a blank, so she reminded me.

"Well, that's not *a* book, honey. That's a trilogy, meaning it's three books. So who am I going as, Gandalf or Frodo?"

"You'll have to wait and see."

"I hope it's not Gollum."

* * *

We were having dinner that night—*enchiladas del camerones*, our first joint cooking enterprise—when Dr. Lunch interrupted us. His eyes were bright with excitement though the rest of his face showed nothing. "Uh," was all he said.

"Yeah?"

"I've got something."

We followed him into his command center, and he turned on a tape.

We heard an old man's voice say, "I'm sick of this bullshit, Allan. I want it taken care of now!"

"That's Governor Coster," Lunch said.

"What do you want me to do?" said another voice.

"That's Allan Forbert," said Lunch, pausing the tape.

He unpaused it. Forbert said, "I have the state police on it, but we haven't been able to find Ed Junior yet."

Another voice came on, said, "The governor doesn't want excuses, Allan. Did the party hand you a load of excuses when you came to us for campaign money, for help making connections in Augusta, for help with your reelection campaign?"

"Christ, Harlan, is this your doing?"

Lunch paused the tape and said, "I think he's talking to Governor Coster's friend and hatchet man, Harlan Rowan."

He unpaused the tape. Forbert said, "First of all, I've kept my part of the bargain. Secondly, Flynn's phone calls have all been made with a nontraceable cell phone. And his personal vehicles are all accounted for. He must have used some kind of—"

"Goddamn it, Allan! There has to be somebody in that podunk little sheriff's office who knows where Eddie is, somebody who can be bought. I don't care how much it takes."

"I've got feelers out on that already. It's going to take—"

Lunch paused the tape again. "Here's where it gets good."

I thought it had already gotten good; I now saw a connection between the Coster family and Henry Chu, or thought I did.

Lunch switched it to play, and we heard Rowan say, "I don't want to hear how much time it's going to take. And when you find this moron Flynn, this loose cannon, I want him shot dead."

There was a pause. Lunch was right; it had gotten good.

"Excuse me?"

"You heard me. Tell your men there's a million dollar price on his head."

Another pause. "Is this the governor's idea or yours?"

"Never mind that. As far as you and I are concerned, you don't need to worry about who's speaking for whom."

"Which gives Coster deniability. I get it."

"Good. And I want you to put the state police on high priority until Sheriff Flynn is found and killed."

"Okay," his voice was more serious, "that's unacceptable. I've already broken the law to push the power plant through, and put Eddie on the payroll. There's only so much—"

"Can it, Allan. You're either with us or against us. You'd better start giving some serious consideration to what that means."

"Yes, sir. I'll do what I can."

Lunch switched off the machine.

I said, "Who is this Harlan Rowan?"

Lunch said, "I did a little research online. He's a hardball type. The kind that would call his own mother a commie whore and provide the documents to prove it if she campaigned against one of his candidates."

"What a piece of work. Whose phone was tapped for this call, Coster's or Forbert's?"

Lunch said, "Both. Coster from his home phone, and Forbert from his office."

Jamie said, "We have to get this to the media."

"Not yet." I was running a plan through in my mind.

"What are you going to do?" she asked.

"For now I don't want Coster knowing we've tapped his phone. Same with Forbert." I turned to Kelso. "You were a lawyer. Can you type up a transcript of this, just Coster and Rowan's side of the conversation, say in ten minutes?"

"It's not that long," he said. "How about five?"

"Good. When it's done I want you and Lunch to go to Augusta and give Forbert a copy. Tell him you're— What's wrong?"

Lunch was shaking his head in a way that reminded me of Dustin Hoffman in *Rain Man*. "I don't . . . I don't do that."

Kelso said, "Yeah, he's not good with the public. I'll go it alone. He'll be more valuable here."

"Fine. Tell Forbert you're working for the Justice Department, gathering evidence on Coster Sr. The transcript is a conversation that you just recorded off Coster's phone. You're showing it to Forbert to get his side of it. See what he says."

Jamie said, "That's a nice fantasy, sweetheart, but Forbert won't just take Lou's word that he's with Justice."

Kelso said, "I'm sure I've got something that'll pass for federal ID," then took the tape deck with the incriminating conversation and a laptop out to the kitchen.

To Lunch, I said, "Can you connect me to Forbert's office?"

He did, using one of his untraceable cell phones.

Forbert answered, and I said, "Mr. Forbert, this is Jack Field. I think this situation with Flynn and your deputy AG has gone a bit too far. I know where Flynn's holding him. Would you mind if I came by your office in an hour and we could discuss a solution?"

There was a surprised pause. "That would be fine."

I hung up and we waited to hear what, if anything, Forbert would tell Coster or his toady Rowan. It didn't take long.

"Sir," he said, once he got Rowan on the line and the preliminaries were done with, "I may have a line on where Flynn is keeping Eddie. I know you wanted him dead, but if I can bring him in, under arrest, I think that's a better solution."

"Not for us it's not."

"We can't just go around killing county sheriffs."

"Who says we can't?"

"Well, *I* can't do it. I won't be a party to it. I suggest you let me handle this my way."

"Fine. When you've got Flynn under wraps let me know where he is so I can have one of our people arrange an accident."

A heavy sigh. "Harlan, come on . . ."

"Just do it. Or you'll be worse off than he is."

I told Lunch, "Get Kelso a tape of this call too and have him type up a transcription. Come on, honey. We're going to be late."

Lunch said, "Wait. Put these on before you go." He gave us what looked like nicotine patches, right down to the Nicotrol logo. "They've got miniature transponders embedded inside them."

"Good," I said. "We may need them where we're going."

"Jack, where are we going?"

On the way out the door I told her we were going to see Tulips, then to the diner to wait for a phone call from Farrell. "He may have some information about where to find Eddie Cole."

"What does finding Eddie Cole have to do with Katherine MacLeary's murder?"

"Probably nothing. But it has everything to do with Brent Pfleger's death."

We took Farrell's truck so Kelso could use the Suburban. On the way to the hospital I said, "I need to tell you something but you have to promise not to yell at me."

"What is it?"

"You have to promise."

"I'm not going to promise you anything, Jack. Especially when you start off by telling me I'll probably yell at you."

"Okay, never mind then."

She was about to hit me, stopped herself and said, "See? I'm learning."

"That's good."

"So what do you need to tell me?"

"Okay, but you have to promise not to get mad when I—"

"What's the point? You're already pissing me off!"

"Fine, then I won't tell you."

This time she *did* hit me. "Sorry. Tell me what it is or—"

"Fine. I know who killed Brent Pfleger."

She took that in. "How do you know that?"

I told her about Tulips saying "we oaken" the other night, then what Farrell had said, and finally what Doyle had told me.

She nodded. "How long have you known?"

"I just found out for sure this morning, when I talked to Doyle. That's one reason we're going to see Tulips right now. I called Tom Shelford earlier. Remember him?"

"Yes, he's a Belfast PD detective."

"Right. He's meeting us at the hospital and bringing some mug shots of Henry Chu so Tulips can make a positive ID. We need to be there because she's scared to say anything, and I think she'll feel safer about making the ID if I can help her through it."

"That's very sweet of you, Jack. Now let's get back to Brent Pfleger. If Tulips saw him get killed, and you found Tulips at Farrell Woods's house Monday night, that means—"

"That's right." I admitted that I'd seen the body that night then explained my reasons for not telling her about it or reporting it to the police.

She shook her head over and over. "I am so furious with you right now. I can't believe you'd be that irresponsible."

"It's not irresponsible. I had to do it to keep Farrell Woods from being—"

"Jack! You're just rationalizing something inexcusable."

"No, I'm not. Not really. Look, sweetheart, I realize that to you the body's location is valuable infor—"

"Damn right it is. It's crucial."

"I agree. But you're a scientist, you're a doctor, you're trained not to jump to conclusions, to look past the obvious. Cops and prosecutors aren't like that. Even most judges aren't like that. As soon as they find a viable suspect, that's where their focus goes. They would've investigated Farrell Woods and built a case against him, brick by brick, until he was totally screwed. They would've never thought to look at Henry Chu *or* Eddie Cole."

"Maybe you're right, but you destroyed evidence! Chu might've left some trace of himself behind—fingerprints, fibers, blood—that could convict him, and now it's gone because of you."

"He didn't leave anything behind, trust me."

"How can I trust you when you lied to me?"

"I didn't lie, exactly. I just kept a few things hidden."

"Same difference. And now we'll never know if Chu left any evidence or not because you destroyed it! You're responsible for letting him get away with murder!"

"Settle down. It's not that simple. I also saved the police

thousands of man hours of building the wrong case against the wrong guy. I saved the DA's office hundreds of—"

"Oh, stop rationalizing your screw-up. You made an error in judgment, then you compounded it by not telling me about it."

"The main reason you're mad at me is because I didn't tell you. And it's not like you've never lied or hidden stuff from me before."

"I have not."

"Yes you have."

"When?"

I was stumped. "I don't know. You're better at remembering my mistakes than I am at remembering yours. That's one of the biological differences between men and wom—"

"Are you serious?" She was really mad now.

"Yes. You know very well that there are differences in how the male and female brains operate. They've done studies—"

"And that's your excuse?"

"It's not an excuse, sweetheart, it's a rational, scientific—"

"You are unbelievable!"

"Wait, now I remember one of the times you lied to me!" I reminded her of a time when she'd pretended that she was thinking about getting back together with her ex-husband Orrin Pritchett. She'd said it in order to make me jealous.

She softened. "You told me you found that appealing."

"It *was* appealing. But that doesn't change the fact that you deliberately lied to me, which is a lot different from what I did, simply hiding the truth about—let me finish." There was a sudden lull in her anger. I decided to take a different tack. "Okay, maybe you're right. I should have told you."

"See? Was that so hard to admit?"

"No. And maybe my logic was a little faulty."

"It certainly was." She thought a bit. "Well . . ." She took the opening I'd given her. "Maybe *you* were right on a certain level to clean up the evidence. I guess I can see your reasoning behind that. But you still should have told me about it."

"I know. I'm sorry, and I won't do it again." I kept a straight face when I said it too.

"Good. So do you think Henry Chu killed Kurt Pfleger too?"

"I doubt it. He'd have no reason to, except as part of his plan to frame Farrell. Plus, if Chu had stuck around, I wouldn't have been knocked cold, I would've been put on ice for good."

"How can you be so sure he didn't kill both of them?"

"That's why I'm your unpaid civilian advisor in criminology, remember? Because I'm pretty good at analyzing criminal behavior and motive."

"Which brings up your crazy idea again that Connie Coster killed her mother."

"Yeah, I know there's no motive for her to have done it, at least none that I can think of yet. In fact, from what I know, Reggie had more of a motive than Connie did."

"What was Reggie's motive?"

"She desperately wanted her mother's money."

"That doesn't mean she would've killed her for it."

"I'm not saying she did. I'm saying Connie did it."

"How can you be sure about that?"

"Because she's a dog lover who was scared to death of Molly, but only after she started digging up the yard. Why? Because she's got a suppressed memory of killing and burying her mother."

"That's a stretch."

"Not if you'd seen her trying to kill her father. She's become totally detached from reality. And I think the reason is she can't live with the guilt of killing her mother."

"Well, if it's true, then maybe Reggie put her up to it."

"I hadn't thought of that." It fit their sibling dynamic, the one I'd picked up from Cord about Reggie being the manipulative "alpha" bitch. "You know, you could be right."

"So, back to our present day murder. If Henry Chu didn't kill Kurt Pfleger, who did?"

"I'm not sure. Were you able to do a tox screen on him?"

She nodded. "We were lucky. The car was parked on a dock. The fire burnt through the boards, and the car fell into the lake. So the bodies weren't burned completely."

"Okay. So? Were there any drugs in his system?"

"Quite a few. Methylphenidate, probably taken as Ritalin, marijuana, cocaine, PCP, and formaldehyde."

I shook my head. "That's not a very healthy high, is it?"

"No. Is there such a thing?"

"Huh? Oh, sure. Looking at you is a healthy high."

She smiled. "You don't have to try so hard, honey. I'm not mad at you anymore."

"I was being serious." I thought it over. "Well, more and more young kids with ADHD are selling their Ritalin to high schoolers. It gives roughly the same high as amphetamine."

"Right."

"And in some cases it can cause psychotic effects."

"Well, yes, but the PCP would be more likely to do that. Plus he'd taken all his clothes off, which is a sure sign of PCP use."

"That's true. And PCP has to be mixed with some kind of solvent to be smoked. Which is where the formaldehyde comes in."

She shook her head. "These kids must be crazy. Smoking embalming fluid? Why? It causes dysphoria, not euphor— Jack, why are you turning left? Bangor's the other direction."

"I know. But the Pflegers live in Searsmont."

"Okay, so?"

"So, we need to tell them that their son Brent was murdered by a bad guy, not by his own brother. It might make his death a little easier to take. And we need to find out if *Kurt's* death was a homicide or a suicide."

"What? You think he purposely set his car on fire?"

"If he had a psychotic break? It's a good possibility."

"I suppose, but how do we prove it?"

"By talking to his parents and going through his room."

She put up her hands. "If you say so, Columbo . . ."

A few minutes later we pulled up to a ranch-style house with two cars, a black Lincoln and a metallic Honda, sitting in a wide carport. The house was partly hidden by tall hedges that rose to and in some cases slightly above the windows. Tall juniper bushes crowded the corners of the structure. We parked across the street, got out, and I noticed a sign next door, PFLEGER AND SON FUNERAL HOME, with flaking paint done in old style letters and HARRALD R. PFLEGER, DIRECTOR, in a newer style.

"There's our first clue," I told Jamie.

"This is going to be pleasant," she griped.

We walked through a narrow space between the carport and the house, then rang the bell beneath a yellow porch light, though there was no porch, just a black rubber welcome mat.

After a few moments the door was opened by a woman in a housedress, in her late forties, with tired brown hair worn loose. Bangs of it nearly covered her cinnamon-colored eyes.

"Yes?" she said.

"Mrs. Pfleger, I'm Dr. Cutter. Remember me?"

"Oh, yes, yes. Please come in."

"Thank you. And this is my husband, Jack Field."

We came into a warm, humid entryway, then followed her to an even warmer and more humid living room with vague, hazy lighting coming from a single table lamp. The television was on, adding flickers of color to the low-level light. Harrald R. Pfleger, balding with a round pouchy stomach, was in a recliner in his stocking feet, a T-shirt, and an old pair of chinos, snacking on Doritos and a Heineken, and watching a baseball game. His team must have been behind because he wasn't in a pleasant mood.

"Harrald, you remember Dr. Cutter?"

He nodded. She introduced me, then waved us to a dark green sofa that curved itself around two of the walls. We sat down.

Harrald flicked his gray eyes at us, then let them wander back to the screen.

"Can I bring you something to drink?" asked Mrs. Pfleger.

"No thanks," I said. "Though it is kind of warm in here. Could we crack open a window or something?"

She looked over at the Barcalounger. "My husband has rheumatism."

She took a seat on the same sofa, close to Harrald, then gave him a look. He turned the volume down on the TV, dropped the bag of Doritos on the floor next to him, and moved the recliner to an upright position. She picked up the bag and folded the top of it down, creasing it several times.

I noticed some photos on the wall of Mr. Pfleger playing with his boys: touch football in the yard, basketball at some gym, and one of him smiling next to Brent, who was in a swimsuit, wet and tired from swimming, wearing a medal around his neck.

Jamie said, "We thought you'd like to have a little more information about your son Brent's death." She looked at me.

That was my cue, so I said, "We have a witness. She's given us a lead on the killer and we're hoping the police can track him down and apprehend him soon."

Mrs. Pfleger said, "Oh, that's good to know."

Harrald said, "What about Kurt?"

Jamie said, "Well, I have some bad news. We found a number of illegal drugs in his bloodstream, so we don't know yet if his death was accidental or—"

"What kind of drugs?" asked Mrs. Pfleger, worried.

Harrald said, "My sons don't do drugs."

Jamie looked at me, which was my cue again. I said, "I understand how hard it must be for you to hear this kind of—"

"They don't do drugs. Brent was on the swim team."

"Sir," I said, "I understand your reluctance to accept the facts, but we know from several sources that your son Brent was not only using marijuana, he was selling it to some of Kurt's classmates. We're pretty sure that's one reason he was killed."

"You're full of crap. And anyway, if my boys *were* involved with drugs, it was probably *your* kid that got them started."

"Excuse me?" I could feel my face burning. With the steam heat and my sudden anger, I felt the need to take *my* clothes off.

Jamie put a warning hand on my knee. "Mr. Pfleger, our sources tell us that Brent's involvement with drugs began long before my husband and his foster son moved to Maine."

"We're sorry to have to tell you all this, but it's going to come out at the killer's trial. It's better for you to learn—"

He said, "And I suppose some punk black kid from New York is totally innocent when it comes to drugs? I don't think so."

"My husband doesn't mean that," said Mrs. Pfleger.

"Yes I do. That kid of his doesn't belong around here."

Quietly, I said, "I can't even begin to imagine the kind of grief you must be feeling, Mr. Pfleger. So I'm going to overlook your remarks. But your sons were the drug abusers, not mine."

He told me to go do something unpleasant to myself.

I said, "Another thing, Kurt had formaldehyde in his blood."

He stared at me.

"It's used to dissolve an animal tranquilizer called PCP so it can be smoked in a marijuana cigarette. Haven't you noticed some of your embalming fluid has been missing?"

"We're done talking here." He was panting softly.

"Okay, but we're going to need to look through Kurt's room."

"Like hell! I want you out of my house. Now. Nadine, show them out." He looked away from us, shifted his chair back to the recliner position, and turned the ballgame back on. Loud.

I got up, quite calmly I must say, walked over to the TV, went behind it, found the plug, and pulled it out of the wall.

"Hey!" He went for the lever on the side of his chair.

I put one foot on it and pinned him in.

He said, "You can't do that."

"I'm doing it."

"Jack . . . let's go . . ."

"No, we're searching Kurt's room. *Then* we'll go."

Pfleger said, "Not without a warrant!"

"Please?" said Mrs. Pfleger. "Can't you just leave?"

"Honey?" I said to Jamie. "Do we need a warrant?"

"Actually," she said to Mr. Pfleger, "your son is a possible murder victim, not a murder suspect. He no longer has any right to privacy. Sorry. And we really do need to search his room."

I stepped back from the recliner and said to the mortician, "You're welcome to watch, if you like." To Mrs. Pfleger, I said, "Which way is it?"

Harrald jumped out of his chair. "I'm calling the police!"

"Good. Ask them how much time the judge will give you for obstructing a state medical examiner's investigation."

Mrs. Pfleger shot her husband a worried look, then said, "It's this way," and led us down a narrow hall past a small bathroom, then to Kurt's bedroom. I noticed another door farther down the hall, probably the master bedroom.

She opened Kurt's door. "What are you looking for?"

Jamie, using her soothing voice, said, "Anything that might help us understand how and why Kurt died, Mrs. Pfleger."

Mr. Pfleger came up behind me. "I want to watch you."

"Fine," I said, "just don't get in our way."

Jamie and I went inside; the Pflegers hovered in the doorway.

It was a typical teenager's room, a desk with a laptop computer, some schoolbooks, and some comic books on top of it, though there were more comic books than schoolbooks. There was also a dresser with one drawer skewed open showing some socks and T-shirts. There was a CD player on top of the dresser.

Jamie put on a pair of pliofilm gloves, then opened one of the closet doors and began going through the jacket and jeans pockets. It reminded me of how I'd gone through Farrell Woods's closet.

I checked out the comics. There seemed to be one series he'd favored. It featured cold steel sword battles between what appeared to be ancient Nordic warriors. The walls were covered with posters featuring similar art work. That was all I needed to see, but Jamie had found something in one of Kurt's pockets.

She held it out to the Pflegers. It was a plastic Baggie filled with marijuana cigarettes, Ritalin tablets, and some other pills I didn't recognize.

"You planted that," said Mr. Pfleger.

I stepped toward him, using my height advantage. "Grow up."

"What?" He stared up at me, his fists clenched at his side. Good; it was time to try my last move.

I put my hand out, flat, and poked him in the chest with all four fingers extended. Softly, I said, "Grow up, Pfleger. Be a man." Poke. "Be a man." Poke, poke.

"Stop that." He pushed my hand away.

"Jack?" said Jamie.

I poked him again. "Admit the truth." Poke. "Be a man." Poke. "Admit that both your sons were weaklings."

He wavered for a moment, his eyes crazy with anger, then he hauled off and punched me in the mouth. And I let him.

I felt my jawbone snap out, then back into place. I tasted copper on my tongue.

We stood toe-to-toe for a moment. Then all the rage left his eyes and they filled up with tears. His face got rubbery as he tried to keep from crying. He turned on his heel and walked toward his bedroom, his head down, his shoulders shaking.

Mrs. Pfleger said, "I think you'd better go now."

"Yeah," I said. "Thanks, we got what we needed. I'm sorry for the trouble. And crack a window once in a while."

Jamie was furious with me. Again.

As we went outside, where it was pleasant to finally feel the sting of cold air on our faces again, she said, "I have *never* seen worse behavior from you. I'm just appalled. I don't even know what to say to you right now."

I didn't say anything; I just walked toward the car, got in and started the engine.

She got in, slammed her door. "What on earth got into you? It was almost like you wanted him to hit you in the mouth!"

"Yeah, that was the point. It was a psychodrama."

She stared. "A psychodrama? What is wrong with you? That poor man just lost his two sons in the most horrible—"

"I know, sweetheart. That's why I did it."

"That's insane! I don't understand this. I mean, I know he said some terrible things about Leon, but—"

"No, that stuff didn't bother me."

"Well, it bothered me."

"Well yeah, me too, at first." I pulled the car away from the curb. "Until I realized what was really going on."

"You're going to have to explain that."

"It's a guy thing." I shrugged it off.

"I don't care what it is! Explain it!"

"Look, he didn't just lose his sons, he lost a part of his man-hood. That's why he was saying those things about Leon. At least it was part of it; he's probably a racist bastard as well."

"He sure sounded like it."

"Well, anyway, I know how devastated I'd be if I lost Leon to drugs. But Leon's not my biological son. He's not a continua-tion of the Field name, if you will. That kind of thing—the need to preserve the bloodline—is important to guys like Pfleger. They feel it's part of their manhood."

"How do you know it's important to him?"

"Because of the sign outside the funeral home. He's his father's son and he doesn't want anyone to forget it."

"I didn't notice anything unusual about that sign."

"It's not *unusual*, it's just indicative of a certain mindset. At any rate, now that both of his sons are dead, a part of his manhood is lost forever. So I got him to punch me in the mouth to give him a little of it back."

She was speechless. "You're serious?"

"Yeah. I had these clients once. They had two Chinese crested dogs, Crowley and Riff. Riff was full of spunk but Crowley was a scaredy-cat. He was scared of the stairs, he was scared of the street, he was scared to play.

"When I came over to meet them, they both jumped up on me and twirled around, happy and excited. But Riff's energy was too much for Crowley, so after a few seconds of greeting me he hopped up on the sofa, turned his back, and curled up into a ball."

"That's odd. And I hope this has something to do with—"

"It does. So I sat next to him and started talking to him: 'Hey, Crowley buddy! How ya doin?' but he kept his back turned. So I started pinching him on the butt."

"You did what?"

"I pinched him on the butt. I was—"

"You were goading him, trying to get him to engage?"

"That's right."

"You could have used a treat, couldn't you?"

"Sure, if I'd wanted him to engage with the *treat*. But it was more than that; I wanted to open him up to his emotions, which he'd shut himself off from, just like Harrald Pfleger has.

"So I pinched him and talked to him, and he still ignored me. So I kept pinching him harder and harder until he finally spun his head around and snapped at me. Then I praised him profusely."

"You *wanted* him to snap at you?"

"Of course. He'd lost the ability to fight, so—"

"You were giving him back his manhood, or his *dog*hood. Still, how was that your responsibility with *Pfleger*?"

"You're right, it wasn't. Or it wouldn't have been if I hadn't had to search his son's room. By doing that I was effectively rubbing his nose in his failures as a man."

"I guess I can see that. And you realize you've just used another dog-training metaphor."

"Yeah, except I'd never rub a dog's nose in anything. So anyway, now, instead of shutting himself off from his emotions by drinking beer and watching a baseball game, he's doing what he should be doing: crying his eyes out over his two lost boys."

"That's what you'd do if you lost Leon, I guess."

"Yeah, or worse."

"Men," she said with a sigh. "You certainly have some complicated rituals, don't you?"

We stopped at a light. I said nothing.

She said, "Let me see your lip." I let her examine my face. When she was done she said, "Well, that'll look pretty tomorrow. We should find a gas station and put some ice on that."

"Good idea."

"And why didn't you dodge his punch? You just stood there."

"Yeah, I had some practice doing that when I was a kid."

She thought about this. "Your father hit you?"

"When he was drunk, yeah. But only with his open hand."

"This is getting even more complicated. It sounds like what you did with Harrald Pfleger was done out of guilt, not out of—"

"Don't psychoanalyze me, sweetheart. If you don't mind?"

"But how long did it go on? How long before he stopped?"

"I don't know." I sighed. "I guess it went on until the day I was big enough to hit him back and win the fight."

"And how did that feel?"

"Beating up my father? It was the worst feeling I've ever had in my entire life, except for the two times you were missing and I couldn't find you. I threw up for hours afterward and couldn't stop crying. I still have nightmares about trying to get his blood off my knuckles." I took a breath. "Anyway, let's get back to the rest of the case."

"Okay," she sighed, "what did you find in Kurt's room that made you say we got what we needed?"

I told her about Kurt's comic books and posters, and explained how comic books deeply affect the psyches of adolescent boys. "I think it has something to do with the way you have to read the word balloons in comics while looking at the artwork. It somehow integrates the right and left hemispheres of the brain."

"So you think he was imitating a Viking funeral for him and his brother? But don't you need a boat for that?"

I shrugged. "He parked the car on a dock, on top of a lake. Maybe he couldn't find a boat. Maybe he couldn't get his brother's body out of the car because rigor had set in."

"You're a strange man, Jack Field, but you *are* brilliant."

"I know I am, but why do you think so?"

"Jerk. Because there *was* a rowboat on the shore, and the cops couldn't figure out why it had been doused with gasoline."

"Now you can tell them why. And now you can write 'suicide' on the death certificate and we can move on to the next step."

"The next step is finding Henry Chu. How do we do that?"

"I don't know. Maybe Farrell or Tulips will have an idea."

She got mad again. "You know, you could've told me some of this before, not just the part about finding the body."

"I know. I'm sorry, but with your phones being tapped . . ."

"But that doesn't . . . oh, never mind." She shivered. "I'll feel a lot safer when Chu is behind bars. And Eddie Cole." She reached a hand over to my head. "I forgot to feel your bump, from where Kurt Pfleger hit you with the baseball bat."

I inclined my head toward her, keeping my eyes on the road.

"I'm going to have an ER doctor examine you."

"That's unnecessary. I'm fine."

"No, you're not. You may *feel* fine, but you have no way of knowing if there's internal hemorrhaging. You could have a subdural hematoma and go into a coma just like General Mac-Leary."

"Oh," I said. "That's another thing I forgot to tell you."

"What is?"

"General MacLeary. He's been faking his coma."

She laughed. "You told me that two days ago!"

"I did?"

"Yes. You don't remember?"

I tried to think.

"At the coffee shop in Augusta? With Kelso and Dr. Lunch? And you tried to get me to promise not to tell his doctors?"

"Oh, right." I was chagrined, then I looked at her. "You didn't tell them, did you?"

"I may have made a phone call that insinuated they do a tox screen to check for anything that shouldn't be in his blood."

"Honey! And you're complaining about me not telling *you* things. And what did they find?"

"The results aren't back yet." She gave me a look. "And as far as I'm concerned, I did the right thing. That Chinese herb, whatever it is, could be very dangerous to that old man."

I drove awhile, then said, "All right, from now on we tell each other everything. Deal?"

"Okay by me, but you're the one who won't live up to it."

"Hah!" I said, though we both knew she was right.

25

When we got to the hospital, we were met with another crisis. Tulips was okay, but the hospital wanted to release her and she refused to go home. In fact, she was clinging to the bed rails with both hands.

"I'm Dr. Cutter," Jamie said to the nurses, one male, one female. "What's going on?"

"She's been discharged," said the female nurse. "But she won't get dressed and let us put her in the wheelchair."

"Jack? Please? Don't let them do this to me!"

I came over to the bed. The nurses stood aside. Tulips let go of the guardrail. I took her hand. "Don't be afraid."

"But I don't have anyplace safe to go." She looked at Jamie, then at the nurses. "Can I talk to you alone?"

"Sure." I gave Jamie my cell phone, told her, "Tom Shelford's number is in the memory. Call him and see when he's coming." Then I gestured everyone out of the room.

Once they were gone, Tulips said that she'd called "her friend" Donald, who I assumed was the married professor she'd been seeing, to see if he would help her, but he'd been cold, distant, unloving: not like the man she knew when they were alone together. "He said we have to stop seeing each other," she said.

Well, it had to happen sooner or later, I supposed, though Donald had picked the exact wrong time to let her down.

"Don't you have any other friends?"

She shook her head. "Just Farrell. And he's gone."

"I know. I don't suppose you could stay at his place."

"Are you kidding? After what happened there?"

"No, I didn't think so."

"Besides," she said, "his place is so . . ."

"What?"

"I don't know; it's so . . . *Farrelly*."

I laughed. "It certainly is. And all that beagle hair!"

"I know!" She laughed along with me.

Jamie came back in. "Tom's downstairs. He'll be right up."

Tulips looked at her and said, "I don't suppose I could stay with the two of you?"

Jamie immediately said she could, even though the spare bedroom was now Dr. Lunch's command center. I pointed this out.

Jamie said, "So? We'll move him into the kitchen."

I agreed she could stay with us till things quieted down.

"Thank you." Her eyes filled with tears; her lips trembled.

I looked at her, held her hand, and saw some things in her eyes, things that were going through her mind. She was afraid that Henry Chu would come back when she least expected it. She felt guilty about her fling with Donald, and she felt lost and abandoned now that it was over. And she needed Farrell in ways she didn't like to think about, but he was in love with her and she wasn't in love with him.

There was something else there, though, some feeling that I couldn't name or put my finger on.

"It's okay, honey," I told her. "You're going to be okay."

"Of course you are," said Jamie.

"No, I'm not." She had a lost look. "The thing is, it felt good." She closed her eyes sadly. "It felt sooooo good."

I thought she was talking about her affair with Donald, then realized: "You mean, when Ryoken gave you that overdose."

She nodded, brushed back the tears. "Why couldn't I have just died? That would have been perfect. Why do I have to go on living?" She tried to laugh. "I know. I'm just being a baby."

"No, you're not," I said. "After everything that's happened, it's no wonder you feel this way."

"But I can't let it drag me down. I don't want . . ." The tears came again. She blubbered through them, "I can't let myself end up like my mother. I don't want to end up working a street corner in Portland or Boston the way she did in Saigon."

Softly, I said, "I don't think she had any choice. Her life was preordained in some ways. Yours isn't."

"I know. But I hate her so much for what she did, who she was. My whole life, I've always hated her."

"Well, now maybe you're grown up enough to understand her, maybe even forgive her."

Jamie put a hand on my shoulder. She said, "And you'll always have Farrell, Amy. He'll always be there for you."

"Farrell," she said with a scornful sigh.

"Amy," said Jamie, "that man really loves you."

"Yeah, that's the problem," Tulips and I said in unison.

We both laughed.

Just then Tom Shelford showed up, followed by the two nurses. Tom showed Tulips some photos. She picked out Brent Pfleger's photo, and Henry Chu's as the man who'd killed him.

"How did he do it?" I asked quietly.

"He, he came behind him and slit his throat."

For Tom's benefit, I said to Jamie, "Does that match the condition of the body in your morgue?"

"To a tee."

"Good," said Shelford. "I'll put out a warrant."

"Now can we get her out of here?" the female nurse said.

"Yeah."

Tulips got dressed, the nurses got her into a wheelchair and wheeled her out to the hall, where I looked both ways, just in case a maintenance man or orderly was out there, acting nonchalant but who also bore a resemblance to Henry Chu.

There was no one there.

I said to Tom, "Can you drive Tulips up to my place? It's Dog Hill Kennels, halfway between Hope—"

"—and Perseverance," he said. "I know. I'd be happy to."

"Good. I'll call the sheriff's department and let them know you're coming. They've got some deputies watching the house."

"Why aren't you coming?" Tulips asked, reaching one hand up for me to hold as we waited for the elevator.

"Jamie and I have to do something. It might be too dangerous for you to come with us."

Jamie said, "This is news to me. Besides, I'm not leaving her
alone. You go to the diner without me."

"Okay." To Tulips, I said, "Other than Donald, does anyone
else know you were here?"

She shook her head. "I didn't even tell him."

"That's good."

To the nurse, I said, "What name is she registered under?"

She looked at the chart on the back of the wheelchair. "Well,
it sure ain't Tulips."

"So what is it?"

"Jane Doe is all I have."

"That's good."

"What kind of name is Tulips anyway?" she asked.

"It's a long story," said Tulips.

It wasn't that long. Farrell told it to me once. He said that
Tulips was the name Amy's birth mother had given her. Her
biological father was an American lieutenant named Terry Merton, who used to bring fresh tulips to the whorehouse in Saigon
where her mother worked. It was the only nice thing he ever
did for her.

Where it gets complicated is how Amy, after working her
ass off to get those two Ph.D.'s of hers, learned Terry Merton's
name, came to Maine to meet him, and finally found out about
her birth name. She also found out that Merton was more of a
bastard than she was.

Jamie and I said our good-nights in the parking lot.

"Well," I said, "we've got Chu for at least one killing now. It
won't be long before he's caught. What's that look mean?"

"This case seems to be bringing up a lot of themes about
mothers and daughters and fathers and sons."

"Yeah, Carl Jung had a name for that kind of thing. He called
it synchronicity."

"So that's where that word comes from."

I said, "I *do* feel sorry for that sorry-ass loser Pfleger, you
know. Sitting there, watching a stupid ballgame, trying—"

"A stupid ballgame? It was the World Series."

"It was? Huh. Shows you how out of touch I am lately."

"No kidding. So tell me something, sweetheart: why do all the sorry-ass losers in the county seem to find their way to you?"

"I don't know. I guess it's because they know that I was a sorry-ass loser myself once."

She looked surprised. "You were?"

"Sure I was, before I met you."

She hugged me. "Ah, yes. I remember now."

"And speaking of fathers and sons, what would you think about us laying some of the groundwork for that kind of thing ourselves?"

"It's a thought," she said, smiling. "But aren't you already satisfying some of your paternal instincts with Leon?"

"Some of them," I said. "But I'm starting to think it's time to send him back to New York to live with his grandmother."

"Why?"

"Are you kidding? With exploding kitchens, crazed hit men, kids smoking embalming fluid, and ex-governors putting out murder contracts on county sheriffs? It isn't safe around here!"

26

On the drive over to the diner, where I was supposed to get a phone call from Farrell that would explain the connection between the discovery of Katherine MacLeary's bones and Eddie Cole, I thought about a couple of previous cases Jamie and I had worked on. The Marti MacKenzie case was the first, of course, since I'd just been remembering Tulips's relationship with Judge Merton, and he'd been at the center of that case. Plus the diner was a central part of that case as well. I also thought about Eddie Cole, since he'd been blackmailing Merton at the time.

Then something else started nagging at my brain. When I'd worked on the Gordon Beeson case, I overheard two Maori hit men, who worked for Miguel Ortíz, talking about Eddie Cole, as if Ortíz and Cole were in business together. That hadn't made much sense to me, though I had a few other things to worry about at the time, like staying alive. I mean, why would a San Diego drug lord be in business with a small-time dealer in Maine?

The diner was on the outskirts of town near the Belfast airport, a small airfield handling mostly agricultural and local commuter flights. I'd always wondered how they sold enough burgers and fries to make any money so far outside of town, and when I pulled up to a stop in the parking lot, I realized they didn't. The place had gone out of business.

I sat there in Farrell's truck wondering how the hell I was going to find him when a dark Buick coupe pulled up beside me.

Uh-oh, I thought. This could be trouble.

The window started to roll down. I put the truck in reverse and was about to punch the accelerator when I heard a voice say: "Nice ride. Did you steal it?"

It was Farrell.

He got out of the passenger side, though I had to look twice before I recognized him; his beard was missing, his hair was cut short, and he was wearing a business suit. He even wore a power tie and a pair of wing-tips. Then a familiar looking guy, late twenties, blond hair, blue eyes, got out of the driver's side. I knew him from somewhere; I just couldn't place from where.

Farrell tilted his head toward his new friend and said, "Jack Field, meet Janwillem van der Dijkstra."

"Hey, Jan," I said.

"Jan*willem*," said the blond, with some sort of European accent. "It's one word. Van der Dijkstra is three."

Oh, I realized, it was a Dutch accent.

"Hey, I remember you!" I said.

He was the bartender from that little shack on the beach in Mexico. I'd forgotten that after Reggie left us that day, Jamie and I sat at the bar and had some more sangria. And this guy, this blond Dutch bartender, had gently prodded us about life in Maine and whether we'd ever heard of his uncle, who he said might be living on an island off the coast again. I was a little drunk but I vaguely remembered that his uncle, whose name I've forgotten if I ever knew it, had lived in Maine a few years back, then had gone to Japan to study with a Zen master, and then moved on to Mexico, which is why his nephew was tending bar along the beach there. He was some kind of journalist, writing a book about his uncle, who was famous back in Amsterdam, for what I don't know. Janwillem had deals with all the hotels in Cabo to hand out free drink coupons to any visitors from Maine, which is how Jamie and I ended up at his temporary place of employment.

"So, did you ever locate your uncle?" I asked him.

He nodded at Farrell and said, "My new friend says I might find him up near Machias." He opened the trunk of the car. Farrell took out a nice piece of luggage and threw it in the back of his pickup. Van der Dijkstra went back to the driver's door.

"It's late," he said. "I need to find a motel. Thanks for your help, Farrell. I'll let you know if I find him."

"No sweat. And thanks for the info on Eddie Cole."

"My pleasure."

He got in the car and drove away.

"Mind if I drive you home?" Farrell asked.

I handed him the keys and said, "Tulips came through okay. She's at my place. She was too afraid to go home alone."

"That's good." He got in, as did I. "Do you think she'd mind if I came in to say hello when we get there?"

"Probably not. She's still a little rocky; I think she could use a friend." I think I may have put a little too much emphasis on the word friend.

On the way home he told me what he'd found out that caused him to go to Mexico, and what he'd learned while he was there.

After our discussion on Sunday, about the joint I found in the ashtray, Farrell had put out feelers about Eddie Cole and quickly found out a few things from various sources around the county, people he knew from his days traveling around, selling pot, and listening to them talk.

The first item of interest was that the Koreans were unhappy with Cole because of a deal that went sour involving Miguel Ortíz and a drug shipment from San Diego.

"That's funny," I said. "I was just thinking about Ortíz. I've always wondered why he'd be hooked up with Eddie Cole."

"Oh, he's connected. Just wait and let me tell you how."

One of Farrell's sources, a girl he knew who was close to Cole, told him that as soon as Cole heard the news about the bones being discovered on General MacLeary's property, he began making some intense phone calls to Ortíz in San Diego, and then to a woman in a little town in Baja California.

"How did your friend know all this?"

"She was with Eddie when the story came on the news. And she overheard his side of the conversations."

"When did she tell *you* about it?"

"The next day, Monday. She also told me that Eddie heard I'd been asking around about him and had sent Ryoken after me."

"You mean Henry Chu."

"Yeah, I like calling him Ryoken. 'Henry' humanizes the bastard; it makes you remember he had parents who named him."

"So that's when you decided to get out of town."

"It wasn't just Ryoken. This chick also told me that Eddie was headed to Mexico, to meet a woman down there. So I thought, screw it; I'm gonna tail him. So I disguised myself—"

"Yeah, I can tell."

"—and trailed him to San Diego, then to this little town in Baja called—"

"I know the place. And that's where you met Dijkstra?"

"Van der Dijkstra," he corrected me, then laughed. "You have no idea how many times I heard him say that on our trip back."

"So what's Cole's connection to Mexico?"

"Well, as fate would have it, in looking for his uncle, Dijkstra has gathered quite a lot of information about this and that and the other. He knows this woman that Eddie Cole went down there to meet. She's his mother."

"Okay." I sat back in my seat. "This is going to be good."

"Oh, it is, Jackie boy. It's real good."

Here's what he told me: in 1950 a young housemaid in Camden, named Margaret Cole, was having an illicit affair with a former navy pilot named Edward Coster. He was married, his wife was pregnant with a child that would soon be named after him: Ed Coster, Jr. Meanwhile, the housemaid also became pregnant.

Coster had a gardener, a Mexican he'd met at the navy yard in San Diego when he was stationed there. His name was Miguel Ortíz.

"Well, that can't be," I said. "Our Miguel Ortíz had to have been less than five years old in 1950."

"True enough. But his father wasn't."

The story went on that Coster, with a little family money to grease the wheels, convinced Ortíz to marry Margaret so the child would be legitimate and no suspicion would be cast on him.

Unfortunately, the county clerk was suspicious. After the wedding it was found that Ortíz had no citizenship papers, so he was sent back to Mexico before the baby was born. He already had a wife, Maria, and three children, Luz, Rosa, and little Miguel.

"How did Dijkstra learn all this? From the old woman?"

"No. He never spoke to her. She's a bit of a recluse. He had a long conversation, though, with Miguel Ortíz, Sr."

I huffed in frustration. "There are too many juniors and seniors in this story! It's like a frickin' high school prom."

"Hah. So anyway, she has the kid, names him after his actual father, Edward Coster. By now she's gone back to her maiden name, so that's how he ends up being called Eddie Cole."

"Well, at least now I understand why Cole keeps getting out of jail. It's because he's Ed Coster, Jr.'s half brother."

"Oh, it gets better than that, Jackie. Remember how Cole was blackmailing Judge Merton?"

"Yeah?"

"That's his M.O. with the justice system; he blackmails cops and judges."

"So he's blackmailing the Coster family?" I thought about it. "I don't know. Fathering an illegitimate child isn't worth being blackmailed for, particularly not so many years aft—"

"Yeah, but he's not blackmailing Coster Sr. because he's the man's illegitimate son. He's doing it because his mother was fifteen years old when Coster was shtupping her."

Now I knew what Katherine MacLeary had been so upset about in the letter to her husband. "Ah, Jesus. Well, Coster can't go to jail for that—unfortunately—there's a statute of limitations, but it would sure as hell ruin his name."

"Wouldn't it?"

"How come nobody knows this? Can't the press dig around and come up with the marriage license or the birth certificate?"

"They could. But she lied about her date of birth. I think Eddie Cole's the only one who's got the real goods on Coster. That's what's kept him alive and out of jail all this time."

"That sounds right. So how'd his mother end up in Mexico? I mean, that's where Mrs. MacLeary is supposed to have gone. That's way too much of a coincidence."

"I don't know. There has to be a connection. You're the one that's good at putting these kinds of puzzles together."

I was stumped. "The only thing I can think of is that she must have been involved somehow in the murder. What else do you know about her?"

"Not much. Like I said before, Dijkstra got all this from old man Ortíz."

"And what's Dijkstra's story again? I was a little drunk the first time I heard it. He seems to be going to an awful lot of trouble just to find some long lost uncle."

"Oh, no. His uncle is a huge legend in Holland, like a combination of Mick Jagger and Billy the Kid. It's quite a story. It involves a billion dollar diamond heist, an affair he had with the prime minister's wife, and a whole lot more. Plus, Janwillem is a journalist; he's been working on a book about his uncle for seven years. He calls it his magnum opus."

"Okay. I get it, sort of. Now about Cole's mother—"

"She raised Eddie in Lewiston, getting hush money from Coster, then she married someone new named Reeves or something, moved to Camden, and that's the last the old man knew of her."

"She'd been writing him letters?"

"Yeah, but mostly the other way around. Old man Ortíz was convinced the baby was his. He still is, according to Dijkstra."

I thought it over and said, "Well, that fits something I've had trouble making any sense of. Miguel Ortíz, I mean the one in San Diego, probably thinks Eddie Cole is his half brother."

"Exactly. And that explains why they're so tight."

I laughed a sour laugh. "Cole must have seen how much mileage that got him with the Coster clan, he found out about Ortíz's father, maybe from the old man's letters to his mother, and he set up some kind of business arrangements with him."

"That explains it, all right."

"I still don't like it. There are too many brothers and half brothers and mixed-up families in this mishegoss."

"That's the way things are these days, Jackie boy. They even have a name for it: blended families."

I snorted. "Somebody ought to *un*blend *these* families, if you ask me. There'd be a lot less trouble around here."

"You're right about that. Though if you think about it, it all comes back to Eddie Cole. He's the source."

"Right. And if that's true, then we've got to find the proof he's holding over the Costers. Once their secret is out, Cole won't be getting a free ride anymore. He'll be toast."

"You've got connections with the press. Can't you just tell Otis Barnes or your friends down in Portland about it?"

"Sure, but they're not going to run a story like this without some kind of proof. And even *I* don't have that yet. All I have is your version of something you heard from a Dutch bartender in Mexico."

He laughed. "Well, when you put it like that . . . So how do you propose to get the proof?"

"I don't know. I'm too tired to think."

We got to the kennel. Sloan's car was in the driveway, even though it was almost one o'clock. She must've heard us drive up because Leon's light came on. Then as Farrell parked, Sloan came running out to her car, throwing her sweater on as she ran.

I got out of the truck. "Hey, Sloan!"

She ignored me, got in her car and started it up. I ran over as she started her K-turn, and ended up in front of her headlights. She inched forward, hoping I'd back down. I didn't.

Finally she rolled down her window. "I need to go home."

Leon stood in the doorway of the carriage house, fully dressed but looking confused. Farrell stood next to his truck.

I said to Sloan, "Don't run off like this again."

"We weren't doing anything. We were just making out."

"Well, that's not nothing." I came around to her window. "Besides, I don't really care what you and Leon were doing or weren't doing." I revised that. "Well, I care, but I'd rather you didn't run off like this. If you two were making out, then you should go back up there and say a proper good-bye to him."

"How do you know I didn't already do that?"

"Did you?"

"No."

"Then you should probably go do that. Right?"

She sighed. "You're right." She turned off the engine.

As she got out I said, "When you're done, I have something I want to talk to you about." She got a cornered look on her face. "Don't worry. It's not about Leon. It's about the murder case."

She gave me a shy shrug. "Okay."

She went to the carriage house and I went over to Farrell. He nodded at the main house. "Seems everyone's asleep."

"So?"

"So, maybe I should just go home."

"It's up to you. But I think she'd like to see you."

"Are you sure?"

"Me? I'm not sure about anything right now."

"That's honest." He looked at the house, then back at his truck. It was going to be a long, lonely drive back to Oak Hill Road if he didn't peek in on her before he left. "Okay."

Leon was walking Sloan to her car, the way a guy should, and the way a girl should let him. They got there, then kissed and said good-night, and she got in.

I came over. "Before you go, I just want to get your advice. If someone had some kind of evidence they'd been using to blackmail someone else, how would you go about finding it?"

She looked surprised. "Why ask me?"

"I don't know. I'm stuck and you're smarter than I am."

"Is that true?" Leon asked.

We both told him it was.

Sloan said, "You know more about criminals and psychology than I do, just like you know more about dogs. I think you'd be better at figuring it out than I would."

"I guess you're right. How's Buster doing?"

She smiled. "It's like he's a different dog. He's so happy; he even plays now."

I told her that was good to know, then walked toward the carriage house, letting the young lovers have their private moment.

After she'd driven off and Leon was headed back to his little room, I stopped him and said, "I hope you're happy with yourself."

"A little. Why?" He gave me a mildly defiant look. "We weren't doing nothin'. We was just makin' out."

"I said you and Sloan could have a conversation, not a date."

"It wasn't a date."

"'Date' is just a nicer way to put it than 'make-out session.'"

"Yeah, okay. So?"

"So, you're grounded for another week."

"What?"

"You heard me. There are rules about this stuff, and you have to pay attention to them."

"But I wasn't plannin' on makin' out with her. We were just talkin', and then stuff just sort of happened."

"Yeah, that's the way it is with girls, Leon, whether it's making out or making love; stuff just sort of happens. There are all kinds of consequences to fooling around that you can't even begin to contemplate when you're wrapped up in those feelings."

"Yo, Pops. You gave me this speech already."

"And I'll probably give it to you again."

"But, yo, man, don't I get to have any fun? I mean, it's my life, ain't it?"

"No, Leon, it's not your life—not *just*. It's Sloan's life, it's my life, it's your grandmother's life, it's the lives of everyone who might get born because of your few moments of fun."

"We wasn't *doin'* it, man, I was just kissin' her."

"I know. But other stuff starts to *just happen* when you're kissing a girl."

Maybe it wasn't Leon, maybe I was just sick and tired of men who gave no concern to where they put their seed. Maybe I was sick to death of dealing with the consequences such men left in their wake, men like Judge Merton and Governor Coster. They were the ones to blame for these deaths, these wrecked lives that Jamie and I were dealing with. Even someone like Harrald Pfleger, not to put more weight on the shoulders, but where was his guidance for those boys? Where's the fatherhood in such a man? In those photographs? Where was he when his kids were falling into the abyss of drugs? Sitting in his hothouse living room, watching a baseball game?

Okay, all right, maybe I'm being too hard on him personally. But seriously, how many men stop to think of the consequences that planting their seed, in that one quick transitory moment of pleasure, brings? Not many, that's all I'm saying.

"I want you to remember this, Leon. It's important."

"Okay. I'll remember it, a'ight?"

"Good. And what do I always tell you about dog training?"

"Yo, I don't know; dogs need to play to get rid of their tension?"

"Well, that's true. But don't I always tell you that the slower you go, the more successful you'll be?"

He shook his head. "I know I ain't as smart as you and Sloan, but I already got that, Pops."

"And you understand about consequences?"

He hung his head. "Yeah. I'm grounded for another week."

"That's right. If Sloan really likes you—and I think she does—she'll still be around."

"Okay. I can live with that."

"Good. You're a good kid, Leon."

"I ain't no kid, yo. I'm a man."

"Not yet you're not. But I will say you're a lot better man than some men I could mention. Good night."

"Good night. And thanks, Pops."

I went inside to the living room, where Kelso was asleep on the couch. Lunch was nowhere to be seen. I poured a shot of scotch, downed it, then poured another and sipped it slowly.

When I was done I walked past the downstairs bedroom. The door was ajar. I peeked in and saw Farrell and Tulips. He'd taken off his shoes, tie, and suit coat, and was lying on top of the covers in his white shirt and slacks. Tulips was under them, with her head on his shoulder. She had her eyes closed and was pretending to be asleep. I could tell she was pretending because she was stroking his cheek and jaw, feeling the bare skin where his beard used to be. She seemed to be smiling.

Farrell saw me and gave me a happy smile and a facial shrug.

I climbed the stairs, pointed Frankie off the bed, then took off my clothes and got under the covers next to Jamie.

She rolled over into my arms and kissed me.

"Mmmmm," she said. "You have whisky breath."

"It's been a long night."

"I don't mind. I kind of like it."

"Farrell's downstairs," I said between kisses. "Softer, honey; that's my split lip."

"Sorry. He came back from California?"

"Yeah. He went to Mexico, actually. It's a long story."

"Is it okay if you tell it to me in the morning?"

I said that was all right.

"Unless you'd rather talk than make a baby?"

"No," I said. "We can talk tomorrow."

She did all the work. My only tasks were to watch her perform her magic and, when it was time, to stifle my screams of pleasure so no one downstairs could hear us. After it was over I was at peace; it felt good to know I'd planted my seed in the one right place.

Whisky can make for bad dreams, though. Halfway to daylight I had the nightmare again—I couldn't scrub my knuckles clean. But a part of me was aware of the dream this time, the same part that had just gone into Jamie, that was still inside her, that connected us forever. That part of me took over, turned it into a lucid dream, so that now instead of the nightmare ending as it usually did, with me waking in tears, trembling, shaking, I reached my hand down to my father, helped him to his feet, and put an arm around him. When I did, I noticed that the blood was gone; my hands were clean.

If only life were as easy as it is in dreams.

27

The morning came quickly, with Doriane Elliot's construction crew arriving around seven. They still had a lot of work to do on the kitchen, mainly replacing the windows and strengthening and rebuilding the door frames. A county inspector came along to make sure the bomb hadn't caused any structural damage.

While they unloaded their equipment, I watched Molly bury a stick. The other dogs ran around, playing or sniffing, but Molly was at the sand pit in the far left corner, with a determined look in her eyes, burying her "bone." While she covered it with sand, I found another one. Then, when she'd covered the first one, I called her, teased her with the new stick, and threw it. I aimed it at the sand pit where she'd buried the first stick, thinking she'd put the second one in with it. But she didn't.

She scooped it up then raced to the other end of the play yard, to the sand pit in the near right corner, and buried it there. This isn't unusual behavior, but I had to wonder at the rationale behind it. On a certain level everything a dog does comes out of instinct and emotion, not strategy and planning. But it sure seemed to me like she'd purposely buried the second stick as far away from the first one as she could; in case one of the other dogs dug that one up, she'd have a backup.

While I pondered how such a seemingly complex, well-thought-out behavior could come out of pure instinct or emotion, I remembered what Kelso had said: Molly was the center of the case. As before, I didn't know what that meant. The only thing that came to mind, oddly enough, was W. C. Fields, and the fact (or maybe it's fable) that he kept all his money in numerous bank accounts under fictitious names (one of the names might have even been Carl LaFong). This seemed similar to Molly's behavior; she was burying different bones in different bank accounts.

After the dogs finished playing and I got them fed, I went back up to the house to see if the kitchen was in good enough shape so I could make breakfast. I found Dr. Lunch sitting at the table, drinking a foamy, dark-greenish concoction he'd mixed up in my blender. A couple of Doriane's guys were removing the sheets of plywood from the outside. And as Lunch drank his green goop, he told me he'd taped Kelso's conversation with Allan Forbert the night before and asked if I wanted to hear it.

"Not really," I said, looking at the carpenters. "Why don't you just give me—you've got a little on your chin." He wiped off the green liquid. "Just give me the gist of it."

He did. Forbert had tried to weasel out of the jam he was in by protesting his innocence, but as he read through the transcript and saw some of his statements to Coster, he caved.

I said, "He's on our side now?"

"Could be. You'd have to ask Kelso when he wakes up. And I need to move my equipment. The sawdust isn't good for—"

The phone rang and I got up to answer it. It was Tom Harris, the FBI's agent in charge. He was in Augusta and wanted me to help talk some sense into Sheriff Flynn.

"What makes the FBI think I can influence him?" I asked.

"Because if you can't, you're in deep shit."

I took a moment, then said, "Okay. Why don't you come up here and we can discuss it."

"How's noon?"

"Noon's fine."

When I hung up I found Lunch giving me a cornered rat look.

"What?"

"You invited the FBI up here?"

"Oh, I forgot." I thought that over. "Okay, we'll move all

your stuff up to the second floor. There's a spare room there. It's full of boxes right now, but we can make you some space."

He still looked frightened.

"And you can, I don't know, camp out across the street until they're gone. I'm sure my groomer won't mind. It's her house."

He seemed relieved. He finished his algae shake then started packing up his equipment for the move upstairs.

The rest of the morning was mostly uneventful. Over breakfast, with Farrell and Jamie and Leon and Kelso, Tulips—who was wearing one of Farrell's old flannel shirts as a housedress, with the sleeves rolled to her elbows—told me how she would explain Molly's Fieldsian method of bone dispersal.

"It has nothing to do with advance planning," she said. "You're the one who taught me dogs don't think that way. You have to take it in binary steps, the way a computer program would."

"Explain."

"Okay. She has a bone or a stick in her mouth, right? But having it in her mouth increases her feelings of tension; another dog or a person might come along and take it from her. She likes the feeling of having it in her mouth, but let's say that the fear of having it taken away is stronger."

"So we're operating under Freud's pleasure principle."

"I don't know about Freud," she said, confused. "I thought this was pure Skinner."

"No. On the most basic level—*instinct*—Freud's psychology is still better than Skinner's. The point is, she likes having it in her mouth less than she *dis*likes having it taken away."

"Right. So digging the first hole reduces her tension."

"Okay, but if it successfully reduces her tension, then why does she bury the second bone somewhere in a different spot?"

Farrell said, "Maybe she forgot where she buried it."

"No," I said. "Most dogs don't forget where their bones are buried."

"Some do," he said. "Brian Wilson used to forget where he buried *his* bones."

Tulips said, "Brian Wilson used to forget a lot of things."

"Who's Brian Wilson?" Jamie asked. "Not the Beach Boy?"

"No," said Farrell, "he was one of my dogs."

"He was eaten by a hawk," I explained.

Jamie said, "Ah, that's terrible."

"I know," Tulips said, "it's sad," then, "Look, all I know is that burying the second bone on top of the first probably doesn't feel as good to Molly as burying it in a new hole. I would imagine that for some dogs that isn't true; they don't bury their bones all over the yard, they bury them all in one spot."

Jamie said, "Given the nature of the murder case we've been working on—with human bones being buried in a yard—doesn't this discussion strike anyone but me as being a little ghoulish?"

"Yo, especially over eggs and bacon," Leon said.

"I know one thing, though," said Kelso. "This may give us a way to trap Eddie Cole."

Jamie said, "I don't see the connection."

I said, "*I* do. We just have to figure out where Eddie Cole likes to bury his bones."

"Ah-hah," said Jamie. "That *would* help, wouldn't it?"

After breakfast I walked Jamie out to her car.

She sighed. "I can't wait till this is all over."

"Me neither."

"Call me."

"I will. Keep your secure cell phone handy."

Farrell Woods came out just as she drove off. He gave me a big smile as he headed toward the Suburban.

"Did you have fun last night?" I asked.

"Huh? Oh. It wasn't like that. We just slept together. You know, nothin' else."

"That's nice."

"Yeah, maybe it'll go nowhere, maybe it'll lead to somethin' . . . who knows?"

"That's a good attitude. And listen, things are coming to a head now, so don't go running off again. I may need you."

He was stung by my words. "Are you sayin' you think I tracked Eddie Cole to Mexico 'cause I'm chickenshit?"

"No, I just don't want you disappearing again."

"I wasn't runnin' away, I was gathering intel."

"Well, you did this before, you know."

"Man, you're pissin' me off." He took a breath. "Look, I wasn't runnin' away then either. I was layin' low, stayin' out of sight so that prick Bermeosolo from the DEA wouldn't be able to trace my suppliers, most of whom were honest, hardworking people who only grew a few extra plants to cover their bills. Okay?"

"Okay. I'm sorry I brought it up, it's just that—"

"And if you remember correctly, I paid them all to destroy their stuff so Bermeosolo couldn't put 'em in jail!"

"I get it," I said, trying to calm him down. "Like they say, sometimes discretion is the better part of—"

"Screw you. I've got dogs to pick up."

He got in the car and slammed the door. The tires spit gravel as he drove up to the county road.

Huh, I thought as I headed back to the kitchen. Maybe I should have worded that differently. After all, Farrell had won medals for his courage in Vietnam—it seems I owed him an apology.

Tulips had cleared the table and started doing the dishes. I came over and saw she had a secret smile on her face. I took a position next to her and we just stood awhile, washing, rinsing, and setting things in the rack to dry.

Finally she said, "Farrell looks a lot different without his long hair and beard, doesn't he?"

"Yep." I looked at her. "You think it's an improvement?"

"It sure is."

After the dishes were done she went back to bed. Kelso and I decamped to my den to hash out a strategy. We asked Lunch to see if he could track down the name of Cole's lawyer and the names of the banks where each of them had a safe deposit box. In just five minutes he was able to find the lawyer's name (Art Fischer) and his bank (Colonial), but not Eddie Cole's.

"Can you keep looking?" I asked.

"There's no point; he doesn't have a bank account under that name. If he did, I would've found it." He went back upstairs.

"That's a dead end," Kelso said. "We'll never get a warrant on his lawyer's safe deposit box."

"Yeah, not without proof that he's been engaging in an ongoing criminal conspiracy with his client."

"Which maybe he is," he said, "but we don't have any proof."

"It's not a dead end, though. It just means we have to find out where Cole is keeping the original documents. It's probably in a safe deposit box in a bank, but under an assumed name."

We were interrupted by a phone call from Jervis. He gave me the account numbers I'd been wanting: one in the Cayman Islands, the other in Mexico. He also told me the general's ruse had been discovered; he was out of the hospital and back at the house in Camden.

"Is he feeling okay?" I asked Jervis.

"Of course. The doctors wouldn't have released him otherwise, would they, sir?"

"I guess not."

I gave the account numbers to Dr. Lunch and asked him to track all financial transactions that looked suspicious, especially those that took place around the time Katherine MacLeary was murdered.

"That'll take weeks," he said.

"Just do what you can," I told him.

A little later Abby Butler called. Regis wanted to talk to me; he was ready to deal. I agreed to go out to the prison later in the day, and she said she'd set it up with the warden.

"Why go to the prison?" Kelso complained, when I told him what was up. "You've got better things to do."

"Yeah, but I'll bet you Regis knows Eddie Cole's aliases. He might even know where the damn evidence is."

He mulled, shook his head. "It's a long shot. Corliss was a dirty cop, so Cole probably has evidence on him as well. If Corliss knew where it was, he'd have it and we wouldn't."

"That's true, but you're forgetting one thing. Regis is a dumb-ass. He isn't as smart as he thinks he is."

"And you are?"

"Most of the time, yeah."

Farrell came back with the dogs for day care a little while later. I met him in the driveway. He was still pissed.

"I've got some things to do," he said. "I'll be back this afternoon to take these doggies home."

"Look, I'm sorry for what I said earlier. But it would be nice to get a phone call from you if you're going to disappear."

"Screw you," he said again, then got into his truck and drove off.

I watched him go, then got the dogs out and played with them for a while, and when they were pooped, I took them up to the kennel. After I got them in their pens I asked Mrs. Murtaugh if Dr. Lunch could spend an hour or so at her place.

"I don't see why not. But whatever for?"

"He's a good guy, but a little shy around strangers and FBI men, both of whom are going to be showing up later."

"Oh, dear. Is he wanted for something?"

"Probably," I said. "But it'd only be for hacking into some government computer somewhere to help someone who needed it."

"Well, then, that's fine. I hope he doesn't mind cats."

Tom Harris showed up at noon. He was tallish with a genial face, and hair like General MacLeary's, meaning he was a former redhead whose hair was going pink. He'd brought a couple of young agents with him: tall, well-muscled, mean-looking.

"Were you worried I might try to beat you up or something?"

"No," he laughed, "but with the kind of shit that's been happening around you lately, you can never be too careful."

"Good point."

We sat in the den and chatted a bit, while his "bodyguards" stood by the door. After a bit of schmoozing he came to the point. It was the same request he'd made on the phone. He wanted me to convince Flynn to release Junior.

"We've got to be able to question him about this bombing."

"Why? He'll only lie to you."

"Don't most suspects lie? We still have to talk to him."

"You're right, but I don't know where Flynn's keeping him."

That was the truth. I knew Flynn had him in a cabin in the woods near Wiscasset, but I didn't know its location.

"I'm sure you're able to contact him if you need to."

"No," I lied, "but if he calls me I'll talk to him about it. Do you know why anybody in a black Town Car with government plates would be following me?"

"When was this?"

"Monday."

"That was probably someone from the NSC. It wasn't one of our people."

I told him about the guy I saw in the state office building.

"He isn't one of ours either. I wouldn't worry too much. I doubt if they're doing anything more than keeping an eye on you."

"It would've been nice if they'd kept an eye on my kitchen. Listen, I have a couple of favors to ask you."

"You're kidding, right?"

I gave him a look. "I figure the FBI owes me at least one for what happened at the wedding. Or don't you remember?"

"Okay, so we owe you one for ruining the ceremony." He sighed. "So what's the *one* favor?" He emphasized the word *one*.

I told him I wanted the FBI to back off for a few days.

"That's not possible. We've got the Pentagon and the NSC breathing down our necks on this one. A three-star general who may have killed his wife? We've got to get this resolved now."

"That part's easy. I can tell you exactly who killed Mrs. Mac-Leary, although I can't prove it yet."

"That's a lot of help. Who was it?"

"It's irrelevant for now. It's gotten more complicated than a simple domestic murder case. If you give me two days I can give you a lot more than Katherine MacLeary's killer."

"I told you, I can't do it."

"Look, give me some time and you'll get Junior, his father, the attorney general, the guy who bombed my kitchen, a drug dealer who's been given a free ride by the judiciary for twenty years, and a crime lord in San Diego. How does that sound?"

"From anyone else it would sound like a load of crap."

"And coming from me?"

"I'd say you might pull it off. What's the second favor?"

"Witness protection for Randall Corliss."

"Are you kidding?" He knew who Corliss was. "No way."

"Look, Tom, I need it to pull this off."

"Okay. If Corliss has information we can't get anywhere else, I'll okay it. But I'm only giving you twenty-four hours."

"It may not be enough, but I'll do my best. Thanks."

With his orange jumpsuit and the apparent lack of his usual tanning and grooming products, Corliss looked a lot different than I'd seen him: a bit pale with a five-o'clock shadow that wasn't very attractive. He no longer had that cocky look in his eye either.

"You gotta get me outta here, Field," were the first words out of his mouth.

"Okay. If you give me enough to nail Ryoken and Eddie Cole, the Feds are willing to put you into witness protection."

"You already talked to them about it?"

"Yeah." I told him about my conversation with Tom Harris.

He scratched his jaw. "Okay. What do you want to know?"

I told him, and he said he could give me all of Eddie Cole's aliases and that his safe deposit box, if he had one, would probably be registered under one of them. He also said that Cole had a ton of dirt, not only on the Costers and several state and local judges, but on Miguel Ortíz, including his drug shipment schedules from Mexico. If true, that was a plum, though I tried to use my poker face when he told it to me.

Finally, Corliss said he knew where Ryoken liked hiding out when the heat was on, though he wouldn't give me the exact location. He said, "Chu and Cole have got some kind of stash of weapons there, handguns, semiautomatics, and a shitload of dynamite and C–4, that kind of stuff."

"Huh. If they can match the explosives with the bomb that went off in my kitchen, that would give you a lot of leverage."

"No shit. When I heard that someone had planted a bomb in your refrigerator, the second thing that came to mind was that it must've been put there by Chu. That's his style."

"Yeah? So, what was the *first* thing that came to mind?"

"About the bomb?" He grinned an evil grin. "Don't ask."

"The thing is, I just asked. And I'm still asking."

"Fine. I wished that *I'd* thought of it first. Anyway, back to Chu's hideout, Cole might have a safe there, downstairs. For him it's better than a safety deposit box, which I figure is why you're asking me about his aliases and bank accounts."

"So, where's it located?"

"Un-uh, not yet. This is off the record. You try to nail me for anything from what I just told you, you're out of luck."

"You haven't given me enough to nail anybody."

"Exactly. If you want Cole's aliases, and the location of his and Henry Chu's hideout, you'll have to talk to my attorney first. She'll call and set up a time to meet so she can give you my computer files, but she'll only provide them if you've got a signed letter from the Feds guaranteeing witness protection."

"You understand they'll only put you in the program if the stuff you've got pans out."

"Oh, it'll pan out; don't worry."

I wasn't worried. In fact, I felt like I was riding a wave.

The trouble is, all waves come crashing down sooner or later.

28

"The building is on Western and Melville," Abby Butler told me. "My office is 511. Can you meet me here around eight?"

"Jamie and I have a Halloween party to go to."

"Fine, then how's five-thirty or six?"

"Oh, sure," I groused, "I just love driving up to Augusta during rush hour."

"Fine," she huffed. "Seven, then. Oh, and bring Frankie!"

"Okay, but why?"

"I don't know. I think Buster would like to see him again."

I thought about it. "How about if I bring Hooch? He's more of a goofball than Frankie. I think Buster might like him better. Plus he's also intact, so that'll give us a chance to do some more work on Buster's social skills in that area."

"Okay," she laughed. "Maybe we can take them for a walk to Capitol Park before we conduct our business. I'm assuming you'll be bringing the signed letter from the FBI with you too."

Now I knew why I liked Abby: dogs first, business second.

"Yeah," I said. "Corliss'll be very happy."

I called Jamie on her secure cell and told her when I'd be in the capital and why. We decided I'd pick her up at her office, then we'd drive across the river to meet Abby, then go back to the crime lab for their big Halloween party.

I also alerted Kelso to what was going on then said, "Have Dr. Lunch find any safe deposit boxes registered under the first

names Ed, Eddie, Edward, Edgar, or Edmund with the last
names Cole, Greaves, or Ortíz."

"Okay, but if he's using Ortíz, he should try Eduardo too."

"Good point."

"And since it's almost closing time at the banks, can this
pseudonym search wait a bit? Lunch is busy hacking into Medicare to fix Mrs. Murtaugh's prescription drug benefits."

I laughed. "That's odd. Very cool, but a little odd."

"Apparently when he went over to her place to avoid the
FBI, the two of them got to talking. Now he's her best friend."

I laughed. "That's great. I'll swing by on my way to Augusta
to get my costume and see how things are going."

"Costume?"

"Yeah, Jamie and I are going to a party at the crime lab. You
want to come? There'll be lots of girls."

"I guess I could meet you there, if I can get a costume together."

"Rent a tux and trade on your vague resemblance to Sean
Connery."

"Ah, you mean I should go as Bond? James Bond?"

"That's pretty good, Lou. You even sound like him."

When the elevator opened onto the fifth floor of Abby's building, Jamie, Hooch, and I stepped into a gray, dimly lit hall with
a dingy tile floor. The paint wasn't chipped and the hall smelled
of bleach, so the building wasn't low-rent, just old.

Hooch wagged his tail, as if he sensed Buster's presence.

Jamie said, "Is that happy excitement or nervousness?"

"All three, I'd say."

We went to the right, around a corner, and saw lights shin-
ing through pebbled glass. The sign on the door said: EMMETT,
BUTLER, AND CHASE — ATTORNEYS AT LAW.

I said, "That's interesting."

"What is?"

"Chase. That's Katherine MacLeary's maiden name. I wonder if they're related."

"It's possible, but it's not that unusual a name."

"I guess you're right." I tried the knob but the door was

locked. I pressed a button on the door frame and heard a buzzing sound and some loud barking, then Abby's voice:

"Buster, quiet! Jack, is that you?"

"Yeah! It's me and Jamie. And Hooch."

"Okay, let me get the leash on him. Buster, stop it! Quiet, please. Now, sit still!"

The door opened and she appeared, leaning over the dog, holding the leash wrapped tightly in one hand and brushing her hair back with the other. "Sorry. How do you want to do this?"

"Uh, let's just see what they do and take it from there."

Both dogs did a play bow at the same time, then began the age old dance of the dogs: "Are you gonna run first, or am I?"

"It's okay," I advised her. "You can let go of him."

She did, and the dogs raced to the end of the hall, then came racing back, did a brief wrestling move or two, then took off down the hall again. This time they went around the corner. We could hear the furious click of their nails on the tile floor and the sound of them panting wildly, with a few play growls to boot.

Abby and I raced after them, then had to jump back as they came whizzing around the corner, back toward her office. We ran back after them, but when we rounded the corner we found that Jamie had hold of both their leashes.

"Well," Abby said, "you were right. He does like Hooch."

Jamie smiled and said, "Yeah. Everybody likes Hooch."

I took Hooch's leash from Jamie and unhooked him. Abby did likewise with Buster. Then Hooch wandered a few feet across the hall and lifted his leg against the far wall.

"Hooch!" I said.

He just looked up at me with a satisfied grin on his face. Buster ran over to the same spot and lifted his leg on it.

"Oh, dear," said Abby.

"I'll clean it up," I said. "Have you got some paper tow—"

"That's all right. I have some enzyme cleaner in my desk drawer. I'll do it later. Though to tell you the truth, for once I'm hoping the janitorial staff sticks to their usual schedule of not showing up except when they feel like it."

"Are you sure?"

"Yeah. It'll be fine. Now that the dogs've had their fun, let's get this over with. I like your costumes, by the way."

"Thanks. Jamie's dressed as Geena Davis from *Transylvania 6–5000*, though she's hiding her cleavage under that cloak."

Jamie hit me. "I'm just your normal, everyday female vampire. Jack's going as Strider from *The Lord of the Rings*."

I put one hand on the hilt of my sword and said, "My true name is Aragorn, son of Arathorn, King of Gondor."

"Really? I never took you for a movie geek."

"I'm not. But I certainly loved the months I spent reading Tolkien when I was in high school."

Jamie said, "Jack has this theory about boys and comic books and fantasy, and how it stays with them into adulthood." She was a little off, but I didn't correct her. "Besides," she squeezed my arm, "he looks awfully dashing, doesn't he?"

"He certainly does," said Abby as she led us inside to a reception area on the left, with a single desk lamp lit.

Jamie said, "Do you always bring your dog with you to work?"

"No," Abby sighed. "But I thought, the way things are going, it wouldn't be a bad idea to have him along for protection. I know he'd rather lick someone to death, but they say just having a dog with you makes some people think twice about bothering you."

There were two offices past the receptionist's desk, one for Emmett and one for Chase. They both had their doors shut. There was a hall leading to the right where you could see a patch of light on the dark carpet. Abby led us in that direction.

"And what do you think they're going to do?" Jamie asked.

"You mean, like plant a bomb in my coffee machine?" She laughed. "Sorry. I shouldn't joke. And I know it's ridiculous, but when you're defending scumbags like Randy Corliss, it doesn't hurt to be too careful."

She led us through a door with a glass pane, into a small office with a smaller file room just to the back. We all got situated, humans in chairs, dogs on a thin layer of gray carpet.

She said, "I should make that 'alleged scumbags.'"

I chuckled, then took Tom Harris's letter out of my Levi's

jacket and tossed it on the desk. Abby opened the envelope, read the letter, and said, "This is great. This will be just perfect."

She put it back in the envelope, opened her desk drawer, which I noticed held a .32 revolver, took out a CD and gave it to me.

I pocketed the CD, nodded at the gun and said, "You really *are* scared."

"Not scared," she said, closing the drawer. "Just careful."

We all heard the outer door to the office suite click open. Abby caught her breath, opened the drawer, took out the gun and said, "Hector? Is that you?"

"Si, señora."

She took a deep breath, then said quietly to me, "Hector's the janitor. He has the key." Then to Hector, "Can you come back later? I'm on the phone, long distance."

"Sorry to interrupt." The voice was moving slowly closer.

"And I'm sorry about the mess in the hall. I'll get it cleaned up as soon as I can."

"Si, señora, but I need to speak to you *por uno momento*."

"All right." She put the gun away, closed the drawer, stood up and whispered to me and Jamie, "Wait here."

I shrugged an okay.

She took Buster through the door, turning out the light as she left. We heard some murmured conversation, then Buster barked, once. Two shadows grew larger as they approached the glass pane in her office door. Abby's shadow had her hands up in the air. The other shadow was off to the left, moving toward her; it looked like he was holding a gun, one that had a silencer.

I leapt for the drawer with the .32.

Jamie jumped up. "What do we do?" she whispered.

"Find a fire alarm switch."

She began searching the walls. I came around the desk and edged against the wall toward the door.

I heard a man's voice say, "We're going to your office to wait for your dog-training friend."

"What do you mean?" Abby asked.

"Knock it off. I know you're meeting him tonight at eight to give him some dirt on Eddie Cole. Now let's move. And keep that dog out of my way."

"I'm sorry, señora," said another voice.

"It's okay, Hector. It's not your fault."

The shadows moved closer to the door.

Jamie signaled that she'd found a fire alarm.

I nodded.

She pushed it down.

The place went crazy with bells.

Buster barked. So did Hooch.

I drew my cape back, pulled the office door open, standing safely to the side, and shouted: "Police! Drop your weapon!"

A pop from the pistol; shards of wood cut my cheek.

"Abby!" I said. "Get down on the floor!"

Beneath the barking and bells there was the faint sound of a scuffle. I couldn't tell if that meant Abby had been able to hit the deck or not. I stepped into the doorway, sideways so as to give the shooter a smaller target. There was another soft pop from the silencer. It sounded just as a man in a janitor's uniform jumped on top of Abby, who was on the floor. The bullet tore the arm of his coveralls; blood spattered toward me.

I looked the shooter in the eye. He was Korean, six-foot-four. His black eyes seemed to be made of cold dark steel.

"Put it down," I said.

He squeezed the trigger. So did I. Only one of our guns went off. That's the problem with silencers. They tend to plug up your gun barrel.

Henry Chu looked at his shoulder. He was dressed all in black so I couldn't see what he saw. All I could see was that he didn't like it, probably his own blood. He squeezed the trigger again. No pop.

I shot him again, this time in the thigh.

His face got ugly. Before I could squeeze off another round he pulled a knife and threw it at me. I jumped back, felt a nick on my ear and a *boing* sound as it hit the wall behind me. I squeezed the trigger. By the time I did, Chu was gone, racing for the door, unscrewing his silencer as he ran.

I ran after him, urging Hooch to follow me. I dropped the gun and the CD as I passed Abby and Hector.

"Jack!" Abby said.

"Keep the gun in case he comes back."

Jamie came out of the office behind me. "Jack, what the hell are you doing?"

"Following him," I said over my shoulder. "Though it's hard to run in these boots, and this sword keeps getting in my—"

"Get back here. Let the police handle it."

"Right now I *am* the police. Take care of these two."

Hooch and I followed the trail of blood down the hall toward the stairs. As I pulled the stairwell door open I noticed that Buster was right behind us.

"You stay here, Buster. Go help Mommy!" I opened the door for Hooch then squeezed through without letting Buster come.

I heard him scratch at the door.

The stairs were dark; a faint light shone from above us, maybe two floors up, but the lights on the floors just above and just below us were out. I held my breath, trying to listen, to hear which direction Chu had gone, up or down. I couldn't tell, but Hooch knew. He started racing up the stairs.

I followed him. We ran up several flights. He stopped on seven and scratched at the door.

I praised him, threw the door open, stepped back, and nothing happened. No knives went whizzing by, no soft pops tore through clothing, only silence. Even Hooch stopped panting.

I told him "Heel," and we moved carefully down the hall, my back against the wall. I told him "Stay," and edged my way around a corner. I heard a ding, and an elevator door opened. I came around just in time to see Chu's lame leg being dragged onto the elevator before the door closed.

I raced to the elevators, looked up at the floor indicator for the second elevator. A car was coming down from nine. I punched Down, told Hooch, "Come, boy!" and he came running.

I looked up at the floor indicator for Chu's elevator. It went past five and I found myself breathing again. Then it went past four just as the second elevator door opened.

It was empty. Hooch and I got on. I pressed the ground floor. It was the longest elevator ride I've ever had.

We got to the lobby in time to see Chu limping his way

through the back door of the building. I ran after him to the alley, but when I got there he was gone.

Maybe he was behind a Dumpster. Maybe he'd made it to his getaway car. All I knew was, he was gone.

"Okay, Hooch. This time we take it real slow." A lone streetlight at the end of the alley cast enough light to see what might've been blood leading in the direction of the street.

I hugged the wall of the building, keeping Hooch right behind me. We moved toward the street.

I heard an engine racing. Crap, I thought, he's getting away. Then it seemed as if the sound wasn't moving away; it was coming closer.

And closer.

And closer and closer.

Bright headlights suddenly appeared at the end of the alley. They stabbed my eyes. The car—I assumed it was a car—stopped. The door opened. A man got out and stood facing me. All I could see was his silhouette. It wasn't Henry Chu. The way this man stood on the balls of his feet, relaxed yet ready, the way he'd sprung out of the car, he reminded me of an athlete, the kind who might wear track shorts under his business suit.

"Sorry, Mr. Field," he said, then raised a gun and shot me.

Something pricked my neck. I put my hand up to feel it. It wasn't sticky; I didn't feel any blood, just something fuzzy with a hard spine, sticking out of my flesh. I heard another shot and heard Hooch grunt. I looked down. A yellow dart was stuck in his shoulder. He groaned, wobbled, and fell to the pavement with a twitch and a whimper.

Tranquilizer darts, I thought as I wobbled, lost my balance, and fell down next to him.

29

The thing that woke me was the smell of wood smoke. My first reaction was panic: the building must be on fire. Then I thought—What building? Where am I?—and noticed that the heat from the fire was coming from my left only. I sniffed a little and detected the old-ashes-and-creosote smell of a fireplace.

I felt something sting my cheek and remembered the tranquilizer dart and the guy I'd first seen outside Compton's office, the one Tom Harris suggested might've been with the NSC.

I felt the sting on my cheek again.

I became aware that I was sitting in a hard chair and someone was slapping me. Hard, very hard; without stopping. My cheeks stung from the blows. I tried to put my hands up to block them but my arms wouldn't move. They were bound to my sides.

"Hey," I muttered, panting.

"So," a rough voice with cigarette breath attached said, "you're awake now?"

"What? Where am I?" I realized I couldn't see.

Another slap. "I ask the questions."

I tried to move my arms again. Another slap. I realized my wrists and ankles were taped to a chair and I'd been blindfolded.

"What do you want?"

Another slap. "I told you. I ask the questions."

"Okay. What questions?"

Another slap.

I could hear the faint sounds of music, laughter, and conversation. A party seemed to be going on not far away.

"Where's my dog?"

Another slap. "You wanna do this all day?"

My cheeks were burning. "No. But I want you to tell me where my dog is."

I prepared myself for another slap—I'd had practice doing this when I was a kid, after all—but the voice said, "He's here, in the other room." There was the sound of a match being struck, then an intake of breath, followed by a puff of cigarette smoke directed at my face. "So, are you ready to answer some questions now?"

"Sure."

"Good. Where's Ed Coster, Jr.?"

"What?" That's *what this was all about?*

Slap. "Answer the question."

"I don't know where he is."

Slap.

I said, "Hey! That wasn't a question."

"Yeah, well it wasn't an answer either."

Another voice, from behind me, said, "Use the stun gun." It sounded familiar. It was a dry, laconic voice. I realized I'd heard it on tape: I was pretty sure it was Harlan Rowan.

"Okay," said the slapper. I heard him move away from me, soft footsteps on carpet. A door opened. The sounds of the music and laughter grew in volume. The door closed and they got soft again. A little time passed.

Rowan said, "Having fun, Mr. Field?"

"Sure," I said. "Where's the piñata?"

"What?"

"You know, I'm blindfolded. I'm guessing that at some point you're going to free my hands, give me a stick, and point me toward a piñata. This *is* a party, right?"

A long pause. "You won't be laughing for very long."

I heard the door open again. That was my cue to scream, to let everyone out there laughing and dancing know that something terribly wrong was happening in another part of the building. I stopped when I heard the sound of a dog panting. A big dog.

"Hooch?"

He whined.

The slapper said to someone, "Help me out here. He's going to pull me off my feet."

A woman's voice said, "Don't do this. He'll tell you what you want to know. Don't hurt his dog."

Hurt Hooch? Hot adrenaline rushed through my face and arms. I struggled at the tape around my wrists. I couldn't get free.

Rowan said, "Just hold the damn leash for him."

"No," the woman said. "Don't do this."

The slapper was struggling to keep Hooch away from me. I could hear him grunting, swearing. I could hear Hooch's paws tearing at the carpet, trying to get to me.

Then the man grunted, as if letting go of or dropping something heavy. A second later Hooch jumped on me, licking my face and knocking me over onto the carpet. It really *was* soft.

"Jesus Christ," shouted Rowan. "Get Toland and Samuels in here. Now!"

Quick, soft footsteps. The door opened again. Hooch licked my face. There were more footsteps. They came toward me. Hooch got pulled away from me. I got pulled upright again.

"Don't hurt him," I said. "He's just a dog."

"We've got him," said another man. He wasn't saying it to me but to Rowan.

Rowan said, "Thank god. Now get on with it."

I heard a click, followed by the spark of an electric charge.

"You ever used one of these before?" he asked.

"Yeah. I was a cop once."

"Good. Here's how this works. You're gonna tell us where we can find Ed Coster, Jr. Do you understand?"

"I don't know where he is."

He placed the stun gun against my neck. "Where is he?"

"I don't know."

Zap!

"Stop!" the woman screamed. It was quick, short, piercing.

I don't know how long *I* screamed. My breathing was heavy, I was sweating, my head was rolling around in its sockets. I smelled burnt flesh. Finally I mumbled, "God, that hurts."

He put it up against my neck again. "Where is he?"

"I don't know."

Zap!

This time I not only screamed—or groaned, they really don't have words for it—I rocked, using my center of gravity to knock myself to the floor. I figured that now he'd have to spend some time getting me and the chair upright before administering the next jolt. It would give me some time to get ready for it.

I heard quick footsteps going away from me, then up some steps. Another door, higher up, opened and closed. I was sweating, panting.

The dry voice said, "Where's she going? Go after her."

One of the other men said, "We can't. Not unless you want us to let go of the damn dog."

"No. Hold him," Rowan said. "I'm tired of this." He came across the room and moved in close to me. He smelled of cigars and old whisky. He said, "Where's Ed Coster, Jr.?"

"I already told you, I don't know."

I felt the stun gun against my neck again and prepared for the jolt, but it got pulled away.

"This time," Rowan said, "use it on the dog."

I struggled to get free, twisted my legs around as hard as I could to loosen the tape around my ankles, pulled as hard as I could with my wrists. I couldn't get loose.

The slapper said to Rowan, "My pleasure."

"Good. Mr. Field will be glad to tell us now."

"Okay." I told them about the cabin in the woods.

"Where is it?" asked Rowan.

"I don't know. Somewhere near Wiscasset."

Rowan said, "Shock the dog."

"Wait, wait," I said, trying to keep my breathing measured and even. "I really don't know where it is but I can find out for you. I can call Flynn. He'll give me the exact location."

I heard Rowan rustling in his pocket.

"What's the number?"

I gave it to him and heard him dial it. He put the phone up to my ear.

"Sheriff," I said, "I'm being held captive by Harlan Rowan, and two guys named Toland and Samuels."

The phone was taken away, the metal got pressed against my neck again.

Zap!

I screamed, lost my mind, my ability to think, for a moment.

"Are you okay?" asked Flynn. "Jack? Are you there?"

"Get cute again," Rowan whispered in my ear, "we shock your dog. For real this time." His voice was toneless, deadly.

"Yeah, okay," I said, still trying to breathe. The phone came up to my ear again. I said to Flynn, "Some people want to know where you're keeping Junior. They've got me and Hooch. They're using a stun gun on me. That's why I screamed."

"Oh, Christ. I'm sorry. Do you know where you are?"

"No. They tranked me in Augusta. I woke up blindfolded."

"They tranked you?"

"Yeah. They shot me and Hooch with a tranquilizer gun."

"What are you, zoo animals? Okay, let me talk to them."

I said to Rowan, "He wants to talk to you."

The phone came away from my ear.

Before Rowan could say anything to Flynn, someone else came into the room. There was muffled conversation, though I heard the words "state police" somewhere in the middle of it.

"Christ," muttered Rowan. "That's all we need. What the hell do they want?"

"They said they got a report that this guy Field is here. They want to search the lodge."

"How the hell did they find out about this? Okay, I'll stall them for a few minutes. Meanwhile, Grunwald, you find that crazy old broad and get her under control. Toland and Samuels, you guys take Field and the dog up the back way to the storage room. Use the tranquilizer on them again to keep them quiet if you have to."

"It might kill the dog," said the slapper, a.k.a. Grunwald.

"You have a problem with that?"

"Me? No, I don't care one way or the other."

"Okay," said Rowan. "Then do it."

I felt a pricking sensation in my neck.

Hooch! I thought, don't die, Hooch! You're a strong doggie! Then I felt my mouth go dry and I fell asleep again.

30

Two things happened at once. I smelled perfume and felt someone pulling the tape away from my ankles. The smoke and heat of the fireplace were gone. I was still in the chair, but I was now in a room with a window cracked open; I could feel the cold night air caressing my face. I could also smell the distant pines, mixed with the closer scent of jasmine and chypre.

I said, "Where's Hooch?"

She said, "He's all right. Aren't you, boy?"

I heard a tail thumping on the floor.

"Ah, good boy," I said. He didn't come bounding toward me. I wondered why not. "Is he tied up?"

"Yes."

"Where are we?"

"It's a hunting lodge. Supposedly."

"The Moose and Eagle."

"Yes, though there's not much to hunt around here. I guess you know, the state police came looking for you."

"For me, specifically?"

"Yes. They searched the lodge, but not here; this is a storage room. Harlan sent them away. But they'll be back."

"That's good to know. Who are you?"

She took my blindfold off and I saw that I was in a room with knotty pine paneling and a lot of shelves with towels and the like. Hooch was by the door, staring at me, head down.

"Good boy," I said, and he slowly wagged his tail.

My liberator was an old woman, though she was costumed in the colorful garb of a young Mexican girl and wore a Frida Kahlo mask, I assumed for the party downstairs.

"Just call me a friend of a friend," she said.

"Why did you come back from Mexico?"

"What? You think because of my costume that I—"

"No, it's not the costume. You *are* Margaret Greaves, though, right? Or do you go by Margarita Ortíz now?"

"No," she sighed, "I'm using the name Margaret Greaves."

"You were involved in Katherine MacLeary's murder, weren't you? That's why you ran off to Mexico."

"No, I wasn't involved. Well, not exactly," she said, pulling the tape away. "Actually, I was the intended target."

Before I could respond, we heard gunshots. She went to the window and looked out.

"That old fool," she said.

"What's going on out there?"

She came away, went out the door, leaving it open slightly. The sounds of laughter and music continued unabated from downstairs. Maybe they hadn't heard the gunfire, maybe they thought it was fireworks or something.

Margaret came back, hurried over to me and put a key in my right hand. "That opens a case in the gun room downstairs, in case you need one. Those two men, Toland and Samuels, they left the tranquilizer gun and that horrible stun gun next door."

"Where's the third man, Grunwald?"

"He's dead. Harlan has more to take his place."

"Who killed him?"

"It doesn't matter. He would've killed me and your dog. And there are five more outside, on the grounds, guarding one of the cabins."

"Guarding it why?"

"Never mind. Right outside the door is a balcony that surrounds the main hall. There are two staircases on either side of the building, but to your far left is a third that goes directly outside. The door to it is hidden behind a framed map of the county. You and your dog can escape that way."

"Why are you helping me?"

"Because if you don't get out of here they'll kill you."

She bent down, finished with my ankles then loosened the tape on my wrists a little.

"What's going on outside?"

"It doesn't matter. I can't do anything to stop it. I thought I could, but I can't. I can't change anything. And it's all my fault anyway. Everything's my fault."

"No, it isn't. Wait!"

She went out the door to the balcony. As she did, the light from outside the door caught an angle on what looked to be a knife tucked into her belt. It appeared to have blood on it.

I looked at Hooch. He was panting, probably thirsty, but he was all right. I pulled hard with my right wrist and the tape came away easily, but my upper arms were still bound at my sides. I was logy, disoriented from the tranquilizer, but kept loosening the tape, or trying to, and had been at it for what felt like half an hour when I heard voices coming from just outside the door.

I stopped and listened. The voices got closer. I had a decision to make: Do I give one last, furious stab at trying to get loose, or do I pull a Jervis, pretend to be passed out?

Then I noticed that one of the voices belonged to Jamie. I heard her say, "I think he's in here."

The door opened and Jamie came in, followed by Kelso. She was still in her Geena Davis costume, Kelso was wearing a tux. Jamie had what looked like a cell phone in one hand.

"Jack!" she shouted as she rushed to my side.

"Hi, honey," I said. "I was wondering when you'd finally show up and rescue me."

"What?" she said, tucking the cell phone or whatever it was into her cleavage. She started pulling the tape off. "You were expecting us?"

"No, that was just an attempt to lighten the mood a little. Besides, I'm the one who's always rescuing you, remember? It's nice to see you taking your turn for once."

Kelso said, "Funny," and untied Hooch.

Free at last, he raced toward me, then tried to jump all over me, knocking over a plastic bucket and impeding Jamie's progress with the tape.

Kelso came over and pulled him off, then told him to sit.

I said to Kelso, "I think he's pretty thirsty. See if you can find him some water."

There was a sink near the door. Kelso went over to it and started the water running, "Hooch!" he said, and the dog ran over to him, jumped up and began slurping at the stream.

"So," I said to Jamie, who was still working on the tape, "how the hell did you find me?"

"The Nicotrol patch, remember?" She pointed to the device tucked into her costume. "This little baby is a locator."

"Oh, yeah. Dr. Lunch's transponders. I almost took mine off when I showered today."

"I'm glad you changed your mind. When you didn't come back to Abby's office, I called Kelso. Lunch used GPS to track you from Augusta to Skowhegan. Kelso drove to Augusta and picked me up. While we were on the way up here, Uncle Horace called and told us what was going on, and about the stun gun." She examined the burns on my neck. "God, that must've been horrible."

"It was no picnic, but the thought of them doing it to Hooch was a lot worse."

"They threatened to shock Hooch?"

"Yeah. I wouldn't have caved and called Flynn otherwise."

"How awful. Anyway, Flynn and I both sent a report to the state police. They kept asking me how I knew you were here, but Lunch said not to tell anyone about the transponders. Still, I insisted they send someone to look for you, and some troopers who were nearby came and searched the lodge but couldn't find you."

"Yeah, I was in here by the time they did their search. Did you see an older woman as you were coming in?"

"No. We came in the back way. We didn't really see anyone but a few waiters. They thought we were here for the party."

I explained about the mystery woman, who was probably Eddie Cole's mother, and how she'd come to my rescue and Hooch's, then asked, "Did you hear any gunfire just now?"

"No," said Kelso.

Jamie said, "If Farrell has a gun, that might explain the—".

"Wait, Farrell's here?"

Jamie nodded. "He was in Vassalboro when he found out what was going on up here. That gave him a good head start on us."

"But how did he find out?"

Kelso said, "He called the kennel. When I told him where you were and why, he said he was going to drive straight up."

I felt a sudden twinge of guilt about what I'd said to him earlier. "Jeez, I hope he's okay."

Jamie finally got the tape unwound. I stood up and stretched my muscles and got the kinks out, then went to the sink and had a long drink of water myself. When I was done, I went through the adjoining door to a small bedroom absent decoration, probably for someone on the housekeeping staff. Jamie, Hooch, and Kelso followed me. I looked around the room.

"What are you looking for?" Jamie asked.

I said, "The old woman said the two goons who brought me here had left the . . . oh, there they are." The tranquilizer gun and the stun gun were on the bed. I went over and picked them up. I said to Kelso, "Did you bring any weapons with you?"

"Just my rapier wit."

"In that case, we're dead."

"Hah, hah."

"Here, you take the dart gun."

We made our way carefully onto the balcony, even though there was no real need for stealth; we were all in costume (except Hooch), so we fit in with the rest of the crowd downstairs.

We looked down at the main hall, constructed of semiskinned lodgepole pines and cut granite, now decorated with cobwebs, dry corn stalks, scarecrows, and jack-o'-lanterns.

We saw twenty or thirty partygoers, in various costumes—zombies, witches, ghouls, a black cat, a pirate, two angels, one devil, Marie Antoinette, a tin man, two guys dressed as Batman—one fat, one skinny—and the like. Some were bunched together, holding drinks, emitting the kind of dark laughter loosened by gin and whisky. Others held on to each other, dancing.

They were all rich. I'd been at parties like this before, at the Yale Club, working a case at a charity event at the Met. Some of the people at those galas looked more ghoulish with*out* Halloween makeup than the ones at this party did *with*.

An old guy in a tux manned a piano in the far corner; his hands seemed more alive than the rest of him. He had help from a youngish bass player who seemed to be in love with his instrument; he curled around it, smiling. No one looked up at us or aimed any weapons in our direction.

Jamie said, "Why are you looking around? Let's get out of here and let the state police handle it."

Before I could agree, out of the corner of my eye I saw something that didn't fit: a man in a business suit. It was my friend from the alley. He stared up at us.

"Uh-oh," I said. "The jig is up."

He moved quickly through the crowd—not running but not strolling leisurely—straight toward the right-hand stairway.

"This way," I said, running left, toward where the mystery woman had said there was a hidden exit.

We passed the stairway and turned a corner.

Jamie said, "Where are we going?"

I explained as we reached a dead end and came to a large, framed map of Somerset County. I pushed against it; nothing happened. I frisked the frame for a hidden button. Nothing.

Jamie pointed at Little Moose Lake. "Does that look like it's raised a little from the rest of the map?"

We heard a lot of footsteps coming toward us.

I pressed the drawing of the lake. The door opened. We quickly went through it and I closed it behind us. A dim, bare bulb illuminated an old dusty stairwell.

As Jamie and Kelso tiptoed down the first step, I heard a voice in the hallway say, "Where'd they go?"

It really *was* a secret entrance.

"They just disappeared," another voice said.

"They can't have."

I stood at the top, listening. I looked down at Hooch—such a good boy to stick by my side. No bounding around, no barking. Then I remembered he'd been tranked twice too.

"Call Harlan," the first voice ordered. "And search the entire second floor." The footsteps moved away from the door.

When Hooch and I got to the bottom of the stairs, we found Jamie and Kelso in a long, narrow hall that ended in a blank wall. It was dark; the only light came from upstairs. The walls were smooth Sheetrock with one-by-four pine spacers.

"There's no way out," Jamie whispered.

"Of course there is," I said quietly. "There has to be. Sshh. I think I hear something."

We listened. A man's voice—it sounded like Harlan Rowan—was yelling at someone to search the rooms upstairs again, and to damn well put a man at the bottom of each stairway. "And don't come back here bothering me until you've found them!"

"How many of these guys *are* there?" whispered Kelso.

"I only know of three inside, and one of them is supposedly dead. I was told there are five outside, guarding a cabin."

"It sounds like they've got a few more than that."

"Never mind. We've got to get out of here." I started feeling the wall closest to me. "Everyone see if you can find a button or something that might open a hidden door."

After a few moments Jamie said, "I think I found it."

One of the spacers had a raised knot. I pushed it, a click sounded, and a wall panel about four feet wide moved away from us on rollers, then slid sideways into the rest of the wall.

We walked into a wider, pine-paneled hallway with green carpet, low cabinets with stuffed pheasants and quail on top, and hunting prints on the walls. I found another raised knot in the paneling, pressed it, and the door slid back into place.

A wooden door with paned glass was to our right. It led outside. Through the glass we could see the black outlines of pine trees and log cabins, and behind them a moonless sky.

Faintly now I heard a voice from behind us say, "This is Rowan. Get the sheriff on the line, we've got a situation at the lodge." There was a pause. "I don't care where he is, we've got people running around here shooting at us."

I followed the sound of the voice to a bark-covered door, though Jamie was tugging on my cape to go the other way.

The door was open slightly. I motioned to Kelso to come next to me, then gave Hooch a look and a hand signal.

He went into a down.

I pointed to Kelso's dart gun, then to my neck, indicating I wanted him to shoot Rowan in the neck with a dart. He nodded.

I quietly opened the door. It was a big room, with several oak gun cases with glass doors sitting against the pine-paneled walls. They were filled with hunting rifles and shotguns. A fire was dwindling in a granite fireplace, which made me think that this might be the room where I'd been tortured earlier.

A smallish fat man, who reminded me of Junior, sat in a big leather chair with his left profile to us, holding a phone to his ear. He was wearing a Superman costume and a pair of glasses. The parts of his face we could see were heavily pocked with warts; they made him look more like the Thing than Superman.

Kelso stepped slowly and quietly into the room beside me. He aimed at Rowan and fired a bull's-eye.

Rowan's left hand came up to his neck. He dropped the phone, spun around and saw us.

I sprinted toward him on the left, Hooch on my heels.

Kelso ran toward him, arcing behind a sofa to the right.

Rowan's right hand came up with a pistol. He shot at me, but his aim was shaky. Before he could get off his second round, I put the stun gun to his left temple and zapped him. It wasn't as much fun as I'd hoped; he was halfway unconscious already.

I grabbed the phone and covered the mouthpiece. I said to him, "How many men do you have here tonight, and what are they?"

He muttered quietly, almost inaudibly, "You're a dead man, Field," then his chin went to his chest and he slumped over.

"Great." I uncovered the mouthpiece on the phone and said, "Who is this?"

"This is the Somerset County Sheriff's Office."

"Okay. And what are you calling about?"

"Uh, we didn't call you, sir. You called us."

"No, I certainly did not. Look, you can't be bothering the mental patients like this."

"Mental patients?"

"Yes, we have a group of mental patients staying here. Oh, don't worry, they're mostly harmless."

"And who are you?"

"The name's LaFong. Dr. Carl LaFong." I spelled it for him, then repeated the name.

"Well, sorry to bother you Dr. LaFong."

I hung up and turned to see Kelso shaking his head.

"Who was that?" he asked, and I told him.

Jamie said, "Well, your little game was very funny, but we could actually *use* some law enforcement here."

"I know that. But it has to be somebody we can trust. For all we know, they're working for Coster and company."

"I suppose," she said doubtfully.

I said, "You two look for something to tie up this little rat bastard. I'm going to get us some guns."

Before we could do anything, we heard more gunfire. It was coming from outside.

"Honey," I said, "you stay here. Call Flynn and the FBI and the state police and anyone else you can think of, and let them know what's going on. You're the chief ME, and you just saw this little prick try to shoot your husband."

"Never mind the burn marks on your neck."

"Yeah, but you didn't actually see that happen. But you did see him shoot at me and you know there's gunfire. That ought to be enough to bring some lights and sirens here and put an end to this crap. Meanwhile, Kelso and I will grab some guns, and go outside, to try and find Farrell and help him out."

"Thanks for volunteering me," he said.

"No sweat."

A man's voice, coming from behind us, said, "Perhaps I could be of some assistance." His tone was calm, mannerly, British.

We turned to see Jervis at the back of the room.

31

"May I approach, sir?" he said to me, with a pointed look at Kelso's dart gun, which was aimed directly at him.

"Put it down," I told Kelso. Then to Jervis, "What are you doing here?"

He strode forward. "I'm here with the general, of course."

"Of course. And what's he doing here?"

"Ah, yes, well, there's a perfectly logical explanation for that, sir."

"No, there isn't," Jamie said. "There can't be."

"Perhaps you're right, mum. It isn't perfect, and it's not very logical. At least not to anyone but General MacLeary."

He explained that the general had had a female visitor at the hospital at a time when Jervis wasn't in attendance. "He's convinced that it was Mrs. MacLeary, and that she's now here, at the lodge. He's also convinced that his daughter Connie is being held here as well. He's come to rescue them, to take both of them home."

Kelso said, "Meaning he's gone completely nuts."

"Not completely," I said. "Connie probably *is* here. He must have dreamed up this stuff about his wife visiting him."

"It's the damn Chinese herb," Jamie said to me.

"Be that as it may," said Jervis, "the general and your friend Farrell Woods—who's a fine shot, by the way, and a good soldier—are pinned behind a low hill, taking fire from a nearby cabin. Woods only has a .22 rifle and is running low on ammo.

I'm afraid we're sadly in need of more munitions. The general sent me here to procure them."

He moved quickly toward one of the gun cabinets. We all followed. "We saw your wife and friend arrive," Jervis said, "so the general knows they're here. If you're interested in helping out, he has a plan of attack."

"You've got to be kidding," said Jamie.

"Okay . . ." I said cautiously; I wasn't sure if I wanted to be taking orders from a loony-tune, but thought it was worth at least hearing the man out. "I know of three men who were working for this sack of nothing in the chair over there. There was another guy, Henry Chu. He came after me earlier, in Augusta. But I shot him a couple times. I don't know if he's with the others."

"Hmm." Jervis stopped, thought it over. "This Chu is a bit of a bother. The general will know how to handle him, though."

"Listen," Jamie said, "that man is not in any condition to be running around orchestrating a gun battle."

Jervis disagreed. "His body may be on the wane but his mind is still a marvelous instrument."

One that's going off the rails, I thought, but said nothing.

"Still," Jamie insisted, "we should wait for the state police, and not go shooting around in the dark."

Jervis pulled out a walkie-talkie and spoke into it. "Sir, it's Jervis."

"I know who it is, goddamnit! Where are those weapons?"

"I'll be out with them shortly. The thing is, sir, Mr. Field, his wife, and friend are here. They tell me there may be three, possibly four more enemy combatants inside the lodge, not just the five guarding the cabin."

"Of course," said MacLeary through the static. "*That's* what they're waiting for. The others will probably circle around from the lodge and come at our right flank. We'll have to reposition ourselves." He seemed to be saying that last bit to Farrell. Then to me he said, "Field, is your platoon armed and ready?"

"I don't have a platoon, but I guess so."

"You guess so? You *guess* so?"

"We were about to go outside with a couple of rifles to help you out, but we got interrupted."

"Good," he said. "That is, it's good you were thinking of helping us out, but not such a good tactic. I'll need one of you to help Jervis run a diversionary out here to block these others from reaching our fallback. Your friend has a sprained ankle and can't move very far or very fast."

"Sorry to hear that. Tell him to hang in. There's only one other gunman that I know of." I explained about Henry Chu.

"He may be with them, he may not even be here. We'll have to leave it at that for now. Have you called for reinforcements?"

"We were just about to do that when Jervis showed up."

"It's probably too late anyway. By the time they arrive we'll have already secured the cabin; either that or we'll all be dead. Who's in command of the opposing forces?"

"Harlan Rowan, I think. But we took him out."

"You killed him?"

"No." I explained about the tranquilizer dart.

"That's good, that's fine. But I'll need you to bring him around. Once we take out some of his men, we'll use Rowan to negotiate a truce. Do you know the dosage of the darts?"

"No. They used it on me, twice. It's pretty strong."

"Well, you may need to give him an electric shock to bring him out of it. Can you strip some wires from a table lamp?"

"Actually," I said, "we have a stun gun."

"Good man! When I give the signal, give him the juice."

"Sir. Are you sure you can handle these guys? I mean, you don't even know where they are."

"Yes, but I know the terrain. Just wait for my signal."

There was radio silence.

I turned to Jervis and said, "Okay, I know he sounds lucid now, but how long do you think he can sustain this?"

"Oh, in greener times he could go three or four days without any sleep and his mind would never falter."

"Yeah, yeah. He was a young Napoleon, a human dynamo back then. I'm talking about now, tonight. He's been in a coma of one kind or another for almost a week. How long can he—"

"I don't know. When will the reinforcements arrive?"

I looked at Jamie. She said, "In about twenty minutes."

Jervis nodded. "Let's pray they get here a tad sooner."

I said, "Okay, get your weapons." While he raided one of the gun cabinets, I said to Jamie and Kelso, "You two stay here with Rowan and Hooch. Jervis and I will—"

"Honey, you're in no condition to fight a gun battle."

"Of course I am." I lied. "Besides, I was a cop for fifteen years. This is my area. It's not Kelso's and it's clearly not yours."

"No, Jack, I insist you let Jervis do this alone."

"I know how to handle a rifle," said Kelso. "I grew up in Colorado, remember? I'll go with Jervis. You stay here."

"That's not going to happen."

Jervis gave me a .30–06 and some ammo. I pulled back the bolt and tried loading the bullets in the chamber, but my hand kept shaking; my fingers were fat, uncooperative sausages. I started to sweat.

"Jack!" Jamie said. "Sit down, now!"

I collapsed in a big leather chair. It felt like it was made of cotton balls. My hands, my arms, were trembling.

"I don't get it. I'm not afraid to go out there."

"Of course you're not afraid. But you've been tranquilized twice, you've been shocked I don't know how many times. Your mind is working just fine—well, not totally fine, but mostly. But your body just isn't up to this."

"Just like General MacLeary."

Kelso took the rifle and ammo from me. He said, "I should have known you were out of it when you started talking about *Napoleon Dynamite*. It was a pretty good movie, but still . . ."

"Cute," I said.

After he and Jervis left, my energy sagged, so to keep things moving I loaded up a couple of shotguns. My hands still trembled but the shells were bigger, easier to handle. While I did that, Jamie made some phone calls. When she was done, we had nothing to do but await further orders from the general on the walkie-talkie. Jamie paced. I sat on the edge of Rowan's chair, doing some deep breathing and conserving my energy.

She said, "Do you think he's really capable of this?"

"You heard Jervis. His mind is a marvelous instrument. Or will be for the next fifteen or twenty minutes."

"Put that in the past tense and I'd agree with you."

"If he doesn't know what the hell he's doing, he sure has me fooled. Was he right about how to wake up sleeping beauty, by using an electric charge?"

She gave me a grudging nod. "All right, maybe he does know a thing or two. *Maybe*. I just hope we both live long enough to find out if that's true."

We *did* live long enough to find out. General MacLeary won his last battle, though it was just a minor skirmish, really.

While Jamie and I waited with Hooch and the unconscious political power broker, the general and Woods repositioned themselves near the lake, surrounded on three sides by water. Jervis supplied them with weapons, then disappeared again to hook up with Kelso. Because Farrell was injured, the general refused to leave his side.

Then Jervis and Kelso, under MacLeary's direction, dogged the third gunman, though they couldn't actually see him. They only had MacLeary's words to guide them past this knoll, behind that cabin, across a certain creek. They fired wildly at various locales at various times, or not so wildly, since their shots were orchestrated by MacLeary from the safety of his "Omaha Beach." How he knew where the man was, no one can say. He and Farrell also got enough shots off to make the man feel surrounded.

The poor fool, not knowing how anyone could see him in the dark, surrendered—threw down his weapon, fell to his knees and gave up. Kelso and Jervis had to ask him to keep talking to them, as if playing Marco Polo, so they could find the bastard in the dark. When they got to him, they found out he wasn't Henry Chu.

That's when Jamie and I got the call.

I used the stun gun on Rowan till he jolted upright, screaming. I thought of using it once more for fun, but remembered the bad dreams I'd had when I'd exacted revenge on my father so I turned it off and tucked it into my belt.

The general told me to take Rowan out to the main room, and give an order to whatever gunmen were left inside the building to surrender immediately and throw down their weapons.

"Are you sure? Can't we wait for the state police?"

"That's a direct order, soldier."

"General," I pointed out, "I'm not a soldier and you're not a general anymore."

"Of course not. I was being metaphorical. But the fact is, your friend and I are still vulnerable out here, and *will* be until everyone from the other side is completely disarmed."

"Okay," I said. "I hope you know what you're doing."

"Honey," Jamie said after the communicator went silent. "Are you sure we ought to do this?"

"I think he's right. If we don't round up these goons and disarm them, something bad's liable to happen."

"Something bad has already happened. Besides, you're in no condition to go out there."

"I'll be fine. I've handled hostage situations before."

"You won't be fine. You could pass out at any minute."

She was right, but I gave her a determined face. "That's not going to happen, trust me. Besides, we've got to do this to keep Farrell safe."

"If you say so," she said, shaking her head.

We got Superman on his feet, I told Hooch to stay, then we paraded our captive out to the main hall, carefully keeping our backs to the wall so none of the goons could fire at us from upstairs. The partygoers paid very little attention at first. Jamie's quite tall, as you know, so she had no trouble holding Rowan up on his feet. It must've looked like he'd had too much to drink and she was just keeping him vertical, never mind that his hands were tied behind him. Still, the aftereffects of the tranquilizer and the stun gun certainly made him *seem* drunk.

I shouted to the men upstairs, "We've got your boss!" This got no response. I wasn't sure if they heard me over the music and conversation, so I fired a shotgun blast at the balcony, in the main direction of the service closet.

Splinters and sawdust rained down on the floor beneath the beam. The hall filled with frantic shrieks and cries.

The similarity between what *I* was doing and a bank robbery wasn't lost on me; I'd been acting too much like a crook during this whole case, but, hell, I thought, why stop now?

"Everybody down!" I yelled, and they all got down on their hands and knees. Then to the goons upstairs, I shouted, "Throw down your weapons, now! We've got your boss! The state police and the FBI are on their way. You can't escape."

Nothing happened upstairs; nothing that I could see, though I thought I heard the sounds of surreptitious movements.

I looked at Rowan. "Say something to your guys. Tell them to listen to me so they don't get hurt. And so *you* don't."

His head was bobbing, his eyes unfocused. "Bamma, gamma," he said, or something like it.

I looked around the room again. We had thirty or so people lying facedown on the parquet, some of whom could have been armed. There were doors all over the place, including upstairs. Plus the two stairways gave our opponents plenty of opportunity to come at us from both sides, or to just hightail it and run home. We were not in the best position to be calling the shots.

"What kind of party are you throwing here, anyway?" I asked Rowan.

"Political . . . fund . . . raiser," he said, swaying and weaving.

He needed a heavy dose of adrenaline if he was going to be of any use. So, even though I'd turned the stun gun off, I pulled it from my belt, put it against his neck, and said, "Okay, tell your men to throw down their weapons."

"Throw down your weapons!" he gasped, suddenly terrified of being shocked again. I didn't blame him.

"That was good," I told him. "Now say it louder."

"Throw—down—your—weapons!" He took a quick, shallow breath between each word, then his body started to sag on Jamie. He'd hyperventilated. Either that or he was faking.

Three men appeared on the balcony. They came out of various rooms, holding their pistols high in the air.

"Eject your clips," I told them, holding the shotgun against Rowan's rib cage. "The same goes for the shells in the chambers. Then throw everything down here."

They did as they were told.

"Ow," said fat Batman. One of the guns landed on his neck.

I said, "Now come down the stairs and join us. Slowly."

They began walking toward the left stairway with their hands above their heads. As they did, I started to feel myself losing energy; my head bobbed, my eyes closed briefly.

"Ow!" I said to Jamie, opening my eyes again. She'd just pinched me.

"Sorry," she said under her breath. "I had to wake you up. We're not going to survive this if you don't get it together."

"Okay, sorry." I shook my head briskly, the way a dog does, to get the blood going.

I looked up at the balcony again. As I did, my pal from the alley moved behind another man. Then he reappeared, but with a gun in his hand. He'd probably pulled it from a holster under his suit. He sprang forward on one knee, using the balcony rail for cover. He fired at me and missed, just barely.

My reflexes were dull, sluggish. Still, I arced the shotgun slowly, lazily, in his direction. "Drop it," I croaked, my head sagging again, "or I'll drop you!"

He smiled, stood up, holding the gun away from his body for a moment, then he quickly aimed it at me again.

My fingers felt slippery. Before I could find the trigger, let alone squeeze it, a shot rang out from another direction.

I swung the shotgun toward the sound and saw Jervis up there with a deer rifle, its barrel smoking.

The shooter had a red hole in the middle of his forehead. He dropped his gun, stumbled forward, and then his body slumped awkwardly across the balcony rail.

His buddies started forward, to help him.

I heard Kelso say from upstairs, "Leave him there."

It didn't matter. The shooter's forward momentum carried him over the rail and he sailed, end over end, down to the first floor. He missed hitting Marie Antoinette by two inches, if that.

I stumbled forward, looked up behind me, and saw that Kelso was on the other side of the balcony from Jervis.

Then Kelso and Jervis waved their weapons at the two remaining goons and got them moving again toward the stairways.

Jervis and Kelso got them downstairs. Kelso tied their hands, using their belts, while Jervis collected the hardware they'd dropped from the balcony. When he was done, he told the party guests they could get up off the floor. Most of them immediately got out their cell phones and began making frantic calls to the police or to their attorneys.

I called Hooch, who came running. Then, with Kelso's help, Jamie and I took the gunmen outside, where I saw several black limousines and a jitney parked in front of the lodge.

I said to Jervis, "What's the jitney for?"

"Oh, there's an airstrip for private jets located a few miles away, sir, on the property. The jitney's for guests who don't care to drive up here. Are you feeling all right?"

I took a deep breath of cold night air. "Yeah," I lied.

I was fading in and out of focus, but I vaguely remember that we took Rowan and his hired guns to the cabin where Connie was being held, with Jamie and Kelso holding Rowan up. Someone, I think it was Jervis, called out to the gunmen, and they threw out their weapons and brought Connie out. Jervis and Kelso tied their hands behind them and then we waited for the cops to arrive.

While we waited, some of the guests came outside to see what was going on, or to tell us we were in a heap of trouble for all the shooting, or to get a breath of fresh, cold night air. Most stayed inside the lodge where it was warm.

I parked one hip on the fender of one of the limos and took some long, deep breaths to get my second wind, which came to me slowly. Then MacLeary appeared from out of the dark pines that lay between us and the lake. He was in a battle uniform and had an arm around Farrell, who was limping beside him.

Jamie immediately went over to see how they were.

The "skirmish in the pines," as it was later called, was hailed by some as a testament to General MacLeary's greatness.

I felt that way myself during the initial flush of victory. I even went over and congratulated him: "That was some piece of strategy, sir. How did you know where the other gunmen would be?"

He pointed to a wide porch at the front of the lodge. "I spent many an afternoon there with nothing to do but imagine what kind of battles might take place here."

As I thought about it later, it didn't amount to much; just two old codgers, an aging Vietnam vet, a forensic pathologist, a former prosecutor for the Manhattan DA's office, a dog trainer and his dog, who got lucky against a squadron of paid goons.

I said to Farrell, "I'm sorry for what I said earlier—"

"Forget it. But I ain't working for you anymore, man."

I felt a shock of pain. "Why? Because of what I—"

"Nah, it ain't that. But bein' around you's dangerous." He laughed and clapped me on the back. "A guy could get killed."

"Sorry about that."

MacLeary, who expected a happy reunion with his daughter, was disappointed. He tried to hug Connie, soothe her, but she just stood there dazed, like he didn't exist, like he wasn't there.

She kept muttering under her breath, "I killed Mama. I remember now. I killed her. I shot her with Daddy's pistol."

We'd finally put an end to the mystery of who killed Katherine MacLeary. But it wasn't a very satisfying conclusion.

"Sweetheart," said MacLeary, "your mother isn't dead. She came to see me at the hospital. She's still alive."

"Liar!" she suddenly screamed at him. Jamie had to hold her back. "Liar! Liar! It's your fault I had to kill her!"

I had to step in to help James.

Jervis put a hand on the old man's shoulder.

Kelso said, "Some family reunion."

"That's the MacLearys for you," I said.

Connie collapsed in Jamie's arms, crying inconsolably, which was good, I thought. At least it was some kind of release.

Jervis gently led the general away. The old man looked around at the costumed people. "She told me to meet her at the masked ball. Here I am. This is it." He was thinking of that night long ago, in Paris. "So where has she gone?"

"That happened a long time ago, sir," said Jervis.

By this time the night air started to tingle with the far-off sound of approaching sirens, so when I caught a ruby red light dancing around the corner of my eye, I thought it was a reflection from an approaching emergency vehicle.

Hooch must've thought it was something to play with because he jumped up and tried to bite at my "Mithril" vest. When he did, the light danced across his back. That's when I realized the beam was coming from the laser sight on a sniper's rifle.

Farrell saw the look in my eye, looked at Hooch, cried "Sniper!" Then he grabbed Hooch and threw him to the ground. As he did, the bullet went through his right lung, exited his body, and grazed one of my left ribs, though I didn't know that at the time.

I stood there wobbling, holding him up as his body sagged. His eyes were fading out of focus.

"Oh, man," he said with a mixture of terror and sadness.

Another shot rang out. This one from close by. It was Jervis, firing into the dark.

We heard a distant crackle of twigs and leaves.

Jamie let go of Connie and helped me ease Farrell to the ground. My knees, my arms, were weak. I wanted to go after Chu—it had to be him—but I couldn't leave Farrell. Besides, I couldn't stand up.

Jamie knelt next to me in the cold dirt, then ripped open Farrell's clothes to look at the wound. His chest was pulsing with blood, making a gurgling sound as his lung began to collapse.

I looked around. Jervis and Kelso were going after Chu, both in a straight line toward where the sound of the shot had come.

MacLeary shouted, "No, no! You have to flank him from both sides. Don't come straight at the bastard!"

His mind was back, briefly; they followed his instructions.

I took off my Levi's jacket and gave it to Jamie. She used it to apply pressure to Farrell's chest.

He said, "This is a funny way for it to end, isn't it?"

"This isn't the end. You're going to be fine."

"I don't think so." He grimaced, tried to gulp some air. "Tell Tulips . . ."

"Tell her yourself. You hear that siren in the distance? That's an ambulance. You're going to make it."

"No, but listen, listen. Tell her she's worth it. Tell her not to give up on herself."

Tears blurred my vision. I said, "Don't you give up either, man. Hooch, stop it!" Hooch was licking his face.

"It's . . . okay . . . I like it . . . I just wish I could see . . . my dogs . . . my little beauties . . . one more time . . ."

"You will. Just hang in there."

He shook his head. "Help Tulips take care of the super group for me," he said, then closed his eyes and was gone.

32

Jervis and Kelso trapped Chu at the lake. Kelso tried to talk Chu into giving himself up, but before the bastard could decide one way or the other, Jervis shot him five times.

When they came back and gave us their report, I said to Jervis, "You couldn't just wound him?"

"Why?" He seemed surprised. "Did you want to kill him yourself?"

I looked down at Farrell's body. "I would have loved to, but we needed him alive so he could testify against Eddie Cole."

"Beg pardon, sir. But just shooting this man just seemed to make him angry. I felt it best to end the threat."

"Good man," said the general. "Good man." Then he said it to Kelso. Then he said it to me. (The pine trees were next.)

When the EMTs arrived to give Farrell some medical attention, Jamie just shook her head sadly, then brushed the tears from her cheeks. She called him dead at the scene.

Hooch barked at the EMTs while they put Farrell's body onto a gurney, and oddly enough, instead of grieving for Farrell or wishing Jamie was wrong, I suddenly realized why Hooch had been barking at the nurses on therapy days: Dr. Stanhope's vet techs had probably been mishandling him during his visits. This had touched a nerve that echoed back to when he was abused as a young pup.

Poor doggie, I thought as the cops arrived. Now I knew how to help him. Funny, huh? That was all I could think about.

* * *

You probably already know how things turned out for Ed Coster and family. It's been in the news. I got some satisfaction out of it for the first day or so, but then I got bored. Coster Sr. wasn't indicted on any charges. His supporters believe the statutory rape never took place, that members of the opposite party had fabricated the whole thing. But his plans for a nuclear power plant in Owl's Head were put on permanent hold.

Junior wasn't so lucky. A direct link was found between him, Harlan Rowan, and the bomb that had been planted in my kitchen by Henry Chu. Their trial should start next year.

All this came about because Eddie Cole's blackmail files were located, thanks to the info we got from Regis. However, the FBI went back on their agreement to give him witness protection because right after my meeting with him at the prison he made two calls, one to his attorney to set up the meeting with me, the other to Henry Chu to kill me. Corliss wasn't happy about witness protection so he'd made a deal with Chu to help him escape. He'd played both sides against the middle, as usual, and lost.

Regis had been right about the hideout that Cole and Chu often used. It was a farmhouse next to an old mill just north of Winslow's Mills. The police found enough weaponry and explosives there to start a small war.

Another item was found hidden there too, one that had the cops baffled. It was a set of plans for a dam on the Kennebec River, one that has since been rebuilt. The paper the plans were printed on was old and musty, as if they had been kept in Eddie Cole's hideout for, oh, say twenty years. The police found a duplicate set of plans when they searched the lodge. I hadn't spoken to or heard from Cord, but wondered if he knew about it.

Tom Harris called me the day before Farrell's funeral. He said, "Thanks, Jack. I guess I owe you another favor or two."

"I guess you do. Let's hope I never have to collect."

"Hah. Knowing you? I'll just keep myself ready."

That night in bed I said to Jamie, "Something's bothering me about that mystery woman."

"Margaret Ortíz? Like what?"

"Like how did she know about that secret exit when Harlan Rowan didn't? Doesn't that seem a little strange to you?"

"I guess. But she'd had an affair with Ed Coster. Maybe when he stayed at the lodge that's how he snuck her inside. Besides, what difference does it make?"

"I don't know. I just have a feeling that she was involved in Katherine MacLeary's murder somehow." I reminded her of the money that was wire-transferred from Katherine MacLeary's bank in the Caymans to Margaret's bank in Cabo, then asked, "Why would Katherine give this woman a quarter of a million dollars? Not to mention the fifty thousand she gave Eddie Cole?"

"Well, we know she wanted to blow the whistle on Ed Coster, Sr.'s secret. If Coster was paying Margaret Ortíz and Eddie Cole to keep quiet, maybe she was paying them *more* to talk."

"Maybe. But I also have a hard time figuring out why she happened to come back from Mexico at the exact same time that Katherine MacLeary's bones were dug up. That can't just be a coincidence. Plus, she probably killed this guy Grunwald."

"Grunwald? Which one was he?" She was thinking in terms of the autopsies; she'd done so many of them.

"The one that was stabbed to death."

"Oh, right." She fluffed her pillow, lay her head down, and threw her arm across my chest. "Well, I trust your instincts. Most of them. So if you're right, you'll find the connection eventually. You just have to trust the wave, right?"

"What wave? I'm feel like I'm paddling around in the—"

"You'll figure it out. Now go to sleep, I'm exhausted."

"Okay, good night." I didn't go to sleep, though. I just lay there, going over it in my mind, and I kept coming up empty. It really *was* like a wave—the kind you can never quite catch.

33

The general attended the service, which was fitting, though he didn't give a eulogy. Jervis wheeled him into the church. The old man didn't seem to know where he was, or why he was there, or why he was anywhere. His face was blank, unfocused, staring: aftereffects of the Chinese herb, I think. Jervis stood at attention behind him during the entire hour.

The crowd was an odd mix, mostly war veterans and stoners, though some were probably a combination of the two. The rest were friends and family, except for six Vietnam vets from Farrell's K–9 outfit, all in dress uniform. Only one of them was from Maine, the others were from Michigan, Alabama, Oregon, all over the country. They didn't have to fly to this man's funeral, a man they hadn't seen in forty years, but they did. They remembered what he'd done in battle, for them and their dogs.

I sat between Tulips and Jamie, toward the front. Tulips kept her head bowed; she couldn't stop crying. Jamie sniffled in fits and starts and held my hand in between.

It felt good to be there for her, to feel her holding onto me. I'd spent most of my life trying to put off being a grown-up. This case had put an end to all that. I was her husband now. I was there for her to hold onto even though she'd been furious at me a few days before and probably would be again.

Me? I didn't cry. Farrell wouldn't have wanted me to. There was more to it than that, of course; tears would have brought a release, a saltwater absolution for my guilt, and I wanted to hang onto that. It would be my memorial to this guy I only sort of knew but whom I came to truly admire in the end.

At one point Farrell's friend Dennis McGregor played guitar and sang a couple of songs, one he'd written called "Angels in This Town" and then "Pancho and Lefty," by Townes Van Zandt—it was Farrell's favorite. It's a folk ballad about a life of crime, about death and betrayal, about no one being there to hear your dying words, and about the Federales who in the end let both Pancho and Lefty slip away, mostly out of kindness, I suppose.

It wasn't true that no one had heard Farrell's dying words. I had. It was a strange, oddly compelling responsibility, one that didn't rest easily on my shoulders.

So after the psalms were read and the hymns were sung and the speakers with cracked voices pondered the meaning of life and told stories about his valor in combat though they clearly hadn't known him that well, it was my turn to sum up Farrell's life.

I got to my feet, shuffled past Jamie's knees, got up to the podium, straightened my tie, and said my piece, which went a little something like this:

"The one thing that no one's seemed to want to talk about here today is that Farrell was a pot dealer." The silence in the already quiet chapel grew deeper. Waves of naked hostility and embarrassed anger began flowing toward me. I withstood them and went on to explain: "I say he *was* because he gave it up a while back to help someone he loved kick her own drug habit."

Tulips, who'd lifted her head up when I started speaking, let her chin drop to her chest again and sobbed loudly.

"The thing is, those of us living in what Farrell would've called the 'straight world,' average people like you and me, we look down our noses at guys like him. And maybe, as a general rule, that's right. Drug dealers are, generally speaking, bad people. But Farrell wasn't. So how do we explain that? In mourning his passing, how do we understand that part of his life, a part that was important to him for over twenty years?

"It seems to me that when we make assumptions about our fellow men, when we put them in boxes, or judge them according to our own views of what's right and wrong, we see them as being less human than we are. The trouble is, when we dehumanize others, we can't help but dehumanize ourselves in the bargain.

"This is one of the great things that knowing Farrell has taught me. He never backed down from being who he was. And in so doing, he forced me to respect him and *accept* him as he was, the good *and* the bad.

"This is a Christian church we're in. And Jesus said, 'Judge not that ye be not judged.' How can we pretend to truly honor Farrell's life if we only remember the parts that we deem right and proper and Christian, and judge him for the rest?

"We've heard about his bravery in battle here today, and that's fine. At times like this we ignore the bad and glorify the good in any man's life. But Farrell told me that when he charged that hill in Vietnam and took out that enemy sniper, it wasn't because he was being courageous or honorable or even protecting the lives of his fellow soldiers. He did it because that Viet Cong soldier had just shot his dog; so he went mad, mad with grief and anger.

"He died the other night doing something similar. He wasn't trying to save my life when he got shot, as some have suggested; he was trying to protect my dog." I had to take a moment before I could go on. "So even if we don't want to look at some parts of his life, the parts we can't accept and would demonize him for, we have to acknowledge that he died a hero.

"He once said about his past vocation that he saw himself as a modern day Johnny Appleseed, spreading his herbal form of happiness all along the Maine coast. I think it's fitting that Farrell always thought of himself as a folk hero because now that he's gone, he'll always be remembered as one."

After the final prayer came the usual shocked hum of faces blending with the smell of flowers and the buzz of homilies. As I looked around, I noticed Farrell's recent acquaintance, Janwillem van der Dijkstra, sitting at the back of the church with an older man who looked like he could have been the lost uncle.

They joined some of us at the cemetery, where in lieu of a twenty-one-gun salute, Tulips had arranged a ten-beagle salute. She'd stopped crying by then. She knew she had to dry her eyes if she was going to give Farrell the send-off he deserved.

She opened the tailgate of his truck, said, "Beagles, formation!" They all jumped out and took their positions next to her. Then she marched them to his grave, said, "Ten-hut!" and they all sat. Then she said, "Beagles, speak!" and they all bayed as one. Their voices rang across the autumn hillside as Farrell's flag-covered coffin was slowly lowered into his grave.

The men from Farrell's unit nearly smiled as they snapped a final salute to their comrade; they were dog lovers, every one. Then they marched to the nearby flagpole and slowly lowered the flag to half-mast, and I thought of the general, who'd been a bigwig in national and local affairs, while Farrell had been a two-bit pot dealer, driving his beat-up truck up and down the Maine coast to sell marijuana to potheads and give it free to cancer patients. I'd still take Farrell Woods over General Mac-Leary any day.

"So," I said to Janwillem's uncle as we headed back to our cars, "you two are going back to Mexico?"

"No, no." He patted Janwillem on the shoulder. "I think we'll try Australia for a while. They have good waves there."

Jamie asked, "How long did you live there?"

"In Baja? Nine or ten years. I'm not good at counting."

I said, "Farrell told me that you actually met the mysterious Margarita Ortíz, face-to-face."

"Ah, yes." His eyes got a faraway look. "We had dinner a few times. She's very enigmatic, very beautiful."

"Is that so?" I said, though it was just my mouth moving. "I sort of met her myself, though she was wearing a mask."

"That's a shame," he said as we arrived at his rental car. "She reminded me of an old movie star. Very beautiful; I forget her name. She was in that movie, *The Adventures of Robin Hood.*"

"You mean the one with Errol Flynn?" I asked.

"Yes. Do you remember her name, that actress?"

"I do," I said, stunned. "It's Olivia de Havilland."

"Yes, that's who she reminded me of. Olivia de Havilland." He looked me over. "Are you all right, my friend?"

"Yeah," I said with a dry mouth. "I was just thinking, I'll have to look her up the next time I'm in Mexico."

Epilogue

Eddie Cole disappeared. He wasn't missing for long, though. By some strange turn of events, a number of drug shipments run by Miguel Ortíz on fishing boats out of Mexico were intercepted by the DEA. Ortíz was arrested, and by another strange turn of events, someone made a phone call to him in prison, suggesting that Eddie Cole was the one who had given him up to the Feds. This person, this tattletale, also pointed out that Eddie Cole and Ortíz weren't actually brothers; Cole had lied to Ortiz about it.

A few days later Cole's body washed up on a beach near La Jolla. He'd been shot forty times. Miguel Ortíz was under investigation for the killing, though there were no real leads.

General MacLeary was back in the hospital in December. He held on till the end of March, proving General MacArthur right: old soldiers never die; they just fade away.

Jervis faded away himself soon after. There were no bands and no smartly dressed soldiers to send him to his reward. Cord was the only MacLeary to attend both funerals. Connie was in a mental hospital. Reggie was in the wind, no one knew where.

Jamie and I didn't attend either man's memorial, although I had an itch to do so, an itch that was easily scratched, I'm afraid. Instead we took another trip south of the border.

We flew to Cabo, checked into our hotel, then rented a car and drove up the peninsula to a dusty village near that tin shack on the beach with the thatched roof.

It was an old Spanish villa that had been partially renovated. It must have cost a lot of money to make it as livable as it was. But then, Katherine MacLeary had a lot of money.

We were kept waiting awhile in a spacious white room with open windows full of light. We didn't talk much. I remember hoping we might be able to get in some waves before going home, but I knew that was unlikely. When the maid brought Katherine in to greet us, her bright expectant smile shattered.

"Oh," she said, then slowly took a seat. "I was told . . ."

"It's time for you to come home," I said softly. "There are some Federales waiting outside."

She shook her head. "I didn't kill her."

"We know," said Jamie. "But you and Reggie covered up Connie's crime. You thought you were protecting her, but . . ."

"You can't prove any of this. And Reggie didn't know."

"Reggie knew. She didn't know where the body was buried, but she knew about the murder; she'd put Connie up to it. Jervis gave me your bank account numbers. It took a while but I found out you've been paying Reggie for her silence all this time."

"You can't prove anything. She's my daughter. Of course I gave her money. And I wasn't involved in that woman's death."

"Katherine," Jamie said gently, "Margaret Greaves was buried in your clothes, wearing your ring."

"She could have stolen those things from me."

I said, "Well, if you don't mind branding her as a thief, you can lie about that at trial. But what about the murder of Grunwald?"

"That was self-defense. He was going to kill me, and you too." She stared out the window. "Anyway, I can't go to trial."

"Chances are slim you'll ever be convicted," I said.

Jamie said, "The jury will be on your side."

"Yes, but . . . no, I can't."

"You have no choice. Think of it this way: maybe if you take responsibility for what you've done, Connie will . . ." I let it hang. There was no hope for Connie and we all knew it.

"Or," she said, with a far-off look, "I could do it for him. In memory of his courage, of the man he once was?"

"No," I said. "That's his . . . that was his journey."

"I still love him, you know. I never stopped loving him."

"I'm sure that's true. And it's a lovely thing. Sad, but lovely. But that's not the point."

"No, it's not, is it? It's not the point."

"No. And besides, your disappearance is what broke him."

"It wasn't me. It was Ed Coster. It was politics, the compromises, the cover-ups. He lost what was best and good in him."

I said, "And so did you."

"But I had to take care of my girls." She sighed, stood up. "I'll just be a moment, then I'll be ready."

I felt stuck in molasses. I knew I should've gone with her but I couldn't move. A look passed between me and Jamie, then slowly perished. A bird somewhere, perhaps in the courtyard, chirped twice, waited, then chirped again.

A few moments later we heard a single gunshot ring from another room. It was a shock, but oddly, it didn't come as much of a surprise.

The Federales rushed in, there was a lot of shouting in Spanish, weeping from the household staff, questions and interrogations from local officials that lasted till the light in the windows had begun to slant and wane, and our flight home was soon to leave without us. Finally, they let us go. On the ride to the airport I kept thinking that I never thanked her for what she did for me and Hooch that night; I should have thanked her.

"Never talk to strangers on the beach," I said to Jamie philosophically, sipping my second single malt on the plane ride home. "That's the lesson here."

"Is it?" she asked with a longing look at my scotch.

"What do you think the lesson is?"

"Who knows?" she said. "That good or bad, it all comes back to family?"

"That's true too. And some families have more good than bad." This reminded me of the next part of our trip, a twenty-four-hour layover in San Diego. "Are you sure you don't mind spending a day in San Diego before we go back home?"

"No, I think you *should* spend some time with your father, especially after all that's happened."

"Not to mention everything that's about to happen, right?" I put one hand against her belly.

She held it, smiled at me, then looked back at my scotch. "Can't I just sniff it?" she asked. "Just smell it?"

"Why torture yourself? You know you can't have any alcohol until after the baby is born."

"I know," she said with a sad sigh that quickly turned to a beatific smile.

Oh. Did I forget to tell you?

That's right. The baby is due in July.

We're busy getting ready to ride the next wave.

Author's Note

Jack's approach to dog training, which is based on the book, *Natural Dog Training* by Kevin Behan, works by stimulating positive, playful emotions in the dog rather than by overusing food rewards, or any use of fear or dominance. Food, markers, even some types of corrections have their place, but food is not the "universal reinforcer" many trainers believe it is. And acting dominant, or alpha (or "calm assertive") is never necessary and can be harmful. The idea of dominance is also based on a complete fallacy. In real wolf packs there is no alpha wolf that controls the pack.

Simonov wrote, "Positive emotions arising in connection with the perfection of a skill, irrespective of its pragmatic significance at a given moment serve as the reinforcement." So it's not food, but positive emotion—usually stimulated by games—that's the *real* universal reinforcer for dogs. Max Von Stephanitz, who developed SchutzHund said, "Before we teach a dog to obey we must teach it how to play." And Nobel Prize winning biologist Konrad Lorenz wrote, "All animals learn best through play."

Finally, the scenes where Jack is helping Buster with his aggression problem are based on real training experiences of my own. But as they say on TV, "Don't try this at home."

Do Jack's techniques work? Absolutely. Can you learn how to do the same thing by reading a mystery novel and then trying it on your own with an aggressive dog? I wouldn't recommend it.

You can try walking the two dogs together, as Jack does with Buster and Frankie. It's an interesting and very helpful training tool. But I'd be very cautious about letting the two dogs loose, as Jack does, to "see if they'll play together." You have to have years of experience to know when to put the dogs in a position like that, and when not to. So I wouldn't even try.

My website: www.leecharleskelley.com
Kevin Behan's website: www.naturaldogtraining.com
My e-mail address: kelleymethod@aol.com
Lou Kelso's e-mail address: louiskelso@aol.com

Recommended Reading

Natural Dog Training, by Kevin Behan. Originally published by William Morrow and Co, 1993. Available again from XLibris. (The best book ever written about dogs and dog training.)

Dogs: A New Understanding of Canine Origins, Behavior, and Evolution by Raymond Coppinger, Lorna Coppinger. University of Chicago Press, October 2002. (Coppinger has said that the logic behind the alpha theory is "just poor." He's also stated that pack social structure "may be related to prey size.")

Play Training Your Dog, Patricia Gail Burnham. St. Martin's Press, 1986. (Shows the importance of playing tug-of-war and teaching a dog to jump up on command.)

Dogs That Know When Their Owners Are Coming Home, Rupert Sheldrake. Three Rivers Press, 2000. (Hypothesizes that some dogs are innately telepathic, and that telepathy is a common biologic function.)

"The Misbehavior of Organisms," Keller Breland, *American Psychologist*, 1961. (An article by the inventor of clicker training, critiquing the philosophy of operant conditioning.)
http://psychclassics.yorku.ca/Breland/misbehavior.htm

Emergence, Steven Johnson, Scribner's, 2001. (This book has nothing to do with dogs but may provide thoughtful readers some insight into the computer program Tulips is writing for Jack.)

Any book by L. David Mech, as well as his wolf studies: http://www.npwrc.usgs.gov/resource/mammals/alstat/index.htm

And visit my blog on Amazon.com.